E-Day Book 2: Bedlam

STACEY LIVINGSTON

ACKNOWLEDGMENTS

When I finally wrote the last word of this novel, I closed the computer and breathed a huge sigh. It was a sigh of contentment and I reflected on all the people who encouraged and supported me along the way.

There are so many of you, that I don't have enough room to name you all here. I only hope that you all realize who you are. I will forever be grateful for your loyalty and help along the way.

1

Jack Denton had been driving for the past three hours. He and Jason Evans were returning from picking up Jason's team just south of Gardiner, Montana.

They had been forced to stay an extra night and Jack wasn't thrilled about it. The older woman, Shirley, wouldn't leave until they had buried her husband, Gerald. He had died when his pacemaker failed after the blast. Shirley had gone a little crazy after his death and just wouldn't budge. Jack knew it was the right thing to do but felt time slipping away. He had to get everyone back to the ranch and be on his way to get Emma.

He was still pondering all this as they came around a bend in the road. Jack saw something about a hundred yards away moving toward them in a rush. He let his foot off the accelerator and eased onto the brake. He quickly glanced back at the group of people in the bed of the truck. As the truck slowed, the people in the back became alert. Jack whipped his head back to the front and tried to make out what was on the road.

"Oh, shit!" he yelled, suddenly realizing what it was.

Beside him, Jason had too. He grabbed hold of the dash with his good hand and roared, "Back up! Back up!"

Jack had already thrown the old Dodge in reverse and was punching the accelerator. They were moving at a high rate of speed back the way they had come. Jack angled the big truck toward the edge of the road, away from the seething mass, and braked along the shoulder.

Jack could see everybody in the back was okay and turned back to the mass. It was a stampede of animals. They were all moving at a dead run past the front of the truck to the other side of the road.

Jason and Jack eased out of the cab and were joined by the three agents. The other three people stayed in the truck bed.

Nobody said a word as they watched the remaining animals dwindle past.

Ray Burch, the lead agent, spoke up next to Jack, "I've never seen anything like that."

Jack turned worriedly to the muscular man and said, "I have. Once. Several years ago we had a wild fire here in Yellowstone. The animals were trying to escape ahead of it."

The female agent, Catherine Simmons, jerked her head around and asked, "Are you telling us there's a fire somewhere up ahead?"

Greg piped up sarcastically and said, "That's just great!"

The three agents and their boss, Jason, were all staring openly at Jack now.

Jack had turned and was intently studying the ridge opposite of where the animals had disappeared. He didn't answer for a moment. Suddenly he turned and said, "We need to go. Now!" He started gesturing everybody back to the truck. As everyone hustled back to the Dodge, Jack continued, "There's a fire over that ridge. How far away, I don't know."

The three agents jumped back into the bed of the truck. Jack got back behind the wheel and tore down the road.

Jason glanced at Jack and asked, "How far away do you think it is?"

Jack's brows were knit in a concerned frown as he told his friend, "Only about two miles, maybe less. The wind is out of the west. I don't know yet if that's good or bad. It depends on how far away from the road the fire is."

Jason looked ahead and told Jack, "Jesus! Now we have to dodge wild animals and a forest fire. How much farther to the ranch?"

"About fifty miles. Once we get into the foothills, there won't be as many trees for the fire to burn. We just have to get past it."

They had just reached the top of a hill and Jack eased up on the gas. Below them they could see the fire in all its fury. It engulfed the gorge on the left side of the road. As they watched, they saw that an extension of the fire had already jumped the road. Jack hesitated for just a second, and then he turned to Jason and said, "Tell them to get under the blankets and for God's sake, hang on!"

Jason didn't bat an eye. He flew out of the truck and relayed the message to the others then hopped back in. He started to say something but Jack didn't give him a chance.

Clenching his jaw, Jack revved the engine, and they were off. He saw that there was only one vehicle that he would have to clear, an abandoned jeep about halfway down the hill. It was angled across the road and Jack eyeballed the distance between the jeep and the guardrail. *Just enough*, he figured. They swooped down toward the fire at an astonishing speed. The old Dodge engine was roaring away. Jack didn't have time to check on everyone but he thought he heard Jason squeak. They bore down on the jeep and were going so fast by the time they passed it, Jack had no time to be worried. They skimmed by it with no more than six inches to spare on either side. Then they were past and Jack was already judging how much the fire had grown. He slowed slightly, studying the road. Making sure to get right in the middle, Jack poured on the speed.

From the top of the hill, their course had looked clear cut. Down here, however, the wind had shifted and blown a wall of smoke right across the road. It looked like they were going full bore into a solid wall. Not knowing what was on the other side, Jack said a prayer and tilted his chin down. As he did, he noticed Jason's knuckles were white as he gripped the dash. There was a split second of complete silence and slow motion as Jack strangled the steering wheel and they punched through the smoke.

Jack let off the gas and coasted as the smoke thinned. They were still moving pretty fast but nothing like their mad dash down the hill. They could see that the road ahead was clear. The fire hadn't made it up the valley wall on this side of the smoke. Jack breathed a sigh of relief and kept going at a reasonable speed.

"How are they looking?" he asked Jason.

Jason took a moment to look into the back and nodded, "Looks good."

Jack nodded and told Jason, "I'm going to get on down the road a bit, then we'll pull over."

Only now did he let himself think about what would have happened had they wrecked the truck. Since the EMP blast, all electronics had failed. That included any automobile with microchips. This 1965 Dodge was the only truck that they found that worked.

Jack thought he heard Jason start breathing again. He smiled to himself, pulled to the side of the road, and stopped. Jack grabbed the map and got out of the truck. Moving to the hood, he spread the map out and checked where they were.

Jason went to check on the others. They were all climbing out of the back. Greg Morrison was rambling on as usual.

"Wow! That was crazy! I didn't know if we'd make it past that jeep." He was bouncing on his toes. Ray just shook his head as he helped the young girl, Ashley Cook, out of the truck bed. Cat was helping Sheila out of the pickup too. The last member of the group, Dai Ji Kuan, had already, smoothly, reached the road.

Jack was covertly watching the group. He had not really studied the group since they had come together the day before. He focused on Kuan first. The Chinese defector stood about five feet six inches tall. He was somewhat slender and Jack could see by the way the man moved that he was confident and capable. He would remember that. Kuan was also quiet, and there was something about the man that bothered Jack. He just couldn't put his finger on it. Moving his attention on to the rest of the group, Jack zeroed in on the agents.

Ray, the leader, was powerfully built. The man was close to Jack's height. He had dark, close-cropped hair, with just a bit of gray, dark eyes and a square jaw. Jack got the feeling that the agent was extremely proficient. Cat, the female agent, was average height. For the most part, she was quiet. She had dark brown hair, brown eyes and seemed to glide as opposed to walk. Greg Morrison. Now there was a character. He had short, wavy blond hair and blue eyes. He came across as a mouthy showoff, but beneath the surface, Jack sensed he was serious and always watching. All in all a good team.

Jason was approaching him so Jack returned his attention to the map.

"What are you looking at? Don't you know all the roads?" Jason asked him.

Jack nodded and told him, "I do. I just wanted to make sure the road I was going to take would be the best."

Jack refolded the map and walked back to the others. "Everybody ok?" he asked the group in general.

They all nodded in the affirmative and he continued, "We're about fifty miles away from the ranch. I'm going to take the back roads so, hopefully, we won't meet any people. It shouldn't be too bad from here on out." The older woman,

Shirley, looked relieved and for a moment he felt bad for her. Jack knew she and Ashley had nowhere to go, so he had brought them both along.

Dismissing those thoughts, he continued, "When we get to the ranch, we'll get cleaned up and rest."

Getting into the old truck, Jack eyed the fuel gauge. Luckily, they still had a quarter of a tank. He glanced at the ugly green cast to the sky and thought about how much he was beginning to hate that color.

He started up the engine and briefly envisioned Emma. Never far from his thoughts, Jack hoped she was keeping safe.

2

Slowly, Emma Hudson came awake. She opened her eyes in the dark and realized where she was. Pigeon Forge. They had made it. It had been a harrowing journey but she and her friends, Lori Bubar and Bryan Peterson, had finally made it out of Atlanta and into Tennessee. She allowed herself the luxury of lying in bed and thinking about all they had been through. The EMP blast, the freak snowstorm, and finally the acquisition of two horses on the last leg here. It was all so dreamlike.

She sobered as she thought of last night and how barren the cabin was. They stayed up late and removed the drop cloths from the furniture and searched for fuel for the fireplace. Bryan had finally found some old wood behind the house, but it had been damp and hard to light. Eventually Lori had found some lighter fluid and they had got it started.

After an inventory, they were surprised to find the cabin well stocked. Their number-one priority today would be finding water. Emma remembered a stream somewhere not far away from the cabin. That would be Lori's and her job. Bryan had already said that he would chop wood with the ax he had found in the garage.

Emma was still listing chores in her head when something jumped on the bed and startled her.

"Bella! Jesus! I wish you wouldn't do that!"

She relaxed and smiled as she caressed her calico cat, then returned to brooding. The cabin had three bedrooms and three baths. Everybody picked a bedroom and her friends told her to take the master since it held so many memories of Jack and her. Her mind immediately jumped to Jack Denton and she cut it off. She had no time for that now. She had a mountain of things to do.

Flipping the covers back she shivered. It was chilly up on the second floor. Snapping on the flashlight, she quickly changed into jeans, sweatshirt and two pair of socks. Emma glanced at her watch and saw it was almost six o'clock. She grabbed the flashlight and headed downstairs. She tried to be quiet so as not to wake her friends. They had all decided not to set a guard, since the cabin had been so undisturbed, but that would change tonight. They had to take precautions.

Downstairs she went immediately to the large fireplace and saw the fire was down to coals. She grabbed some of the crumpled newspaper that Bryan had left over from last night, along with some of the old wood, and began to build up the fire. Thankfully, the wood had dried out overnight and the fire reignited right away. Before long, Emma had a nice blaze to take the chill off. She brushed her hands off and turned to the kitchen. She needed to check on the horses. They had brushed them down as best they could with some old rags then tied them up under the back balcony.

As she walked out the back door, the horses raised their heads and looked at her. She walked over to them speaking gently. As she spoke, she realized they'd have to build a place for the horses. She felt overwhelmed by all she and her friends had to accomplish. Emma sighed and then consoled herself by thinking it would help make the time pass quicker. She knew it was eighteen hundred miles from Wyoming to here. It could take Jack a long time by horse to get here. She glanced at the sky and saw by the growing light that the ominous green glow was still there.

Giving each horse one last pat, Emma went into the house to start her morning. She found Lori and Bryan dressed and standing by the fire to get warm. Bella had made herself at home on the couch and was grooming herself daintily.

"So how did you guys sleep?" Emma asked her friends as she got some cat food from her bag.

"It was beautiful!" Lori said, "After the last few nights, a real bed felt like heaven!"

Bryan was a little less enthusiastic. "I'm going to have to find some more blankets. I was freezing."

Emma nodded and then changed subjects. "I've got a mental list of things to get done today. Are you game?"

Her friends said they were, and Emma filled them in.

Hours later, Emma, Bryan and Lori, exhausted, were sitting in the living room admiring their handiwork. All of the old wood that was left outside was now stacked next to the fireplace drying out. They located the creek less than five minutes away, where it cut through the property. They had discovered that the property was fenced and probably covered two acres. Bryan rode Leroy along the fence line to make sure it was intact. They had even hauled water up in buckets to have a supply. They had gone through the house and found that it had everything they needed to survive.

All of a sudden, something caught Emma's eye from the front porch and she grabbed her Glock.

Lori saw the quick movement and asked, "What?"

Emma said, "Sh!" and motioned her friends over by the fireplace. Bryan had grabbed the rifle and was covering the front window where Emma had seen the movement.

"What'd you see?" Bryan whispered.

"I'm not sure," she answered. Emma saw that Lori had her knife in her hand.

They saw another shadow move and heard footsteps pause on the front porch. Before she could think about what she was doing, Emma quickly strode to the door, twisted the knob, jerked it open, and pointed the gun at the person's head.

She heard Lori gasp behind her as she studied the man on the porch. He was about Emma's age with red hair and a full beard and moustache. He had a cap on and camouflage coveralls. His boots were muddy and he carried a rifle pointed at the porch. He clearly was surprised, but he had been looking at the friends' muddy footprints on the porch.

"What do you want?" Emma demanded.

The man swallowed, then tried to speak. He wasn't successful, so he cleared his throat. "My name is Anthony Moore," the man stammered.

He hadn't moved a muscle since Emma had confronted

him.

"Larry asked me a couple of years ago to keep an eye on his place," he added. He remained standing, looking down the barrel of the pistol. Emma was waiting for more but it wasn't coming.

Suddenly, she remembered that Larry was the name of Jack's rich friend who owned the cabin.

"I want to believe you, Mr. Moore, but you'll forgive me for being just a wee bit skeptical in our present circumstances," Emma stated, and saw the man pale further. She continued, "Do you happen to have your ID?"

The man looked confused but nodded vaguely and slowly reached in his back pocket. He slipped his wallet out and handed it to Emma. Emma handed it to her friends without looking, and said, "Would you check this man's ID, Lori?"

She felt Lori take the wallet but continued to hold the gun on the man. They stood like that for a moment until Lori spoke up, "Yep, it says Anthony Robert Moore. Looks like him too."

"Well, that's good. I tell you what. If you'll put that rifle down on the porch, I will too. Then we can talk," Emma stated.

Anthony looked behind Emma and she presumed he was looking at Bryan's rifle pointed at him too.

"He'll put his down too. I promise," Emma said.

Anthony looked doubtful, but what choice did he have? He slowly kneeled and placed the rifle on the porch. Emma followed suit and she could hear Bryan also laying down his weapon. Once that was done, they all relaxed a little.

Anthony spoke up first, "Who are you people? Are you friends of Larry?"

Emma took a deep breath and replied, "I don't know Larry, but I am friends with Jack Denton." She looked to see if this name registered with the man. When it didn't, she went on. "Jack went to high school with Larry." She watched hopefully as Anthony seemed to be deep in thought.

All at once, the man snapped his fingers and smiled. "Jack! You must mean Jacky! That's what we all called him in school. His mother called him that in grade school and it just stuck."

The nickname was so unexpected that for a minute Emma didn't say anything. She then regained her composure and said, "I'm sure that's him. I didn't know about the nickname, but I just met him ten years ago."

Anthony was smiling and then reached out his hand for Emma to shake. "Any friend of Jack and Larry are friends of mine."

Emma smiled back and shook Anthony's hand. "Why don't you come in and sit for a while? I'm sure you have questions and we do too."

Anthony agreed. They all gathered their weapons and entered the house. Introductions were made and they all took a seat.

"Just call me Tony. I haven't gone by Anthony in years." They all agreed.

Before Emma could open her mouth, Tony asked, "Where is Jack? Or Larry?"

He looked genuinely confused and Emma organized her thoughts before she spoke. "Like I said before, I don't know Larry. I know Jack. Look, let me start at the beginning."

He got comfortable and she began, telling the shortened version about meeting Jack and falling in love. She skipped the part about breaking it off and, instead, just said they took a break for her nursing career. Emma went on to tell him about Jack's previous military experience, and his vague phone call about this very cabin, and that he would come for her. She ended by explaining how she knew Bryan and Lori.

He was looking at all of them wide-eyed and said, "You came all the way from Atlanta? After the blast?"

All three friends nodded at the man. He shook his head incredulously. "By foot?"

The friends looked at one another and Emma spoke up, "Actually, most of the way we rode horses."

Tony asked, "Where are they? I didn't see any horses."

Bryan spoke up. "We have two of them. They're out back, under the balcony."

Tony slowly nodded, letting it all sink in. Meanwhile, Emma had questions of her own.

"Tell us about you and Pigeon Forge. I've only been here once, briefly."

Tony agreed and started. "I live just up the road with my wife and two kids. I was coming past the property on my way to go hunting, and I thought I would check on the place. It's been awhile. Nobody bothers anything around here usually, and I haven't heard from Larry in a year or more. That's when I came across your footprints on the porch. I was shocked. I sure wasn't expecting you to stick that pistol in my face." He grinned at Emma and then continued, "As for Pigeon Forge, we're a small little town. For the most part, we watch out for each other. Don't get me wrong, we have our share of nuisances and people who cause problems, but we ran those out of town after they tried to make trouble on the third day. We don't put up with nonsense around here." This last part was said as he steadily looked at Emma.

Alarm bells were mildly going off in Emma's head. Something wasn't right about this guy. She had been watching Tony closely. It was something about the man's eyes. She saw Lori open her mouth to say something and quickly cut her off.

"What has been going on in town since this crisis?" she asked in a friendly manner. She eased her hand closer to her handgun when Tony wasn't looking. She saw Lori had a puzzled and slightly hurt look on her face as she glanced at Emma. Emma knew she was still looking at her and tried to signal her with a slight shake of her head.

She didn't know if Lori had seen her as she returned her attention to what Tony was saying.

"The day it happened was a nightmare. You probably saw the same thing, or worse, in Atlanta. There was a flash of white light and a loud rumble like thunder. I was talking on my cell phone and I heard a sizzle before it went dead. The lights went out and the electricity. We had a lot of airplanes crash, though luckily, none in town. Those airplanes caused a lot of fires, and without fire trucks, it took us a while to get them under control. We had wrecks in town that caused deaths and we're still finding people that just dropped dead for unknown reasons after it happened." He looked haunted at the memories and bowed his head. Emma took this moment to ease her hand over the Glock. When he looked back up, Emma smiled encouragingly at the man. He continued, "We thought, at first, that it was something just around here. A glitch or something. We were waiting for the government to come in and help out."

He was shaking his head again, this time in disbelief. After a moment, Tony went on, "The water plant up at Douglas Lake didn't work anymore. We had water for the first twenty-four hours. After that, you had to find your own." His eyes were haunted at the memories, but Emma kept her guard up. She still didn't feel right.

He went on, "After two days, everyone knew this was going to be the way it was for a while. We had no idea what had happened, but knew that since we hadn't heard from the outside by then, it must be a problem all across the U.S. The troublemakers that I told you about started banding together after the water plant quit. The next day they started looting. The good folks in town were forced to come together to stop them. That night, along with local law enforcement and the mayor, we all met at the First Baptist Church and got organized. We were told to bring our firearms and that night we formed a search party." After he said this last bit, Tony smiled cruelly. The hair stood up on the back of Emma's neck and she fought to keep a straight face.

"Needless to say, we don't have any problems with the looters anymore," Tony finished.

Emma wished he would continue, so she could get more information. It was apparent, however, that he would say no more.

She took the lead to keep her friends quiet. "Well! We sure are glad to have met you. Thank you so much for filling us in." Here Emma smiled to keep Tony off guard. She did not want the man to know she didn't like him. It seemed to work and she continued, "If you don't mind, we would like to stay for a few days and then we will be moving on."

She felt both her friends look at her with surprise. She hoped they wouldn't say anything until Tony had left.

Tony appeared not to notice anything and, in fact, seemed pleased that they would be staying a while. "That's no problem, no problem at all." He stood up while he said this last part and made to leave. "I have to tell the sheriff that you three are out here. It's part of the new town policy. I wouldn't worry, though. He'll probably just come by to meet you."

He had his rifle in his hand and Emma had gripped the Glock inconspicuously as she saw him out.

She kept up the ruse until Tony left. After she shut the door, the wide grin slid from her face and she narrowed her eyes while surreptitiously watching him walk down the steps.

Behind her, Emma heard Bryan and Lori start asking her

questions at the same time. Without looking at them, she held up her finger signaling her friends to wait.

Emma continued to shield herself from the outside as she quietly moved from window to window, watching Tony as he circled the cabin. He didn't walk away as an innocent man would. More like he was plotting something.

He went directly around to look at the horses. Tony didn't just glance at them and walk away. He walked up to them, ran his hands over them, and even checked their legs and teeth, for all the world looking like he was about to make a purchase.

By now, Emma's friends had quit talking and were sneaking around room to room following Emma and watching Tony too. When they saw he went right for the horses, they understood what was going on and inhaled sharply. Emma saw the man nod to himself with a pleased look on his face. He then turned and walked away.

Emma stood at the window a while looking at the sickly green sky and thinking. Her friends were behind her talking about what was going on. She wasn't listening to them. This changed everything. She should be scared, but she wasn't. She was pissed. They'd worked so hard and had gone through so much to get here, and now they had just been threatened. Subtly, to be sure, but threatened nonetheless. Emma didn't take kindly to threats. She turned from the window and looked around. Her friends looked angry too.

"We need to figure out what we're going to do," Emma stated. She walked past them into the living room.

"What do you mean?" Bryan asked. "I say we stay right here! We have gone through a shit storm to get here! Didn't you say this Jack person is military? Why don't we just tell them that and claim squatter's rights? Everything has gone to hell anyway! What happened to 'possession is nine-tenths of the law'?"

Emma let him run out of steam. She waited to see what Lori said, and she didn't have long to wait.

"I don't understand. I guess I missed something. Why did Tony go check out our horses like they belong to him? Why does he have to report us to the sheriff?" Lori was clearly confused.

Emma let out a deep breath and put her hands on her hips. "Look, I don't like Tony. There's something about him that feels off." She looked at her friends and saw that they now felt the same way. She continued, "We have to start thinking differently. We are living in a crazy, messed up world now. What motivated people before does not motivate them now. Think about it. Right now, people are not thinking about day-to-day jobs. They're thinking about food, water, and shelter. At whatever cost. There will be little, if any, punishment to people for what they do in their pursuit to survive."

Emma finished and looked at her friends. Lori looked sad and worried. Bryan's expression was anger mixed with disappointment.

"I think we have two basic choices. Stay here and see what the sheriff has to say. It could be that I am just overreacting to Tony and there's nothing weird going on. Or we could leave. If we leave, I have no idea how to meet Jack. It would take at least a month to get to Cody. Jack, meanwhile, would be on his way here. Not to mention the fact that it's chaos out there."

Emma could tell that Lori was remembering what happened to the woman back in Kennesaw. The woman's assault by the group of men had hit her friend really hard.

She went on to get her friend's thoughts away from those memories, "I like it here. It hadn't occurred to me that anybody would bother us. I guess I should—"

There was a loud knock on the door that interrupted Emma and startled them all. The friends, standing in the living room, immediately had their weapons out again. Lori looked questioningly at Bryan. Bryan shook his head in puzzlement and Emma was about to whisper something to them both when the person who knocked spoke up, "Open the door! I'm here to help you, but I don't know if Tony will come back or not!"

The friends all looked at each other in surprise. Before they could answer, the voice spoke again, "Come on, dammit! You can trust me!"

Emma went to open the door. If the person outside had wanted to hurt them, he wouldn't have knocked on the front door. Besides, she had her Glock.

She looked back at her friends before opening the door and was surprised to see they had moved to more strategic positions. They were learning.

She unlocked the front door and pulled it open. She had

her gun leveled at the young man's nose before he could blink. He wasn't surprised. He just looked at Emma and said, "If you're going to shoot me, do it now. If you aren't, then let me in and close the door. We're wasting time."

Emma looked deep into his brown eyes and knew he was being honest with her. She glanced around behind him and then waved him in with the gun. He quickly entered the house and Emma shut the door. She turned, held the gun ready by her side, and said, "Why don't you tell us who you are?"

Emma could see the stranger wasn't armed. He was about an inch taller than Emma, which put him at five feet eight, and probably weighed no more than a hundred and fifty pounds. He looked to be in his mid-twenties and had dark hair and a dark, wispy moustache.

"My name is Matt Carroll. I was following Tony when he came across your tracks. I kept following him when he came here. After he left, I waited until he was gone, and then came to find out who you are and to warn you."

Emma cocked her head to the side. "Warn us? About what?"

Matt pointed to a chair. "Can we sit? I'm tired and this may take a few minutes."

Emma nodded and everyone sat. When they were comfortable, Matt resumed, "Before I start, please tell me what Tony said to you."

Emma hesitated but saw no way it could hurt them. "He said he had been out hunting and decided to check on the cabin. He said Larry, the owner of the cabin, asked him to keep an eye on it." She looked up and saw he was paying close attention. She relaxed and went on to recount the conversation word for word.

As she finished, Emma noticed that Matt looked mad and was slightly shaking his head.

"Unbelievable. I can't believe that ass had enough nerve to say that we were looting!"

The friends were really confused and Bryan said so. "Wait. Who said you were looting?" Then it dawned on him. "Oh! Tony was talking about looters. You were one of the looters?"

"Tony was lying! We were not looting!" Matt was agitated and stood up to pace. After a minute, he stopped and turned back to them. "I need to tell you what is really going on in Pigeon Forge. If nothing else, it will let you decide if you want to stay here or not." He said this last part with such conviction that Emma could do nothing but ask him to continue.

He sat back down now and said, "I'm going to tell you the short version, since I don't know when the sheriff will arrive. Believe me, he will be out as soon as Tony tells him you're here. So listen up.

"I had walked to town on an errand the third day after the blast. There was a large group of people in front of the Kroger on Wears Valley Road. I was trying to fill a prescription and pick up some food. I had money and the prescription. I knew there would probably be a line, but I needed those things!"

Emma saw that Matt was getting angrier the more he told the story. She encouraged him to go on.

He took a deep breath and continued, "As I walked up on the back of the group, I could hear they were yelling questions toward the front of the store. I was standing on my toes and trying to get a look at who they were yelling at. "It turned out to be the sheriff and a lot of other men with guns. The mayor was there too. The sheriff and his men were on horses and were blocking the store. The more I listened I began to understand what was going on. The crowd was wanting to know why they couldn't go in and get food and supplies. The sheriff was yelling back that he and the mayor were declaring martial law, locally, until they could contact the government. There was to be a curfew starting that night at sundown and it was to be until dawn. The group would disperse and there was to be no unauthorized gatherings.

"You could only get permission for gatherings or to be out during curfew from the sheriff's office. As I looked around, I noticed that the people in the group were just regular folks. They were scared and worried. They weren't there to cause trouble. It was then that the sheriff told the people to go home. He told us that the sheriff's office would be open the next morning and they could come then to apply for things they needed. That was when he told us that the sheriff's office would have the final say on who would get what supplies. He also said we needed to bring something to barter with. No paper money. He wanted silver, gold, or things of value.

"This didn't go over well with the group. Somebody yelled that the sheriff couldn't do that. I saw several people start walking toward the front of the store. The sheriff's men yelled at the people to step back, but they kept walking. They didn't have guns like the sheriff's men did. They weren't being threatening. It looked to me like they were trying to get close to the sheriff and plead their case. Then they shot them!" Matt stopped and rubbed his face with his hands.

Emma wasn't expecting him to say this. She felt all the blood drain from her face and leaned forward. Lori and Bryan were equally shocked and Lori asked, "What? Did you say the sheriff's men shot them? In cold blood?"

Matt had drawn his hands down from his face and now he nodded. "Yes. They shot the four men that were in the front. They were unarmed and just wanting to get supplies for their families. After the shooting, there was a stampede. The people that were left in the group scattered. I was almost trampled before I came to my senses and ran too.

"The reason I wanted to tell you this is because the man Tony that you met today? He was one of the shooters. I saw him."

Bryan exclaimed, "Oh my God!"

Lori grabbed Bryan's shirtsleeve and her jaw dropped open.

Emma closed her eyes and shook her head. Her eyes quickly popped back open as she remembered something. "You said you wanted to warn us about something. Is this what you were talking about?"

Matt replied, "Yes. That and something else. For the past few days the sheriff has been sending his men out to all the residents to let people know there are some changes that have been made. Until things get back to normal, the mayor, the sheriff, and local judge Byron Washington will be the new legal system in Pigeon Forge. He also said that all strangers showing up in the area were to be reported to the sheriff's office. Supposedly they want to keep criminals from coming into the area causing problems, but I'm not so sure."

Emma furrowed her brow. "What do you mean?"

Matt sighed, "Before all this happened, there were some rumors around town about the mayor and sheriff. They were said to be corrupt and to take bribes, but were never caught. They both go to the same church, by the way, and so do a lot of the sheriff's men. Tony is actually a deacon at the church. First Baptist Church is the name of it. If you meet someone that goes to that church, I would be careful."

Matt had been acting nervous for the past few minutes and now he stood up to go.

Emma and her friends stood too and followed him to the door. Emma reached out gently and grabbed his forearm, "Wait. We have some more questions."

The young man looked at Emma and her friends and shook his head, "I do NOT want to be here when the sheriff comes by to check you all out. I haven't done anything wrong, but you don't want to be on that man's radar."

Bryan started to say something but Matt cut him off, "I'm staying with my family on their farm that's south of here about two miles. If you go due south for a mile, you'll hit Little Cove Road. Turn west and go about another mile and you'll see a driveway on your left with a mailbox with a 225 and the name Carroll on it. That's us. If you decide to stay here, make sure no one follows you or is watching you and come see us. I can tell you more then. Please don't tell anybody I was here."

The last thing Emma saw before he left was his haunted eyes. He disappeared down the steps and quickly blended into the trees.

Emma realized that Matt's visit had not made their decision to stay any easier. If anything, it was now more confusing.

"Well, shit!" Bryan exclaimed, "We really needed some more info!"

Emma was looking at the floor and mumbled, "We'll just have to make our decision based on what we know. That's all we can do."

"Please don't tell me we're going to ride all the way to Wyoming. I don't think my ass could take it!" Lori said.

Emma grinned at her small friend, knowing she was trying to lighten the mood.

Bryan just rolled his eyes at the two. "Come on, you guys! Quit joking around. Do we stay and wait on this asshole sheriff? Or do we ride off to Wyoming? Are there any other choices that we might have?"

Emma turned serious again and contemplated his question. They had to make a decision in the next few minutes. A plan had formed in her mind and she told her friends.

"I think we should hear what the sheriff has to say, but I don't want us all to be in here like sitting ducks. Bryan, I want you to take the rifle, go out into the woods on the east side of the cabin, and find a hiding place. Make sure it's a spot where you have a good line of sight of the front of the house. Saddle the sorrel and take him with you. If they ask, I'm going to tell them you went hunting. This way, we won't all be in one spot, and at least one of the horses will be protected. Lori and I will have you watching us in case anything goes bad."

Bryan looked dismayed. "Do we really want to do that? What if he just fricking shoots you two? I can't help you if I'm out in the woods!"

Bryan was looking back and forth between the two women and was frantic.

Emma stepped up and grabbed his bicep. "Bryan!" she said, to get his attention. "These are good ole boys. They would believe that a man went hunting before they would believe that a woman did and left the man at the cabin. We need you out in the woods to watch out for us. You're a good shot and I can handle the sheriff!"

Bryan thought about what Emma had said for a few seconds and realized she was right. His shoulders slumped and he nodded.

Emma let her hand drop and smiled. "Good. Now, let's get ready!"

3

Jack pulled the Dodge up to the house. He was glad to be home. Grady Hudson, the ranch foreman, was walking out to the truck. Jack turned the truck off and slid out of the cab. Jason opened his door and went around to help the others out of the back. Jack saw him wince and reminded himself to look at the field dressing on Jason's left arm. Jeez! The only time Jason is out in the field, and he gets shot. He shook his head as he joined Grady at the front of the truck. Grady was looking at the group getting out of the back of the truck.

"Found a few strays?" Grady asked.

"Long story," Jack replied and stretched his arms. It had been an exhausting drive.

"You can tell me later." Grady had turned to Jack with a serious face and said, "Had a visit from some of the townspeople."

Jack waited him out. He'd known Grady long enough to be patient. He saw Danny and Scott Hudson were walking over and smiled at them. They were Grady's sons and also lived and worked on the ranch. Jack had gotten so close to the Hudsons that they might as well be his family.

Scott slapped him on the back and said, "Hey, where've

you been? I thought we were going to have to come find you!"

Jack grinned and answered, "You couldn't find your butt with both hands!"

Danny chortled when he heard this and Jack turned serious. "What happened, Grady?"

Grady smoothed his gray moustache and beard and replied, "Some of the city council came out wanting to talk to you. They remember that you were in the military. They also know about the 'crazy' things you've done to the ranch." He paused and looked at Jack meaningfully, and then said, "I told them that you were out on the ranch."

Jack quirked an eyebrow at the old man and the old man shrugged. "I didn't know what else to tell them, Jack. I didn't want them snooping around here. They seemed to buy it, and they asked if you'd come into town and see them when you got a moment."

Jack nodded at Grady and said, "They'll just have to wait."

They were following everyone up to the house and Grady continued, "The water finally quit yesterday, but not before we filled all those containers you got at that auction. The boys and I got the outhouses dug and the showers set up. I never could, for the life of me, figure out why you bought all that lumber. Now, I'm glad that you did."

Jack watched as the newcomers went into the house.

Jack and the others had stopped out on the porch to talk in privacy. "Thanks, Grady. As you can see, we're going to need all of it. I'm just glad that movie star I bought the ranch from wanted such a big house. Plenty of room for our guests.

"I'm going to go clean up and get something to eat. By the way, I'm sure you've seen the smoke. There's a wildfire up in the park. The wind's sending it this way, but we should be okay. There's not that much fuel for the fire between here and the woodlands. We need to keep an eye on it, though. "

Grady mumbled agreement and Jack went in the front door. As his eyes adjusted, Jack could see that Maria, Grady's wife, had everybody seated at the large dining table and was offering everyone food and drink. She was calmly making small talk with the guests to relax them.

Denise was helping her mother-in-law with the refreshments. The two women glanced over at Jack and he mouthed "thank you" to them both. Maria acknowledged him and he dashed up to his room. He grabbed his things and went out back to the new showers to get cleaned up. He wasn't looking forward to a cold shower, but beggars couldn't be choosers.

* * *

Ray had seen the exchange between Jack and the two women. It reassured him that Jack Denton seemed to be a good man. His years in the agency had taught Ray not to take a person's character at face value. He had been starving and now that he and the other two agents were through eating, he wanted to talk to them alone. Ray scanned the area for

Jason. It wasn't that he was keeping anything from Jason, he just had a couple of things to discuss with his fellow agents.

He saw Jason heading up the stairs. Ray got Cat's and Greg's attention and motioned them to follow him. As they rose from the table, they thanked Maria and Denise for the meal. Ray went back out the front door and his fellow agents followed.

When they got to the truck, Ray stopped and put his hands on his hips. He glanced around to make sure they were alone before he spoke. "We haven't had a chance to talk much, and so I wanted to go over a couple of things with you two."

Cat and Greg both looked a little confused so Ray explained, "Now that we've done what we were supposed to do and gotten Kuan to Jason safely, our assignment is done. I figure Jason has a new assignment in mind. He may just want us to help escort him to wherever he takes Kuan. Anyway, you two know I don't have any family since my wife passed away years ago. Both of you still have families."

They were really looking confused now and Ray tried again. "I guess I'm asking if you two had thought about going to check on your families. If you did want to, I would be glad to talk to Jason for you. After we left that town in Montana, I got to thinking about how worried I would be if I did have family." Greg and Cat seemed to understand now, but both of them were already shaking their heads.

Cat spoke first. "I haven't been back to visit my family in years. Besides, they have a large farm and are better prepared than most to take care of themselves during this." She waved her hand up at the green sky.

Greg spoke up then with a snarl, "The best thing to happen to me is the agency. I don't ever want to see those people again!"

Ray was surprised at Greg's strong emotion but nodded and replied, "Okay, I just wanted to make sure. The second thing I wanted to ask you, Cat, what have you heard about Jack Denton. I saw how you reacted when you found out who he was. You looked stunned."

He was looking at Cat and saw she was uncomfortable. "It was just rumors. When I first started at the agency, I was paired with a veteran. He'd worked with Jack in the Middle East. He told me that Jack had an uncanny sixth sense. He was legendary in the agency for knowing and sensing things. Against *any* odds, Jack and his team always made it out unscathed. But my partner wouldn't tell me what happened to Jack. That's why I looked startled when I met him."

Greg looked thoughtful and thanked Cat. He filed the information away for later.

"I guess that's all I wanted to ask. Do you two have any questions?" Ray asked his friends.

Cat mumbled no, and Greg shook his head. They all returned to the house. As they walked in the front door, they saw Jason coming from the back of the house where the showers were. His hair was wet and he looked refreshed.

Jason saw the agents. "Grab your bags and I'll show you to your rooms. They've already taken Ashley, Shirley, and Mr.

Kuan to theirs. Afterward, you can take showers. There are two of them out back and you can take turns."

* * *

Sometime later, Jack and Jason sat alone at the table. They were waiting for Kuan to get dressed after his shower. Grady and his family knew that the two men wanted to question the defector so they were keeping out of the way. Jack had just rewrapped Jason's left bicep and put antibiotic on it.

Jack looked at Jason and said, "We need to talk about who all is going to Tennessee with us. I know it'll be you, me, and Kuan. What about your agents?"

Jason nodded. "We need to bring them for protection. With the way things are, we need to give ourselves every chance to succeed. The stakes are just too high."

Jack agreed. "I'll get Grady to hitch up the trailer. I'll be right back." He got up to leave then turned back to Jason with narrowed eyes. "Don't start without me."

Jason lifted his eyebrows with mock innocence and said, "I wouldn't think of it." Jack stared at him for a minute more, then turned and left.

Kuan was coming down the stairs when Jack returned and they all headed to the den. Jack asked Kuan if he would like something to drink and the man declined.

Settling onto one of the chairs, Jack spoke first. "I haven't talked with you directly, but I guess you know my name is

Jack Denton. I worked with Jason a few years ago. If it's okay with you, I will be helping him out with this." He waited until Kuan agreed and then looked at Jason to continue.

"First of all, I would like to take thank you for helping us. We know you didn't have to and you gave up everything to do this for us."

Jason waited for Kuan to answer him and when the man just looked at them he went on. "I want to let you know that when this is over and things get back to normal, the American government will give you a new identity and set you up in a new life."

Again, Kuan just looked at the two men. Jason looked at Jack. Jack had been watching Kuan the whole time. For the first time in his life, Jack could not read a man he was questioning. This bothered him a lot. He'd had this feeling before with Kuan.

Jack tried not to show his irritation as he asked quietly, "Can you tell us why the EMP bombs went off sooner than they were supposed to?" Jack didn't expect an answer, so he was surprised when Kuan did spoke up.

"The bombs went off before their designated time, for the simple reason that the men in charge of the People's Republic of China are intelligent but paranoid. That is a bad combination. They surely realized that my death was a ruse. As soon as they did, they started the countdown." Here Kuan shrugged.

Jack was perplexed by the man's nonchalance. Jason stared, but then he shook it off and asked the next question,

"Why were you not able to sabotage all the bombs? You told us that you could."

Kuan was already shaking his head before Jason finished. He said, "I told you that I would try! I am only human, and I simply ran out of time!"

This outburst clearly surprised Jason, but Jack was studying Kuan intently. He too was startled but realized that this man was hiding something. Since Jack's ability to read people did not work on him, he could only guess.

Kuan quickly controlled his emotions and Jason resumed his questions. "Can you help us fix what has happened to the atmosphere? Is there anything we can do?"

This was the crucial question. Dai Ji Kuan was the recognized expert in electromagnetics and nanotechnology, and if anyone knew how to change things back, he would be the one to do it.

Kuan zeroed in on Jason and replied, "I cannot explain to you what I can do. I do not know what you have built. If you take me to your shield I will examine it and do what I can. You can be assured that I put my home country's shield out of commission. I made sure that was done first."

Jack could sense that the man was telling the truth, but was confused. There was still something bothering him about Kuan, as if he was holding something back. Jack was familiar with interrogation techniques that could make the man tell them everything, but Kuan had the knowledge they needed to put things right. They couldn't just force the man to cooperate.

Jack sighed with frustration. He tried a different route.

"Jason said there were nuclear bombs to be deployed after the EMP devices were detonated. Are you sure you disabled all of those?"

"I know I deactivated all the nuclear weapons," Kuan said. "I did that immediately after sabotaging our shield. I also must tell you that I have no idea how many other EMP devices were detonated around the world."

This revelation opened up a whole new set of worries for Jack. He hadn't even thought about the rest of the world being in the dark. He had been so engrossed in America's problems he had failed to consider the other EMP devices circling the globe.

"Wait." He held up a finger. "Originally, there were twenty-five bombs in all, right?"

Kuan nodded and Jack continued, "It took only one to wipe out our electricity coast to coast." He was thinking out loud now. "If you were able to disarm some of them, then we have to assume there are countries out there that are still functioning, right?" He was staring at Kuan.

Kuan was staring right back, "Yes. Possibly. However, you must remember that everything from the moment the bombs detonated is purely guesswork. They never even allowed us a test bomb, so we had no idea what to expect. There were many theories, but nothing was certain. At least you Americans tested the atomic bomb. You knew the effects by studying what happened afterward. My government was too afraid America would find out and be able to stop them.

So, to further answer your question, yes, there were probably some areas of the globe that did not get hit. They could be driving their cars and listening to their radios as we speak, but I don't think they are. Do you want to know why? I will tell you. Because of the green color of the sky. In all the theories there was never any conjecture about the sky turning green. Remember that I am *the* expert on electromagnetism and this result never occurred to me. I have had a lot of time since the blast to think about it. My conclusion is simple and complex. No scientist has ever studied perpetually interacting particles. We don't know what they will do." Kuan was looking earnestly at Jack but Jack was semi-lost. Jason was completely left in the dust and apparently their expressions told Kuan this fact.

The defector shook his head and tried again, "You know those perpetual motion toys that you have on your desk—the one with five silver balls in a line hanging from a wire." Here he saw recognition dawn on the two men's faces.

He went on. "You grab one of the silver balls and lift it and drop it, setting the balls in motion! It is the same way with the particles in the atmosphere. Once the electrons are set in motion, they just keep bouncing into one another and generating electrical currents. It isn't perpetual, but it could be years before it goes away." He stopped here and waited for the two men to talk.

Jack understood what Kuan was saying, but he was impatient and wanted to ask one question. "Can we reverse it?"

The very air in the room seemed to stand still as all three men stood in a circle and stared at each other.

Kuan hesitated just a bare second before he said, "Yes, if what you have told me is true, Agent Evans."

Jack looked questioningly at Jason. This was new. Narrowing his eyes at Jason, Jack asked, "Okay, little buddy. What have you told our Chinese friend here?"

Jason was looking at Jack with a blank look and Jack was having none of it. He turned and squared his broad shoulders at the agent.

Jason broke and said, "Okay, okay! I didn't tell you because I didn't have time!"

He rubbed his forehead and then looked at Jack. "This is going to sound crazy, but we have a device—though we are not really sure how it's going to work." Jason looked defiantly at Jack with his hands on his hips.

Jack blinked twice and then asked, "You don't know how this 'device' is going to work? What the *hell* are you talking about?"

Jason got that stern look on his face that Jack remembered seeing in his years of service under the man.

"All I am allowed to say is that another secret department of the government has collaborated with my scientists and has loaned us a device developed with reverse-engineered technology that may be electromagnetic repulsing technology."

Jack was flabbergasted. He opened his mouth twice to say something, then thought better of it and finally asked in all seriousness, "Will it work, Jason?"

Jason focused on his friend and stated, "In theory it should. There are some final issues that my scientists can't figure out. That's why we need Kuan."

Jack looked worried for a few moments, then realized they had no choice. He heaved a sigh, crossed his arms, looked over his shoulder at Kuan, and quietly asked, "If we can get you there, will you try to help us?"

Kuan had intently been studying the communication between Jack and Jason. He realized that these two men were not on the same page, but after a second he nodded. "Yes, I will try my best." After this, he smiled and saw the men relax.

It was getting dark in the room so Jack went in the other room and retrieved a lantern.

After lighting it he turned to Kuan and said, "I have a couple of more questions, if you don't mind."

Kuan still had a big smile on his face when he replied, "Certainly, I will do my best."

"Since you are the expert, tell me what other effects we can expect. I've read a lot of the theories, but I have no idea what's true."

Kuan sighed and then began, "Of course, you know about the total destruction of the electrical grids. All of your electrical plants are fried. Anything that required electricity to operate has been annihilated. Computers, refrigerators, washers, and dryers. None of those things will work. Then you have the secondary things that have been disabled. The automobile is one of these items. Even though it doesn't plug in to an electrical outlet, the new ones do have microchips.

These microchips are extremely sensitive to electromagnetic pulses. As for older vehicles that do not have microchips, it was my theory that when the bombs went off, that they would be disabled also. Because of the electrical wiring and parts throughout the older vehicles, I did not think they would work.

"The bombs we designed and built were much more powerful than the bombs used back in the testing period during the fifties and early sixties. But again, it was all conjecture. I was surprised to see the Dodge truck still worked. Did you keep this truck in a garage?"

This last part surprised Jack but he answered, "It belongs to a friend of mine, and yes, it was in a garage."

Kuan looked thoughtful as he slowly nodded. He then asked another question, "What was the garage made of?"

This question really confused Jack and he had a baffled look on his face as he answered, "It has a metal roof and wooden doors and the walls are made of cinder block."

As Jack finished telling Kuan this last bit, the Chinese man's expression cleared up and he was intensely interested.

"Cinder block? As in concrete?" he asked.

Jack still looked puzzled and nodded.

Kuan was smiling again and was looking at Jack as if he should understand.

Jack rolled his eyes and said, "Tell me what I'm missing."

Jason was really out of the loop now and was just looking back and forth between Jack and Kuan as if he were watching a tennis match.

Kuan took a breath and explained, "One of the things that can be used to shield against electromagnetic pulses is conductive concrete! If the truck was in the concrete building during the pulse, it explains why it still works. It also tells me something else."

Here, Kuan seemed to be talking to himself as he mumbled, "If that is true, then it means that the green glow of the sky will not interfere with electronics once the initial pulse has occurred."

Jack heard him but didn't think Kuan meant for him to. He kept quiet and filed the words away for later reflection. He didn't know what this man was up to, but he would watch him very closely.

Jack stated, "Okay, let me get this right. Only older vehicles are spared. Out of those vehicles, only automobiles that were shielded during the blast will still run?"

Kuan had refocused on Jack and nodded.

Jack blew his breath out and saw that Jason had caught back up.

Jack was back to asking questions. "Let me ask you something else. Cell phones. Are they fried because of the electronics in them? Or is it because of the satellites?"

Kuan didn't hesitate. "Both. The smart phones don't work because of the electronics, and the sat phones don't work because the multiple EMP bombs, orbiting the earth, detonated. When they did, they laid down a fog of radiation in the atmosphere around the globe. As the satellites come into contact with this radiation, it fries the sensitive circuits."

Jack saw Jason start as the knowledge sank in.

"So," Jack said, "even if you get the shield to reverse the EMP effects, and you rebuild to the point of having new cell phones, you would have to launch new communication satellites in order to use the cell phones."

Jason finished the thought, "That would take years!"

Kuan nodded as Jack and Jason sat dumbfounded.

After about two minutes of mulling this over, Jack shook his head and leaned forward. "Let me get this straight. In order to set things back on the right track, we have to first get this 'device' working." Here, Jack glanced at Jason. "Then, we have to use it. If it does work, then we'll have to rebuild the infrastructure. Get the water and sewage going. Then, replace parts and get the vehicles going to haul…"

Jack just quit talking. He was so overwhelmed trying to figure out what to do first, that he couldn't comprehend it all.

He finally shook his head and refocused. He looked at Jason, who was still examining everything, then glanced back at Kuan. He opened his mouth to ask Kuan something else, and then stopped. Kuan had a far-off look on his face.

Jack narrowed his eyes and watched the man for a minute and then spoke. "It looks like we have our work cut out for us. I don't have anything else to ask you right now. Do you, Jason?"

Jason seemed almost back to normal and sighed before he

said, "No. I think that's about all I can take right now."

Jack agreed and, thanking Kuan, watched him leave to go back to his room.

After the man left, Jack and Jason sat alone in the den.

Jack looked sharply at Jason. "This device. Will it work?"

Jason sighed and said, "Like I said before, there are some problems with the finished device. The scientists tried it out on a small scale in an underground chamber a week ago. It should have worked, but it didn't. We thought we had some time before we would need it, if we ever did. That's why I was retrieving Kuan."

Jack looked at Jason doubtfully. "Tell me you didn't pin everything on this guy Kuan."

Jason closed his eyes briefly and said, "Of course not. The plan was to get Kuan and fly him to the facility in Knoxville and question him. We had another expert that was flying to Tennessee from Maryland. He has a PhD in electromagnetics from MIT. Our intention was to get both men together and, between the two of them and you, we hoped to have this EMI device ready by the time we needed it."

Jack interrupted him. "EMI. Electromagnetic interference shielding." Nodding to himself, he mumbled, "I've read about that."

Jason nodded and continued, "Yes, well, that was the plan. As you can see, it didn't quite work out as I had wanted." He waved vaguely at the ceiling.

Jack ignored the sarcasm and asked, "This expert from

Maryland. Where is he now?"

"He should have arrived at the facility the day this all happened. I hadn't been notified by the time the bombs went off. Best-case scenario? He made it and is there now, working on it as we speak. Worst-case scenario? He crashed on the plane as the bombs went off. So, your guess is as good as mine. My job right now is to get Kuan safely to the facility in Knoxville and see if he can do anything with the device."

Jason was steadily looking at Jack.

Jack rubbed his hands across his face. He was so tired. He still had to go talk to Grady and set up a watch schedule. Tomorrow he would have to get everything in order before they left. Jack was estimating that he wouldn't have everything ready to go until the day after tomorrow, but it couldn't be helped.

He related all this to Jason and to the man's credit, he just nodded. They both rose slowly and walked out of the den.

4

Bryan had been out in the woods for about two hours when Emma noticed movement out on the road. She had been going room to room, covertly looking out the windows to keep the sheriff from sneaking up on them. Lori had started out helping Emma watch for the sheriff, but then started worrying so much about Bryan that she said she had to go do something else. Currently, she was dragging things out of the storage room she found above the garage. She was keeping her mind occupied by making a list of what she found. Bella was intensely curious and was following Lori back and forth checking out each item.

"Lori!" Emma hissed, "They're here!"

Lori had just returned with what looked like a tent. She quickly dropped it and rushed to Emma's side.

"How many are there?" Lori whispered back.

They both peered out past the curtain and could see three people on horseback. The sheriff was easy to spot. He was a big man riding a stout horse between the other two men. Emma studied him intently as the men rode closer. He had close-cropped steely gray hair and a thick mustache of the same color. He sat on his horse with authority and ease. Emma could tell that the man knew how to ride. She could also see the sheriff was checking out the area all around the cabin. She prayed that Bryan was paying attention and was staying out of sight.

Emma and Lori had already talked about what they were going to do and how they would act. Quickly, they slipped from the window and went into the kitchen. They had their bags on the floor next to them and appeared to be sorting through foods.

The two women only had a few minutes to wait before they heard a knock on the front door.

Lori looked nervous and Emma grabbed her hand to calm her before she walked to the front door. She had asked Lori to let her do all the talking and Lori had readily agreed. Emma looked around for Bella before opening the door, and saw the end of the cat's fluffy tail disappear into the garage. Good, she thought; that was one less thing she'd have to worry about.

Emma took a deep breath, said a silent prayer, and then confidently opened the door.

Smiling, she looked up at the sheriff and said, "Well, Tony said you would be coming out here." Emma had her Glock holstered on her right hip to make sure he saw it.

The man saw it right away but didn't miss a beat as he smiled widely and said, "Hi there! My name is Frank Green. I'm the sheriff in Pigeon Forge."

He hesitated, waiting for Emma to invite him in. She knew she shouldn't but she made him wait a couple of beats.

As they both stood there with smiles on their faces, Emma

studied the man close up. He had gray eyes that went with the steel-gray hair, and he exuded charm. It made you want to trust the man. However, Emma felt that same underlying vibe that she'd felt with Tony. The sheriff felt "off" somehow.

Knowing she was pushing her luck now, she opened the door wider and, still smiling, asked, "Would you like to come in?"

His smile had slipped a little as the big man waited but now it was back in full force. "Why, thank you, ma'am! I appreciate it."

Frank stepped in and Emma closed the door behind him. She noted that the sheriff's two men stayed on their horses and was glad. She needed to focus on Frank and his reactions as they talked.

She walked past him and saw the man scrutinizing everything.

Lori chose that moment to walk into the living room, and the sheriff zeroed in on Emma's friend.

Emma stepped in front of him and said, "Sheriff Green, my name is Emma Hudson and this is my friend, Lori Bubar." She stuck her hand out and Frank shook it. By this time, Lori was standing confidently next to Emma.

Frank offered his hand to Lori and said, "Ma'am. Nice to meet you both."

Emma saw Lori hesitate and knew her friend was thinking about what Matt had told them about the sheriff.

Bravely, Lori squared her shoulders and shook the man's

hand. Thankfully, Frank didn't seem to notice.

They all sat and the sheriff seemed to look around before he said, "So, Tony told me he talked to you. He told me that there was a man with you. Where is he?"

He still had a pleasant look on his face but his eyes were sharp and in that moment, Emma knew this was not a man to mess with. She needed to be very careful.

Keeping her own expression pleasant and relaxed, she replied, "Oh, you mean Bryan. He said he was tired of canned food and was going hunting." Emma kept her face carefully blank as she studied the sheriff.

He nodded and looked away for a moment then asked, "Has he been gone for a while?"

Emma had to think quickly without acting like it. She felt like she and the sheriff were playing a mental game of poker. *Should she tell the truth? Why does he want to know? Would he use the information against them?* It was nerve-racking!

"He's been gone about an hour," Emma replied keeping it short.

The sheriff was nodding and said, "Well, Tony told me you all talked and he told me most of it. He said you know Jack Denton. Is that true?"

Emma saw that the man wasn't smiling anymore and his eyes were hooded. It hit her then that this man had history with Jack. She was on high alert now.

"I was friends with Jack a few years ago and he called me right before this happened. He is good friends with the owner of this cabin and since I had been here before, he told me to come here if anything happened."

Something she said got the sheriff's full attention. He looked at her sharply and asked, "He called you before this happened?"

Emma mentally backpedaled and, nodding, said, "Yes, he left a voicemail for me."

That was all she would say and she could tell he wanted more answers. "Did Jack know this would happen? What else did he say? Where does he live?"

He was asking these questions one after another and Emma was really getting nervous.

She calmed herself and tried to diffuse the situation. "Jack didn't sound like he knew this would happen. It sounded more like he thought there was a possibility something might happen. He lives in Wyoming and he said if anything *did* happen, if I got here, he would come for me. That's all the voicemail said."

This seemed to satisfy the sheriff for the moment, and calmly he went on. "I know Tony told you a little about what has been happening here and I want to let you know where we stand. We sent riders to most of our neighboring towns in order to try to see if they've been in contact with the government. Apparently, all the surrounding cities are in the same boat we are. No electricity, no automobiles, and no contact with any government authority. We've had some trouble with looting and people causing problems, so the mayor and I have declared a local form of martial law."

He went on to tell them some of the same things that Matt had told them earlier. It just confirmed that Matt was telling the truth. The sheriff left out the part about the shootings and instead said that he and his men ran the looters out of town. He emphasized that the mayor, the judge, and he himself were just trying to keep civil order until things got back to normal. As Emma was listening to this, she realized he was saying all this by rote. Like he was repeating something he said a lot.

Something Frank was saying got her attention and she refocused on the man.

"For the good of the community, I have to ask if you and your friends are staying."

Emma decided to stick with her story. "We're going to ride on out. We'll probably stay here tonight and rest up, then leave tomorrow morning."

The sheriff's face was hard to read as he said, "That's good. I'll be out to check on you all the day after tomorrow. If you do decide to stay, we'll have to register you at the sheriff's office. Tony said you have two horses, is that right?"

Emma nodded and the man went on. "Deciding to stay will make you part of my jurisdiction, and I will have to confiscate one of your horses as well as your handguns."

Emma felt Lori shift and take a breath to say something, so she smoothly leaned forward to cut her off.

"We understand," Emma said with a brilliant smile.

Frank Green was clearly a man who was accustomed to getting what he wanted, and Emma realized they would get no more information out of him. She just wanted the man to leave.

The sheriff seemed mildly perplexed that Emma was being so pleasant but then she stood, still smiling. Lori scrambled to stand too and finally the man got the hint.

He stood but when he reached the door he hesitated before saying, "Don't make trouble in my town." He was staring straight at Emma when he said this. Then he was gone.

As Emma shut the door, Lori let out her breath and started talking. Emma shushed her as she peeked past the curtain, waiting for the men to leave.

When she saw the men round the fence at the end of the driveway, she turned back to Lori and Lori stepped back. The look on Emma's face was not one that Lori had seen very often. Her friend was pissed.

Before either one of them could say anything, Bryan came through the back door in a rush.

"What'd they say?" he asked.

Lori gestured to Emma. She could sense her friend needed to vent and she was right.

Bryan had just gotten close enough to see Emma's expression when he raised his eyebrows at Lori. Lori briefly shook her head at Bryan and turned toward her friend.

Emma was pacing, she was so mad. "Everything Matt said is true. The sheriff is taking advantage of this situation. He's pretending to be the official taking care of the town.

Meanwhile, he's taking care of himself and maybe his friends." She stopped.

Looking at Bryan and Lori, she said, "We can't leave. It's too far to travel to Wyoming, so we have to stay here. We need to go see the Carrolls. I want the sheriff to think we've left and we need more answers to survive until Jack gets here." She was looking at her friends.

Lori and Bryan looked at each other and back at Emma. Bryan was the one to speak. "I don't see where we have much choice, Em."

Emma sighed, then said, "I'm sorry, you guys. It wasn't supposed to be this hard once we got here. I was really looking forward to finally relaxing in one place."

Lori spoke up softly, "We're alive when others are dead, Emma. We're all just trying to do our best. This isn't anything we could have predicted. I, for one, am glad you took us with you. Can you imagine what Atlanta is like right now?" She looked at Bryan for confirmation and he nodded.

Emma had gained some of her resolve back as Lori spoke. She hugged her friend and then rallied. "Okay. You're right. The sheriff says he'll be back the day after tomorrow. Let's get some rest and pack tomorrow. We'll take turns keeping watch tonight. When we leave, we'll lay down a false trail to make them think we're headed out of town. Then we'll double back, cover our trail, and go talk to Matt and his family."

Exhausted after the long day, her two friends agreed and they began to make their plans.

5

Jack couldn't believe they were really on their way. Just as he had suspected, it had taken all of yesterday to plan, prepare, and then execute the packing. They had discussed every tool and item that might be needed along the way. As he handed that task over to Jason and the agents, he then had to have a meeting with Grady and the family. The meeting had taken longer than he had planned. Scott and Danny had to be convinced that they were needed on the ranch.

Jack had put Grady in charge and told him what to say to the townspeople that had come looking for him when he was out retrieving Kuan.

There was also the very serious discussion of what route to take to Tennessee. They had to consider what the conditions might be in different towns along the way and reroute accordingly. Finally, last night at about seven o'clock, they were packed. They were all tired and knew they would wait until morning to leave.

Jack glanced in the rearview mirror at the enclosed trailer. He was glad he had bought it two years ago. It was now carrying some containers of gasoline from his bunker, as well as tow straps, axes, picks, and a slew of other items they might need.

He glanced again in the mirror but this time at the people

in the bed of the truck. The three agents had decided to go with them as well as Kuan, of course.

They were a motley crew, but seemed to be a good group. Jack was satisfied.

They had put a mattress in the bed of the truck to cushion them on the long ride. The group also had plenty of blankets and jackets.

Jack also brought along extra weapons and ammo. Everybody except Kuan had some type of handgun on. You couldn't prepare for everything, but you could damn sure try.

Loading up just as the sun cleared the horizon, they had pulled out into the gloomy green dawn. It had been slow going on the back roads until it had lightened enough to see obstacles better.

They had been driving for three hours and encountered no problems. However, Jack was a worrier. He would be on high alert for the remainder of the journey.

Just as they came around a bend in the road, he saw people on horseback. Thankfully, Jack had learned his lesson on the first trip in the truck. He was now going slower at blind spots in the road.

He pressed the brake and eased to a stop about thirty yards down from the group.

Jack could see the group was surprised to see the truck. He and Jason had discussed this and he looked over his shoulder to see Ray had already covered Kuan up. The ruse wouldn't work if the group ahead saw the Asian man.

Jack saw that Jason had his hand on his handgun and said, "Easy. Let me talk."

He made sure his own gun was ready just in case. He saw the group ahead of them had overcome the shock and were moving toward them. Jack counted three men and two women on horseback. All were armed.

The group was ten feet in front of the truck when they stopped, and the man in the center said, "Hello there!"

Jack hung his elbow out the window and said, "Hello!" with a smile.

The man in the middle seemed to be the leader and was about fifty years old. Wearing a white Stetson, jeans, and a denim cowboy shirt. He asked the same thing Jack would have if their roles were reversed.

"How is it you found a truck that runs?"

Jack kept smiling and answered, "Just got lucky, I guess. I think it has to do with older cars. For some reason, newer autos won't work."

The man seemed to accept this with a nod and then asked, "Where are you from?"

Jack expected this too and said, "Cody. Some of my neighbors are coming with me. I gotta go check on my sister down in Rawlins. Where are you all coming from?"

He was still grinning and asked this last question with an offhand, friendly manner.

The man answered, "We're coming from Thermopolis heading to Cody. I'm the mayor and these are some of the city council. My name's Guy Woods. Do you know what's going on?"

Jack let a look of concern cloud his face as he shook his head and said, "Nope. We've been trying to figure it out. At first, we thought it was something local happened to Pacific Power and Light. Since then, we've figured out it's a lot more than that. That's why I'm worried about my sister. What's going on in Thermopolis?"

The group had all relaxed by now and were just drinking in the information.

"Not a whole lot. We thought it was something local too, but when we went a couple of days without hearing from the outside world, we got together and decided to ride to the nearest city." He was waiting for Jack to tell him more, but Jack was trying to be vague.

"Well, I sure hope they get things going again. I'm about tired of this green sky," Jack replied and let out a chuckle.

Guy laughed with him and then Jack went on, "Had any trouble?"

Now Guy turned serious, "Yeah, we had a group causing some trouble and had to lock them up. I don't even have a judge to do a trial. Things are just going downhill and we need to see what other cities plan on doing."

Jack looked out the front windshield and nodded. "Yep, I know what you mean. Hey, good luck in Cody. I hate to run, but I have to get to my sister." He started up the truck and gave a smile and a brief nod to the mayor and his group and they eased on down the road.

"That was smooth." Jason said.

"Yeah, I hated to lie to them but the less they know right now, the better."

Jack looked back at the truck bed and saw Kuan was back up above the cover. He saw Ray looking at him and Ray gave a curt nod.

This part of Wyoming was pretty flat. He was able to see a ways ahead and Jack increased his speed a little.

The sun was up enough to see clearly and there were just a few cars stalled in the road. These were easy to drive around and he did so carefully. Jack and Jason both knew, now, what was at stake if they wrecked so Jason would point things out and Jack would maneuver.

When they first started out, they had stopped and checked the first couple of vehicles they came to. Now they just drove around them. It would take forever to get to Tennessee if they stopped at every one. You picked your battles.

Over the next two hours, Jack and Jason talked about old times and caught up on the last ten years. Jason asked about Emma and Jack asked about Sarah and Jay Jr.

Soon, they were coming up on Casper and Jack decided to pull to the side. Everybody needed to stretch and pass around some food and water plus, Jack needed to look at the map. He had decided that they needed to take back roads around major cities and he needed to see what roads would take them around Casper and meet back up with I-25.

Jack had stopped on a straightaway and he could see there

was no one for miles. He got out and stretched.

"Jeez!" Greg said, "I thought you'd never stop!" he told Jack.

Jack was learning that Greg was just that way.

"I could've let you stay back at the ranch," he told the youngster, and had the pleasure of seeing him gape like a fish.

"Don't encourage him," Ray said.

Too late. Greg started off on a rant.

Jack ignored them and concentrated on the map. It was about one o'clock in the afternoon and the sun was glaring through the green haze.

He and Jason looked at the map. Jack pointed to some routes around Casper and Jason agreed. They put the map away and shared some lunch.

When everyone seemed satisfied, they all got back in the truck and away they went. They had stopped maybe twenty minutes and in all that time, saw not one human being. It was eerie. Plenty of birds, lizards, and a turtle making its way slowly across the road, but no humans. Actually, Jack could get used to it.

Back on the road, Jack suddenly asked Jason, "If we get this shield going, what then?"

Jason turned to Jack and said, "What do you mean?"

Jack glanced at Jason and saw that he had a blank look. There was a purpose to his question. Jack tried a different angle. "Where is the President, Jason?" He asked this last part offhanded.

Jason hesitated just a fraction of a second, and that was all Jack needed to know he should beware of Jason.

He let the hesitation slide as he listened to the man's answer, "I guess he's in the bunker, underneath the White House. That was the procedure!" He sounded indignant and Jack let it go. For now.

They had driven another hour when they saw smoke on the opposite side of the road and as they got closer, they could see several people sitting around a fire. Jack debated going on but decided to stop. He pulled over when they were about thirty yards from the group. Several people in the group shot to their feet.

Jack told Jason, "Have your gun ready. I'm going to go check them out."

Jason looked at Jack and said, "Why?"

Jack looked back at Jason and said, "Because it's the right thing to do." He slammed the door and walked toward the group.

As he got near, he saw that there were children in the group. Everyone had stood now and looked like they were seeing a vision. Jack continued up to within fifteen feet and stopped.

Before he could say anything a man about forty years old, with a belly and a beard, said, "Wow, did you just drive up in a truck?"

Jack smiled and nodded, "Yep. I did. How long have you all been out here?"

He counted seven people. Four adults and three children.

The man with a belly spoke up again, "Ever since that bright light flashed! The cars just quit." He motioned to the four cars Jack could see up and down the road.

"Everyone got out and after a while, the owners of the other cars started walking. They didn't have kids like we do." He emphasized this by indicating the group.

On closer inspection, Jack saw that they all seemed to favor the man with the belly and the woman by his side.

The speaker confirmed this with his next words, "We were traveling up to see Yellowstone. My name is Craig Runnels." He went around the circle introducing his family. The other two adults were his twenty-year-old son and the boy's girlfriend.

The introductions had given Jack time to think. "I'm from Cody," he said. "My family and I happened to get this old truck running and now we're going to check on my sister in Nebraska. If you're waiting for some help to come by, you might be waiting a long time. Everything is down. Electricity, phones, computers, and of course automobiles. Do you have enough food?"

Craig shook his head. "We ran out yesterday and I was just getting ready to hike back to Douglas."

Jack knew that Douglas was about twenty miles down the road. He wished he could give the man a ride, but didn't want the man asking questions about Kuan.

He made a decision. "I can spare some food for your family to have until you get back. I wish I could give you a ride, but I don't have room. I do want to let you know something. There are a lot of bad people out there. Now that the power is out, there are groups of people causing trouble in the cities and towns. Go to the smallest town you can. You might be able to appeal to farm or ranch owners. Be careful, it's dangerous out there."

The family had looked more and more concerned as Jack spoke. Now Craig's wife asked Jack, "What about the police?"

Jack said, "Ma'am, the police are there, but they have their hands full. Just be careful. I'll be back with some food."

He didn't give them a chance to answer. He turned and went back to the trailer. Opening it, he grabbed some dry food supplies and returned to Craig and his family. Jack handed the man a small bottle of water purification tablets and pointed toward the North Platte River. Explaining how to use the tablets, he set the rest of the things down. He wished the family well and returned to the truck. Starting the truck up, he headed past the group and gave them a short wave. It bothered Jack that he couldn't do anything more for the family. He knew, however, that there would be many more people that he would have to pass by. He had to look at the bigger picture. The longer it took him to get to Knoxville, the more society would degrade.

Jason interrupted his thoughts, "Where do you want to spend the night?"

It was a good question, and Jack answered, "There's an interchange that we have to turn off on at highway 26. We're going to go around Douglas here in a minute and we should make it to that interchange in about two hours. I thought we would shelter there."

Jason nodded and turned to look out the side window.

Jack was slowing down to go around two cars blocking the road when he noticed a low rumbling. He bunched his eyebrows together and stopped the truck. He thought it was something in the engine until the rumbling grew louder and the truck started to shake. Jack noticed the cars next to him were starting to shimmy as well, and it dawned on him what was happening. He quickly pressed the accelerator and got the truck into the clear. Jason said, "What the hell? Are we seriously having—?"

He wasn't able to get the question out of his mouth before a violent shake jerked the truck and trailer sideways, and Jack stomped the gas and wrenched the steering wheel to keep them from sliding into the ditch. The deep growl of the engine warred with the growl of the earthquake as the back tires tried to grab the edge of the pavement. Finally, they caught hold, and Jack quickly eased up on the gas and spun the steering wheel back the other way. Jack allowed the truck to come to a stop as he realized the earthquake had gone as quickly as it had come.

Jumping out of the cab, Jack briefly checked on the four in the back before striding to the back of the trailer. He felt sure the gasoline was okay, as it was in sealed plastic containers, but he just wanted to double-check. He made sure to check all around for strangers before opening the trailer door.

Jason joined him as he swung the door wide. "The gas?"

Jack didn't smell anything and that was good. He looked at the containers and confirmed they were still sealed. He sighed with relief and looked at the rest of the supplies. It all looked secure.

"It looks okay," Jack said for Jason's benefit.

Jason let out his breath as the rest of the group gathered at the back of the trailer.

"Was that an earthquake?" Greg asked.

"Yeah," Jack answered as he closed the trailer door.

Everybody but Kuan started asking questions at one time. Jack raised his hand for silence.

"Ray, could you, Cat, and Greg check around and make sure there aren't any people in these cars? Might as well, since we're at a standstill," Jack said.

Ray nodded and took the other two with him.

Jack wanted to talk to Kuan without the others around. He and Jason turned to Kuan.

Dai Ji Kuan looked back at the men serenely.

Once again, Jack wished he could get a feel for the man.

Mentally shaking his head, Jack stated, "You don't seem to be very surprised."

Jason stood a little to the side and Jack saw him twitch in alarm.

Kuan, however, didn't move a muscle. Jason slowly looked over at Kuan.

Jack narrowed his eyes at Kuan and quietly said, "Why don't you tell me why we just had a substantial earthquake here in Wyoming, and why you aren't surprised."

While he waited for Kuan to speak, he studied Jason out of the corner of his eye. Jason seemed genuinely surprised, but there was another expression that Jack didn't expect. Cold calculation. The kind of cold calculation that one man would give another if he thought that man was cheating.

Jack returned his attention to Kuan; he'd have to think about Jason later. He needed to know about the damn earthquake right now.

Kuan cleared his throat and said, "There have been some studies recently that stated it was possible that large earthquakes could be caused by massive coronal mass ejections."

Jack and Jason were blinking, waiting for elaboration. When it was clear that Kuan was not going to say more, Jack motioned for him to provide more info.

It was clear that the defector was reluctant to say more, but he sighed and continued, "I am aware of ongoing studies that were tracking CMEs from the sun and their connection to major earthquakes here on earth. Most people think that solar flares are the same as coronal mass ejections. They are not. Solar flares are, technically, a large release of light. Coronal mass ejection is the release of billions of particles from the sun. CMEs are magnetic shockwaves that, when directed at earth, can have an effect on earth's magnetic field.

"Supposedly, in the past, when the sun released a major CME, two to three days later there would be a major earthquake or volcanic eruption. These studies were just starting last year, so they were not complete. The possibility was there, yes. That is why I was not surprised."

Jack said, "You're telling us that, because of the overwhelming manmade electromagnetic field, the earth is now reacting to this?"

Jason was studying Kuan closely.

Kuan looked resigned. "Earth is responding to the accumulating electromagnetic field surrounding us now."

Jack shook his head. "Will the earthquakes increase? And what was that about volcanoes?"

Kuan shook his head sadly. "I am at a loss, just as you are. I knew of some possible effects. However, as I have said before, we are breaking new ground here."

Jack realized that Kuan either could not or would not say anything more. He sighed and looked around. Seeing that the three agents had returned, he knew they needed to get going.

"Did you find anything?" Jack asked the three.

Ray spoke up. "No. All we saw were abandoned cars."

Jack nodded and they all headed back to the truck. As Jack climbed back into the driver's seat, a thought hit him, and he hesitated. Yellowstone was a caldera. The thought hit him so hard, he hesitated with one foot in the truck and one on the ground. He had known for several years that Yellowstone was considered a sleeping super volcano. He had studied it on the Internet, but concluded that, even though it had had violent eruptions in the past, it was not considered an eruption hazard. But now? With the massive electromagnetic overload in the atmosphere, there was no predicting what could happen.

Jason and the others were already loaded up and all eyes were on Jack.

Jason said, "What's wrong?"

Jack came to the swift and awful conclusion that there was nothing he could do to help his extended family back at the ranch. He was now in the race of a lifetime to get to Knoxville and try to set things right. It was all he could do.

To Jason he said, "Nothing. Let's go."

With a new sense of urgency, Jack got in, put the truck in gear, and weaved his way through the rest of the empty automobiles.

In the back of the truck, Ray was worried. He had been standing behind Jack long enough to hear the end of the conversation. Cat and Greg hadn't been there long enough to get the information. He was debating whether to tell his fellow agents about the new dangers. After a silent internal struggle, Ray decided to tell them later, when they stopped for the evening.

Suddenly, he felt Cat's hand on his arm and looked sharply at her. She was looking up at the green sky with awe on her face. He followed her stare and felt his own jaw fall open. As they watched, there were sparks of small reddish light high up in the sky. It lasted for just a minute. Glancing quickly at Kuan, he saw that the man was smiling to himself after seeing the display. *There's a lot more he knows that he's not telling*, Ray thought to himself, and resolved to keep a closer eye on the defector.

Ray asked Kuan, "What was that?"

Kuan replied simply, "Red sprites."

With exasperation, Greg asked, "And what in the hell is that?"

Luckily they weren't going very fast, so it was easy to hear Kuan. "It is a discharge of electricity. Before the bombs, it was a rarely seen phenomenon only visible high in the atmosphere during electrical storms."

Ray asked the obvious, "So why are we seeing it now?"

Kuan shrugged, "I assume it is because of the still highly charged atmosphere." He said nothing more and the three agents were left with their own thoughts.

They drove two more hours before they stopped for the evening. They made a lot better time than they thought they would, so Jack drove on past the overpass.

When they had made it past Torrington, it was almost dark. Jack found a secluded field and pulled far off the road. Everyone was tired but got out and started to set up camp. Jack had brought some military surplus tents and Ray sent Greg to help start handing out gear.

Ray took Cat and scouted the perimeter. They needed to keep an eye out. Even though they were off the beaten path, they still needed to keep watch. Ray pointed to his eyes and carved a half circle with his fist. Cat was about fifty yards away and he saw her head off into the night. Ray took the other half of the circle and started walking the boundary.

As he walked quietly, he looked for anything unusual. He thought back about the red sprites and knew he would have to tell Jason about them. He had no idea what the damn sprites were, he just had his gut instinct telling him that events were accelerating.

Ray was still brooding when he thought he saw something moving out by the road.

Instantly, Ray went down on one knee and had his weapon pointed at the moving shadow. The green glow lent him some light, but he had to wait to make sure. All of a sudden, about twenty-five yards away, Ray saw the shadow shift, and then a horse snorted. Ray was zeroed in with his handgun and moved quickly in a crouch toward the target.

Adrenaline pumping, he calmed himself and said, "Show yourself!"

There was a brief pause, then Ray heard someone on the horse say quietly, "Hey man, I'm not your enemy."

Switching on his flashlight, Ray replied, "I've got you covered. Why don't you just ease off the horse and lay down any weapons."

The man had his hands up and nodded. He slowly dismounted and eased his six-shooter out of its holster before tossing it to the ground. Ray edged up closer to the man and looked him over. He was in his fifties, with a blond mustache sprinkled with gray. He wore a black flat-brimmed cowboy hat, jeans, and a black long-sleeved t-shirt. Battered black cowboy boots adorned his feet and with a matching leather holster on his hip, he looked for all the world like what Ray pictured a modern-day gunslinger would look like.

Ray stood about fifteen feet from the man and asked, "What's your name and what are you doing here?"

The man smiled easily. "Samuel Harding is my name. As to what I'm doing, I've been watching you all from across the road. Your group is the first I've seen that's going somewhere with a purpose, not to mention you have a truck that runs."

Ray sensed Cat arriving at his side and made a quick decision. The stranger was visibly curious but hadn't made any threatening moves. Jason and Jack would definitely want to talk to the man.

Ray asked Cat, "Could you pick up the man's gun? And grab his horse." Cat nodded.

To Samuel, Ray said, "My name's Ray and that's Cat. We'll take you to see Jason and he can figure out what to do with you."

Samuel surprised Ray by tipping his hat at Cat, then held out his hand for Ray to shake. "Nice to meet you. Just call me Sam."

Ray shook his hand awkwardly and said, "Sure thing, Sam."

The two men walked toward the truck while Cat followed with the horse.

As they arrived, Ray saw that the group had set up camp on the side of the truck away from the road.

Jason turned and Ray said, "This is Sam Harding. We found him near the road watching us set up."

Cat handed Sam's gun over to Jason and passed him the reins. The two left to finish checking the perimeter.

Jason raised his eyebrows and asked, point blank, "What are you doing out here, Mr. Harding?"

The stranger took his hat off and ran his hand through his mid-length dark hair.

"I'm a friend of Nebraska governor, Craig Manning. He's sent me on an errand," Sam said, vaguely.

Jason looked at the man and then over at Jack.

Jack shrugged then spoke. "Well, we were about to eat. Are you hungry?"

Sam smiled gratefully and said, "I could eat something."

Jack saw that Greg was listening and that Kuan was resting against the trailer tire.

Jack already had some food out and went back to the trailer to get another MRE.

Jason had already parceled out the rest of the food, saving two meals for Ray and Cat. Jack took a seat next to the newcomer.

Sam opened his meal and dug in. Jack and Jason did the same and all was quiet.

When they were almost finished, Jack said offhandedly, "Are you military?"

Sam calmly looked at Jack. "I used to be. Back in the nineties. Desert Storm."

Jack saw Jason start to say something and he spoke first. "I guess you've figured out that we're military too."

He saw Jason look startled and ignored him.

Sam looked at Jack and grinned. "Yep, I did." He said nothing more and Jack thought for a moment.

Jack decided to continue and looked straight at the man. "Look, to be honest with you, we're trying to set things right. We're on a mission, and if we do this right, we might be able to see America back on its feet."

Sam looked at Jack, unsurprised, and said, "I hope that works out for you."

Jack had told the man as much as he had, in the hopes that Sam would share info with him. He was a little bewildered that the man didn't seem more curious than he did.

"You don't seem surprised." He stated this to draw the man out and it worked.

"To be up front with you, I'm not," Sam replied. "I knew there would be people out working to get things going again. I just think you're wasting your time."

Jack could understand the man's feelings. The EMP blast was a huge blow to mankind and the advances that had been made. Then again, Sam didn't have all the information they had.

He started to ask another question, but Jason spoke up instead. "You said you were on an errand from Governor Manning. Can you tell us what's going on?"

Jack sensed that Jason was trying to steer the conversation away from their purpose. Jack sat back and observed.

Sam took his time finishing his meal, then replied, "Craig and I have been friends since we served together in Iraq. When we got back, he became ambitious and finally got elected governor. I was a lot more laid back and just wanted to see America. We always kept in touch and I finally settled back down here in Nebraska. I would visit Craig and have a few beers. He read a whole bunch and knew all about conspiracy theories and such, so when that bomb went off, he suspected what had happened and filled me in."

Here Sam stopped and looked directly at the two men. "He didn't like the way the federal government was going in the last few years, and he wasn't alone. The South Dakota governor and the governor of Wyoming are friends of Craig and they had all felt the same way for the past few years. Of course there was nothing they could do about it before this happened. It was just blind luck for Craig that this happened when it did."

Jack and Jason froze as they listened to Sam openly talk about how three governors did not like the federal government. For the two men, this was surprising. It was one thing to read people's opinions on the Internet from a warm, comfortable living room. It was another to hear about it during a catastrophic event when most people would be trying to contact federal emergency management to help them get things organized.

Jack recovered first and asked, "What do you mean, 'blind luck'?"

Sam sat for a minute thinking about how much he should say. Gathering himself, he said, "You guys seem to be decent men, and I know you can't call anyone and tell them, so I will tell you this: Craig and the other governors are quickly joining forces. They are taking care of their own people and getting organized. They remember Hurricane Katrina and are determined that will not happen here. They tried, at first, to contact the National Guard armories in their states, but quickly found out that communication with these facilities was useless. The commanders had their hands full just trying to keep their soldiers from going home to their families, and weren't having much success. Those soldiers know what an EMP blast is and the reality of how deep we are in trouble. When it comes down to it, you want to be home defending your loved ones, not fighting for a system that has no leadership."

Sam's eyes were on fire as he paused and looked at the two men and then continued. "I believe in Craig. He's a good man who loves his country and his state. When he asked me to be his courier between him and the other two governors, I agreed. So, you two go ahead on your 'mission' and I really do wish you well, but we are not waiting for the feds to come save us. From what I understand, even if you get rid of the aftereffects, it will take years to rebuild all that has been destroyed…if it ever is.

"Craig and the others have enough resources among them

to take care of their own people. He is already gathering the Nebraska citizens that need his help, and moving them to the Lincoln/Omaha area. He is forming his own militia, and they're calling themselves the Husker Army—after the Cornhusker nickname."

Sam finished talking, stood up, and stretched. Jack and Jason stood with him.

The cowboy had seemed to calm down and said, "I appreciate the food but I'd like to get going."

Jason looked at Jack and Jack shrugged.

Jason let out a sigh, but handed Sam back his gun. He thanked the two men and walked to his horse.

Sam got on his horse, tipped his hat to the men, and then he was gone.

Jack was behind Jason and as the man rode off into the dark, Jason turned to him and said, "Maybe we should have held him."

Jack looked at the man in surprise. "What for, Jason? Don't you think this is going on all over the country? What would we have done with him? Keep him tied up and lug him to Tennessee with us? It came to me while Sam was telling us about those governors, it has been a week now and nothing has changed, except to get worse.

"Where is our government? I have yet to see any troops or hear anyone we've come across say anything about word from our military. You haven't said anything and you're part of the government. Why don't you tell me what the federal plan is for this kind of emergency?"

Jack had been getting more irate the more he spoke, and his anger was directed at Jason. He had moved within six inches of the man's face.

Jason looked irritated at Jack's burning questions, and Jack saw a fleeting look of alarm before Jason replied, "You know the government is compartmentalized, and I wasn't made aware of all that was happening. I only know of one other thing that the committees were doing and had accomplished just last year. They made sure that all the nuclear power plants were hardened against an EMP and are now self-sustained. At least there won't be a nuclear meltdown in the next few months, but we have got to get this fixed so we can keep a meltdown at bay. The self-sustainability will not last forever."

The idea of a meltdown hit Jack like a physical blow. He hadn't even thought about the multiple nuclear power plants across the United States, and it was welcome news that at least the government had bought them some time before the shit really hit the fan.

Jack saw that Greg and Kuan had been listening but it didn't matter. Mentally Jack reorganized what his priorities were. He had always put Emma up near the top, if not at the top of the list. With what he had heard from Sam, Jack had a better understanding of what would be happening in America and how he needed to proceed.

Jason was trying to talk to Jack, but Jack waved him off and walked away, organizing his thoughts.

He walked down to a creek about thirty yards away. He

eased down next to the turgid water and zoned out. He closed his eyes and thought about all that had happened.

When Jason came to him a week ago, Jack believed it would be a relatively easy trip. Go down to Tennessee, get the shield up and running, grab Emma, and come back to the ranch. The government would clean up the mess, while he and his extended family defended and lived off the ranch until things got back to normal. How stupid of him.

He had not figured in the human nature factor of people taking serious advantage of the situation. This was happening and was happening, surprisingly, quickly.

Jack thought about Emma and what she could be going through. As he did so, he stood up and began to pace. After a minute, he stopped and took a deep breath.

He closed his eyes and focused on slowing his breathing. He thought about Emma and centered on his love for her. Everything came into sharp focus. He could feel Emma was still southeast of him and he sensed she was safe. His concentration broke then and he stumbled. He didn't do this often and for good reason. It always gave him a bad headache and made him feel nauseated.

He stumbled to the side and threw up his supper in a bush. After a minute, he wiped his mouth and sat down on the ground, winded.

He slowed his breathing as he had done for many years, and after about five minutes, he was calm. He still had the headache and knew it would stay with him until tomorrow some time. He didn't care. He knew Emma was still alive.

He allowed himself a few more minutes to firm up what he was going to do. It was still important to get Kuan down to Knoxville and try to start the shield. Now, however, it was imperative not only that he watch his ass around Jason, who he was convinced had an alternate agenda, but also against militias that would be getting organized and more dangerous.

No matter what happened in Knoxville, he had to find Emma and return to the ranch. Everything he cared about was there, and whether he lived or died, he swore it would be on his own terms with his loved ones.

He tested his legs and when he realized he was good, he walked back to camp.

As he reached the truck, he saw that Cat and Ray were back eating supper and that apparently, Greg and Jason were taking their turn at guard.

Ray's mouth was full, so he nodded at Jack and Jack nodded back.

Jack walked over to Kuan and asked how he was.

Kuan looked up from where he still sat against the trailer tire and smiled pleasantly. "I am good, Jack. Thank you for asking."

Jack acknowledged the man and continued to the back of the trailer where he opened it up and found the first-aid kit. He retrieved some aspirin and a canteen of water to wash them down.

As he finished, he heard something, whipped his revolver out with lightning speed, and pointed.

Seeing that it was Ray, he relaxed; and the big agent walked toward him with one eyebrow raised. "I know the feeling. I'm a wee bit jumpy myself."

Jack mumbled agreement as he holstered his weapon and replaced the water canteen.

"What's up, Ray?"

Jack sat down on the edge of the trailer and Ray eased down beside him. He had checked Jack out in the firelight and saw that the man looked pale. He asked Jack, "Are you okay? You don't look so good."

He watched as Jack rubbed his face and then the man looked at him and said, "I'll be fine. What is it?"

Ray let it go and said, "I'll be telling Jason, but I haven't had a chance yet. On the drive here, after the earthquake, Cat and I saw some red streaks up in the sky. When we asked Kuan about them, he said they were red sprites. Do you know what they are? He wouldn't elaborate. He just said the atmosphere must still be highly charged."

He waited while Jack thought. Jack was rubbing his head for a minute, then dropped his hand. He looked sideways at Ray and said, "You haven't had a chance to talk to Jason, huh?"

Ray shook his head. Jack sighed and because he felt Ray was a good person, better than Jason, even, he related everything Sam had told them. When he was done, he was exhausted but felt better having told Ray something he felt sure that Jason never would have.

Ray sat for a minute then asked Jack, "Why did you tell me that?"

Jack stood up and said, "You're a good guy, Ray. I just feel like you need to have all the pieces to the puzzle."

Not waiting for Ray to answer, Jack went on, "I have a bad headache and need to rest. Tell everyone I'll take extra shifts of guard duty tomorrow, but I can't right now."

He was too tired to say more. Saying a prayer for Emma, he dragged himself to the truck, shut himself in the cab, and passed out.

6

Emma had been up since Lori woke her at two. Thankfully, it had been quiet outside. Bella had kept her company
for a while as Emma walked from window to window. Emma
had quickly become bored, so to make the time go by faster,
she had started going through things and packing.

She had not realized how noisy the world had been until
the blast happened. The noise of refrigerators humming,
clocks ticking, heaters and air conditioners kicking on—none
of that could be heard now. It was eerily quiet.

Emma had just finished placing the last of the packed
items by the door when she saw Bryan. She had kept the
fire going and rigged a grate in the fireplace to boil a pot of
water.

Bryan stretched. "How'd it go? Any problems?"

Emma smiled and shook her head. "Nothing. I went
outside a couple of times. I was just thinking how quiet it
is without all the technology. It makes you focus on nature.
Crickets, frogs, and other animals. No car noises. It was just
nice."

The water was starting to boil so Emma went to the
kitchen for two mugs. She found some instant coffee and
spooned some into the mugs.

Walking back into the room, she handed one of the mugs to Bryan and grabbed the pot with a rag. After pouring some of the water into the mugs, she placed the pot on the hearth. Bryan wrapped his hand around the mug and thanked her.

Emma waited until he got them some sugar and then asked, "What do you think about going to Matt's?"

Bryan blew on his coffee as he thought, then answered, "I don't think we have a choice. We're new here. If the sheriff is not going to play by the rules, we need to be with the people who know what is going on. I think we are good folks. We have to wait here for Jack, right? So, I think we should be on the side that helps each other. Matt felt right to me. I don't know how to explain it, but, the sheriff felt bad…not right, you know?"

He took a sip of his coffee and looked at Emma over the cup.

Emma nodded and agreed. "I felt the same way. Tony sat wrong with me and so did the sheriff. If we were in the old world, I would play by the rules. This is a brand new world. We're going to have to feel our way through this with gut instinct. I don't trust Tony, and I don't trust Sheriff Green. I think if we stay here we will have to do what they say because he has the power, the guns, and the men. I don't like it. He has control and, if he is bad, we will be under his control. I won't do it."

She saw Lori coming down the stairs. Emma set the pot of water back on the grate to boil for Lori.

"Hey, Lori, Bryan and I were just discussing going to

Matt's. What's your opinion?"

Lori put up a hand to stop Emma. "Wait. Let me get some coffee first."

Emma smiled and retrieved a cup with coffee granules for her.

Lori thanked her and poured some hot water. She stirred in the sugar then sipped.

Emma saw Bryan was watching all this with an amused look on his face—and maybe something else. Bryan was falling for Lori, and it made Emma happy. Lori had secretly liked Bryan for quite a while now, but Bryan had wanted to go out with Emma until he'd found out just how much Emma loved Jack.

Lori brought Emma back to the present by announcing, "We need to go to the Carrolls'. Something's not right with this sheriff."

Bryan nodded. "Emma and I were just saying the same thing. So it's unanimous."

Emma nodded and said, "I packed while keeping watch, so go through your bags and see if there's anything else you want to take. I'm going to saddle the horses."

* * *

Two hours later, they were mounted and packed and had determined which way to head to lay down a false trail. It had taken her a while to find Bella, but she had finally located her in the basement and the feline was safely in her backpack.

Emma was in the lead and her friends were riding double on the sorrel. At least they had a name for him now. As Lori had been trying to straddle him earlier, he kept easing away. Lori kept telling him to scoot toward her, so now his name was Scooter.

Emma grinned thinking about it. Leave it to her little friend to come up with the perfect name.

She was still grinning as she led them off to the north. They had only gone a few steps when a man stepped out from behind a tree pointing a rifle at the trio.

After her initial surprise, Emma sighed, *What the hell now?*

The friends had come to a stop and the man asked, "Who the hell are you, and what are you doing in my house?"

Nobody moved and Emma blinked twice before realization dawned on her and she stammered, "L-Lar-ry?"

The man visibly started then slightly moved the gun away from his face. "Do I know you?" he asked.

"Not personally, but you know a good friend of mine, Jack Denton."

The man hesitated again but then refocused. "How do you know Jack?"

Emma said, "We almost got married a few years ago. He might have told you about me. I'm Emma."

This seemed to jar his memory as recognition dawned on

the man's face.

"Emma? Jack brought you here a few years back, right?"

He had lowered his rifle during this exchange and Emma relaxed a little. "Yes. That was me. To answer your question of why we're here, Jack had called me just before this happened." Here she waved at the green sky, and then continued, "He said something might happen, and if it did, I should come here."

"Here?" Now the man slung the rifle over his shoulder. "I thought you and your family lived on Jack's ranch."

Emma opened her mouth to answer when a woman with a long blond braid stepped out behind Larry.

Emma raised her eyebrows at Larry. He looked back at the woman and said, "May I introduce my wife, Rita." He smiled and his blue eyes softened. Emma could tell he loved the woman.

This reminded Emma of her own bad manners and she introduced Lori and Bryan.

With everyone acquainted, Larry asked again why she wasn't in Wyoming.

Emma realized she was anxious to get out of the open. She also knew she owed this man and his wife some explanations. After all, it was his cabin.

Trying not to sigh, she looked back at Bryan and Lori. They understood and Bryan rolled his eyes. Hoping that Larry hadn't seen Bryan do this, she turned back to the couple, "Can we go back in the cabin? I think we all need to talk."

Larry and Rita agreed.

As Emma dismounted, she studied the couple. For some reason, she expected Larry to be taller. He was an inch taller than she, putting him about five foot ten. He was also very muscular, like he worked out. His brown hair was cut short like Jack's, but that was the only thing that they had in common.

Emma turned her attention to Rita. The same height as Larry, her blond hair was in a messy braid that reached about four inches past her shoulders. The woman had brown eyes and was lean and tan.

Larry and his wife looked disheveled and dirty. Emma had the impression that they had traveled a long way.

Bryan told Emma that he would take care of the horses and keep a lookout. She could fill him in later. She thanked him and followed the others in the house.

Closing the back door, Emma saw that Lori had grabbed the pot from the hearth and was filling it with water.

Emma asked, "Would you two like some coffee?"

She saw their eyes light up and smiled as she said, "It's the least we can do since it's your coffee."

She added wood to the coals and stoked the fire. Lori placed the pot of water on the grate to boil and Emma turned to the couple.

They all sat and Emma took a breath and started, "I haven't seen Jack in a long time. Several years, in fact."

At this, Larry looked puzzled and opened his mouth to say something.

Emma held up her hand and he stopped. "That being said, I kept in contact with my family. I've been living in Atlanta for the past few years, getting my nursing degree. I would have finished next week and was going to move back home when all of this happened. I don't want to get into why I was living in Atlanta when I obviously love Jack. That's a long story. Let's just say I had my reasons and what's done is done. The night before the bomb went off, Jack left me a voice mail saying to come to the cabin if something happened. I had no idea what it meant until the next day."

Lori was nodding throughout the story, and Larry and Rita had settled in to listen.

Emma continued, "Lori and Bryan are my friends and worked with me at the hospital. We were having lunch together in downtown Atlanta when the bomb went off.

"We had no idea what had happened, until we made it back to my apartment. It was then that I remembered a TV show about an EMP bomb. It all made sense. I also remembered Jack's cryptic message and asked Lori and Bryan if they wanted to come with me. I hope you don't mind."

Larry and Rita had been listening intently, and at Emma's last words, he said he was glad they had all made it.

Emma waited as Lori got the two some coffee, then asked, "Where have you two come from? It looks like you've been through hell."

Larry and Rita looked at each other and he answered, "We

pretty much have. We flew in to McGhee Tyson airport about an hour before the bomb went off. We were at the counter to pick up our car rental to come here and spend a few days, when it all went down. Rita and I are lucky to be alive.

"There was a flash of bright light and a rumble like thunder. Everyone stopped and looked around. The power went out and people on their cell phones were trying to get them to work. Then the planes started crashing. There were explosions and screams. I grabbed Rita and we started to run toward the front of the airport. I didn't understand what was happening at that point, we just ran on instinct.

"We had almost made it out the front door, when TSA locked down the airport. I guess we all were thinking planes had been hijacked again. We didn't think about the power going out until later.

"Security rounded everybody up and took us to the middle of the airport. We could tell they were as scared as we were, but at least they had a plan. People get used to listening to authority, so we all just did what they told us and sat tight.

"A few hours later, we could tell that the lights weren't going to come back on and this weird green glow wasn't going away. All of us civilians were getting restless. The TSA workers were getting anxious too. You could tell they hadn't been trained for that.

"After people started begging the guards to let us go, the guy in charge finally realized there really wasn't any reason to keep us there, so he released everyone."

Rita looked distraught, and Larry put his arm around his

wife to comfort her. He continued, "It was awful. When the planes were crashing, we could see airport workers trying to take fire trucks and ambulances out to the runways but the vehicles wouldn't work. Eventually, the workers ran out to the wreckage and tried to help whoever might have survived, but the fires were too hot and large. All they could do was watch.

"When they finally let us go, Rita and I walked down to baggage claim and got our luggage. The whole time we sat there, I had been thinking about what had happened and came to the conclusion that it was an EMP detonation. I had read up on it years ago after talking to Jack. Since the nature of my business is dependent on electricity and computers, I knew I had to find out all I could. Nothing ever happened, so I thought maybe Jack was wrong."

Here, Larry looked at his wife then back at Emma. "I should have known. Jack is rarely ever wrong. Anyway, after they let us go and we got our luggage, Rita and I waited until everyone else left and then we went through our luggage and the other bags that were there. I wanted to supply ourselves with what I knew we might need for the walk home. I had told Rita what was going on, but didn't let anyone else know. I didn't want to set off a panic."

Emma and Lori were captivated by the tale, so both of them jumped when Bryan opened the back door and yelled, "Riders!"

Emma stood up and ran to the back window. She saw that there were three riders and two dogs, and the leader was Tony.

"Shit! Shit! Shit!" she said viciously.

Larry and Rita were right beside her at the window, and he was surprised at her tone. "What the hell is it?"

She rubbed her forehead, thinking, then quickly said, "Listen, these guys are not good. They're deputies for the sheriff and I can't explain it all now, but just trust me! You don't know what's going on here. It's complicated and I'll explain it after they leave, but you two need to hide. Now!"

As Emma spoke, Larry and Rita became more alarmed at her tone of voice. To their credit, though, they didn't argue. Larry quickly pulled his wife away from the window and into the depths of the cabin.

Emma returned her attention to the riders and composed herself.

Lori had caught on to Emma's plan and grabbed the couple's cups and hid them.

Emma mumbled her thanks as she opened the back door and stepped out.

The riders had made it to within twenty feet of the back door and stopped. The dogs were German shepherds and were sniffing around, excited. Emma tried to ignore the dogs and concentrate on Tony.

"What can I do for you, deputy?" She was trying to be cheerful and appear helpful.

Before he answered, Emma glanced to see where her friends were and saw that Bryan was a little off to the side with the rifle pointed halfway between the ground and Tony.

Not quite threatening, but not exactly relaxed. Lori was slightly behind Emma and she could feel her friend was tense.

Tony leaned over the pommel and said, "We were on patrol this morning, in my sector, and the dogs got a whiff of something. We followed them and, well, here we are." He finished with a grin on his face that Emma didn't like.

Thinking quickly, Emma said smoothly, "I'm sure they came across Bryan's trail. Didn't Sheriff Green tell you that Bryan went hunting yesterday?" She secured an innocent look on her face, but made sure the man knew she was amazed that the sheriff forgot to tell him this.

Tony looked at the two men with him, quickly, and sat back on the saddle, "Yeah, he told me about the hunting. I just wanted to check everything out and see what you all had decided."

This verbal game put the ball back in her court, and Emma was ready. "Well, as you can see," here she spread her hands at the bags left around, "we're about to head out to Wyoming." She shot him the brightest smile she could.

Tony expected this and nodded knowingly. "I'll be sure and tell Sheriff Green." He pulled his horses reins and signaled the other men with him.

Emma kept smiling and acting dumb. She even waved at them and she saw Lori follow suit.

She reached down and busied herself getting the bags ready as the men disappeared into the woods. She was glad to see the dogs had given up sniffing around and had gone with the riders.

Under her breath, Emma said, "Look like you're getting everything ready to go!"

Bryan slung the rifle over his shoulder and started loading the bags on the horses. Lori just tried to look busy.

Emma kept watching the riders to see if they were suspicious. It looked like they bought the story, but Emma wanted to make sure.

"Bryan!" she whispered, "watch which way they go, then circle around and follow them. I want to make sure they don't come back."

Bryan mumbled his agreement. After they had been gone about five minutes, Bryan quickly took off to the east in a circular path toward the deputies.

Emma was impressed as she watched Bryan leave. For a California boy, he sure knew his way around the woods.

As the group disappeared, Emma stopped what she was doing and went into the cabin. As she reached the living room, she ran into Larry and Rita coming down from the second floor.

Before Emma could say anything, Larry spoke up, "What the hell is going on? I know that man, that's Tony Moore. He's a deputy now? I'm sorry, tell us what's happened."

Emma was glad he had stopped talking. She sat the two down and rapidly told them what had happened to the trio since their arrival here. She even told them how she felt as she talked to the sheriff and Tony. She also let them know about the visit from Matt Carroll, and what he had to say.

When she finished, Larry and his wife looked horrified. She knew how they felt and said, "Look, we didn't expect to have to decide whether we wanted to stay here or go to Wyoming, but we were put in this situation.

"You would think that people would be willing to pull together and help each other, but apparently that's not the case here. We can't go to Wyoming. It's too far and Jack is coming here. We only told the sheriff that because I don't trust him and his deputies. Matt said to come see him if we decided to stay, and that's what we're going to do.

"We'll see what they have to say and go from there. I've told you everything we know. It's up to you two, now, to decide what you're going to do."

Larry seemed to be thinking, so Emma gave him some time and walked to the back porch. She was worried about Bryan, and Lori was right there with her.

"I'm sorry, I shouldn't have sent him out."

Lori looked amused and said, "He'll be back. He loves doing this crap, apparently."

Emma looked at her friend and chuckled, "Maybe he missed his calling. He's a pretty good guy. Pretty smart, too. I guess you could do worse."

Emma was teasing her friend and Lori knew it. She put her hands on her hips and jokingly said, "You could have had him, if you didn't love this Jack guy so much."

Emma had a wide grin as she said, "Just wait until you meet him. You'll just melt!"

Lori laughed and shoved her friend's shoulder, "Whatever."

Emma sobered and decided Larry and Rita should be finished talking and went back in the living room.

Larry looked at Emma and said, "I didn't get a chance to finish telling you what we went through to get here, but Rita and I just need to rest a while. You've bought us some time by hiding us from Tony and we appreciate it, but I think we're going to stay here at the cabin. You may be right about the sheriff and his men. I don't know what is really going on around here, but I hope, since I own the cabin and they know me, they'll leave us alone."

Emma didn't think Larry was right about that, but she had to respect his decision.

"I understand. Please do me a favor and don't tell anyone where we went. Matt was pretty serious about that. Let me get our bags and we'll leave the things we took when we thought nobody would be here to use them."

Lori followed her out to the back porch to help. As they were grabbing the bags, Bryan walked out of the trees and joined the two women.

"Last I saw of Tony and his men, they were riding away from us toward town," Bryan said breathlessly.

Emma nodded and thanked him, then let him know that Larry and Rita were staying.

Bryan had a puzzled look as he asked, "Doesn't he understand what's going on here?"

Emma sadly shook her head as she once again picked

Bella up. "I don't think he does. They're both adults, though, so they get to make their own choices. At least someone will be at the cabin when Jack gets here. They can tell him where we've gone."

Bryan still looked baffled as Emma handed Lori the bag of things they would leave and asked her to give them back to the couple.

Lori agreed and Emma finished getting Bella in the backpack.

Bryan thought of something and quickly asked, "Did you say you told them where we're going?"

Emma nodded, "Yes, I did. That way, we won't miss Jack." She continued checking the horses.

"What if Sheriff Green finds out? Matt was pretty direct about the man not finding out."

Emma sighed and said, "I know. I told him how important it was not to say anything, but it's just a chance we'll have to take."

Bryan looked resigned.

Lori came back out with the couple trailing her.

With Leroy's reins in one hand, Emma reached out the other to the couple. "I sure wish you would change your mind, but I do understand. When you see Jack, send him my way." This last part Emma said with a huge smile.

Larry and Rita shook her hand and told her they would.

Looking for her friends, Emma saw they were already

aboard Scooter and ready to go. Taking a big breath, she swung her leg up over Leroy and the three rode away.

7

Jack snapped out of sleep with a whip of his left hand and grabbed a wrist just as his eyes flew open. He had heard a noise and reacted.

Now he looked at the face belonging to the wrist and saw it was just Jason. Apparently he had reached across to shake Jack awake.

Jack released the man and said, "You should know better than to sneak up on me like that."

Jack rubbed his temple as he sat up.

"Sneak up on you?" Jason sputtered, "I knocked on the window twice before opening the door!"

Surprisingly, Jack felt refreshed with just a slight throbbing behind his eyes.

Jason had stepped back and Jack slid out of the truck. Jason fell in step with him as he walked toward the back of the truck where the rest of the group was gathered.

Glancing skyward, Jack saw the sun was almost up, and, of course, an emerald sky. He looked around at the group and saw everyone was breaking camp. Apparently everyone else had eaten, so he grabbed some crackers out of his bag and a canteen of water.

As he chewed, Jack reached back in the bag and dragged out the map.

He traced a finger down the route he wanted to go. If everything went okay, four or five more days. Maybe less.

He finished up and went to help everyone out.

* * *

After driving all day, Jack began to notice the sky getting darker as they drove east. They were just outside of Columbia, Missouri, and he was about to say something to Jason when he noticed movement in the sky about five miles down the road.

Jack didn't slam on the brakes like last time. He just eased to a stop.

Nobody moved for a moment as they looked off down the hill.

Ahead of them, the group saw a wall of angry clouds that stretched to the north and south in a sinuous line all the way to the horizons. Behind them it seemed almost a different world. Patchy clouds with the usual green sky.

In front of them it almost looked as if a weatherman's map had come alive, and you could see the jet stream moving along the defining line of clouds.

Jack had never seen anything like it and neither had any of the others.

They all got out of the truck to stare at the sight.

Greg was the first to say something. "Are you kidding me? It's not enough we have stampedes, earthquakes, and forest fires; now we have to drive through some kind of fricking hurricane on land?"

Nobody responded, since that was exactly what the clouds looked like. Jack noticed, as he looked closer, that, although the clouds looked like the leading edge of a hurricane, there didn't appear to be the accompanying winds below them. As they watched, the trees, bushes and grass that should be whipping in the winds were absolutely still. It was the damnedest thing Jack had ever seen.

He looked up at the edge of the slowly moving clouds for a minute to make sure it wasn't advancing toward them. When he made sure it was just moving south, he reached for the map and spread it on the hood.

Behind him, he heard Ray quietly giving orders to Cat and Greg to spread out and keep watch. He was also aware of Jason asking Kuan his opinion on the clouds. Jack dismissed that conversation, since Kuan seemed to not know much more than they did at this point.

Returning his attention to the atlas, Jack looked at where they were and where he had planned to go. They had traveled all day and he knew everyone was tired. The Missouri river was just ahead a few miles, but with those clouds hanging over them, he decided they should find someplace to bed down for the night and get a fresh start in the morning.

He was looking at a spot on the map, off to the south. No

roads, no houses. Probably a pasture.

He glanced up over the hood and saw they would have to cut the fence but the bushes were small enough to drive through.

He put the map away, turned to Jason, and said, "I don't want to drive into that tonight." He gestured toward the clouds.

Jason had his hands on his hips. "Yeah, I don't either."

Pointing toward the pasture, Jack began, "Let's go through that fence and—"

Before he could finish, there was a rustling in the bushes on the north side of the road, and out walked a man zipping up his pants.

Jack whirled around at the noise and before the young man knew it, there were several guns pointed at him.

Ray had been on that side headed toward those same bushes, so he was closest to the newcomer. "Put your hands up!" the agent stated loudly.

The man did so instantly and Jack looked him over. He was about five foot ten inches tall, with curly black hair, green eyes, and had a backpack on.

Ray had eased up to the man and was patting him down. Jack heard a noise come from Jason and looked over at him. For just a split second he thought he saw recognition on his friend's face, but then it was gone and Jason was looking back at Jack with a neutral expression. Maybe Jack was seeing things. How could Jason have recognized this man? He must be getting paranoid.

He looked back at the man and saw that Cat and Greg had joined Ray and the newcomer. Greg stood a little way off keeping watch.

Jack heard the man ask, "What's up with you dudes?" As he noticed the truck and trailer, he went on, "Whoa! You guys have wheels! Nobody has wheels! How'd you guys do that?"

He directed this last question at Jack and Jason, since they appeared to be the leaders.

Jack shook his head and stepped up to the young man. "My name's Jack, Jack Denton, and this is Jason Evans. What's your name?"

Jack tried to be non-threatening and just appear curious.

The young man had stopped staring at the truck and looked into Jack's face.

"I'm Chris Black." He grinned easily and for some reason Jack felt like he'd seen the man before, yet, at the same time, he knew they'd never met. He combed his fingers through his hair in a gesture of dismissal and refocused on Chris.

"So, where are you headed, Chris?"

Chris didn't hesitate, "I'm headed to Asheville. I can't find a car that runs so," he shrugged, "I walk."

Jack wanted to know a little more. It was just in his nature. "Do you have family in Asheville?"

Chris said, "Yeah, I have some family near there." His face

lit up then and he asked, "Are you guys heading that way? I could sure use a ride."

Jack sensed he wasn't lying but was being evasive about something. Well, hell. During this crap, everyone was being evasive about something.

He left the man with Ray and Cat and stepped over to Jason.

"What do you think?" Jack was watching Jason's reaction but Jason raised his eyebrows and said, "Why not? It's getting to be quite a party. One more won't hurt!"

Jack heard the sarcasm in Jason's voice and sighed. He couldn't just leave the man out here and they were going close to Asheville anyway.

He'd made his decision and turned to let Chris know, "Alright. We're headed to Pigeon Forge so we can take you that far."

As the young man's face lit up, Jack spoke up to tell him the rules, "You'll keep out of our way and do what you're told. I don't want any questions about what we're doing. You will help with chores and whatever else we need you to help us with, understood?"

The man seemed so grateful for a ride, he was bobbing his head and nodding yes at each point. "Thank you, Mr. Denton! You won't be sorry! I'll help with whatever you need help with, I promise!"

Jack slowly shook his head and silently wondered if he was doing the right thing. Everybody else seemed to be covertly wondering the same thing. All except Jason, that is. Jack saw out of the corner of his eye that Jason was already heading back to the truck.

He hooked a thumb at the truck to let Chris know where he'd be riding and turned to walk back to the map. On his way, he again studied the line of sullen clouds. He noticed something and stopped.

As he did, someone ran into him from behind and knocked him forward a few steps.

"What the hell!" Jack turned to see who had run into him and saw it was Chris.

"I-I was going to tell you something about those clouds. I'm sorry." The young man stammered.

Jack regained his composure and tried not to glare at Chris. At the same time, he noticed that the agents were studiously finding something else to do and wandered off.

He took a deep breath and asked, "What about the clouds?"

The youngster looked chastised but determined. "The clouds seem to be following an invisible line like you would see on a weather map. I think it's a powerful jet stream."

He waited for Jack to say something, and when Jack nodded, the young man continued, "If it is, that means it is flowing down from the north and dipping in an arc to the south."

Jack had his hands on his hips and now he dropped them and turned to the swirling clouds with new eyes.

It did look like a virtual weather map with the clouds darker to the north but slowly moving south. As he watched, a funnel cloud tried to form on the edge of the clouds about fifteen miles to the north and then dissipated.

That did it. Jack knew they would have to turn south where the weather looked less severe.

He quickly turned back to the map and plotted a different course south and then east. They would have to go south through Arkansas down to Memphis. It was going to take them about six hours out of the way.

"Shit!" Jack kicked the tire on the truck.

Jason was there and looked over his shoulder, "What's wrong?"

Jack heaved a sigh and, tucking one hand under his arm, he stepped back and gestured with the other at the map, "We're going to have to drive three hundred miles out of our way to get around this crap!"

He turned and faced the angry clouds. Slowly, he calmed himself. Knowing he had no choice, Jack relaxed and after a few minutes, he took a deep breath.

Turning to the group he said, "Look. I hate it, but we're going to have to go south, around this. It's going to take us five or six hours out of our way, but we have no choice. If you all are up to it, I'll drive us through the night and we'll stop when we get closer to Tennessee."

Ray and Cat were facing out but he saw them nod. Kuan was still quietly sitting in the truck bed and Jack saw he didn't care. Jason just blew out a breath and the newcomer, Chris, was bobbing his head. Greg was blinking at Jack and opened his mouth, but then, thinking better of it, he just closed it and walked off.

Jack went around to check the tires and used some gas from the trailer to fill the gas tank. After everyone had loaded up, they took off to the south.

They decided to take back roads, and a few times they had to get out and push cars to the side of the road. This made Jack think about possible ambushes that people might try using stalled cars. He told Jason his thoughts and Jason agreed they needed to be careful.

Jack had been getting more anxious as the hours wore on. After driving steadily for five hours, it was fully dark and Jack had switched on his lights. With no electricity, they felt very conspicuous.

He had been looking for a place to pull off for a while when he noticed they had just passed into the University Forest Conservation Area. They were just outside Poplar Bluff and Jack sighed with relief. There would be no houses in the federal area and hopefully, nobody camping out. He slowed down and had Jason help him look for a turn off to a campground.

Jason spoke up, "There! Pinewoods Lake campground."

Jack relaxed somewhat and turned down the gravel road.

He was hoping for a secluded area and a more relaxing sleep tonight.

As they arrived in the turnaround by the lake, he put the truck in park and killed the lights.

The dark engulfed them and Jack sat for a moment looking off at the lightning to the north.

He thought about what they needed to do and heaved a big sigh. Glancing at Jason, he opened the door and stepped out.

They needed to get everyone fed and settled down. He headed to the trailer as Jason set up the security.

The three agents had already jumped out and gathered around Jason. Chris stretched as he wandered over toward Jack. Jack ignored him as he flicked on his flashlight and opened the trailer. He put Chris to work helping him unload the tents and other equipment.

Chris seemed surprised at the contents and said, "Man! What are you doing with all this?"

Jack turned to the young man and scowled at him, "I told you earlier. We're giving you a ride. Don't ask questions. You don't need to know. You just need to be thankful for a ride."

He had said all this quietly. Before he had finished speaking, Chris had held up his hands and was nodding, "Okay, okay! No need to get all defensive. I was just curious, dude."

Jack just shook his head and turned back to the task.

Chris, surprisingly, kept quiet and joined Jack in grabbing the rest of the things.

They carried the equipment over to where Kuan was standing. Jason was next to him clearing the ground of sticks and rocks.

Jack noticed the three agents had spread out to patrol the area and he started setting up the tents. He showed Chris what to do and left him to it as he retrieved some MRE's from the trailer.

Jason helped him set them out on the tailgate and since they were alone, Jack asked, "Do you know Chris from somewhere, Jason?"

He watched Jason carefully but saw nothing suspicious as his friend looked at him and replied, "Now where would I have seen him before? I was shocked to see someone casually walking out of the bushes. Don't you find that just a little bit coincidental? What if someone heard us coming and planted him there? I don't think we should have brought him along." This last sentence was whispered just loud enough for Jack to hear.

Jack didn't agree and told Jason so, "There is no way anyone could have been fast enough to place someone at that exact place at that exact time!"

He whispered this back at Jason. The two men stared at one another and Jack was convinced Jason had just been surprised by the young man's arrival.

The staring contest ended as they heard shouting on the far side of the campground. Both Jack and Jason had their guns out in a flash.

Turning off his flashlight, Jack wheeled toward the voices. He noticed that Chris was only two steps away from him and was in a defensive stance facing toward the disturbance.

Jack briefly scrunched his eyebrows together but quickly forgot it as he quickly strode to the edge of the trailer to find out what was happening.

Jason eased past him, hesitating every few steps and pointing his gun arm stiffly in different directions.

There was still shouting about forty yards away. Jack could see the agents had some bodies on the ground. He could make out Ray and Cat holding guns on whoever they had on the ground. There was no sign of Greg.

Ray said something to Cat and she slipped into the trees.

Jack forced himself not to rush up to the commotion. He needed to stay with the truck in case it was a ruse. Jack quickly reverted to his military training and scrutinized the area surrounding the truck and trailer. The keys were in his pocket and he silently commended himself for removing them from the ignition.

He saw that Chris was staying by him and he motioned to the man to stay here at the back of the trailer.

Chris shook his head and motioned that he wanted to follow Jack. Jack inwardly sighed, and to save time, motioned sternly for the man to stay behind.

Returning his attention to the surrounding area, Jack allowed his senses to reach out around him and he became aware that the night sounds had stopped. Not good.

He moved in a silent crouch along the edge of the passenger side of the Dodge. Jack's eyes darted everywhere and he was aware that Chris hadn't listened and was right behind him. There was nothing he could do about it, so he focused back on his task.

As he neared the front of the truck, Jack had a split second when he heard, or sensed, something move about twenty feet up the road. He turned quickly and leveled his gun in that direction. Opening his mouth to ask who was there, he never got the question out. A body hit him from behind just as he saw a muzzle flash come from the direction of the noise. As he went down, he heard the bumblebee sound of a bullet whiz by where his head had just been.

He was shocked to find himself on the ground and of all people, Chris had been the one to tackle him.

Jack quickly reassessed Chris and his being a possible threat, but as he thought this, he realized that if the young man had wanted to harm him, he wouldn't be looking fearfully out from behind the bumper toward where the shooting had come from.

Jack jumped up and crouched by Chris.

"That was pretty timely!" he hissed.

Chris just shook his head, still looking out at the dark.

Jack left the questions for later as he heard Greg shout out in the direction of the shooter, "WE'VE GOT YOU SURROUNDED! LAY DOWN YOUR GUNS!"

Jack heard some movement and low voices.

Cat spoke up, "I think we got 'em all, Jason!"

Jack and Chris slowly stood up and started walking toward the agents. Jason had cut across and was already with Cat and

Greg. They were surrounding three people who had their hands up.

Jack looked over at Ray, who had his two people still covered and laying on their stomachs.

Returning his attention to the three men in front of him he saw that two of them were in their forties or fifties and the other man was about half their age. He could be the son of one of the older men.

Jason started the questions. "So why don't you start by telling me who you are and why you're shooting at us?"

One of the older men had the decency to look ashamed but said, "I'm Henry and this here is Bob. The youngster there, that's Joshua, my son." He stood a little taller and then said, "We're on our way back from trying to hunt something down to eat. It hasn't gone very well, so when we saw your truck lights going down the road, we followed you. Being the only lights around, it was a very obvious temptation. We were raided yesterday by a group of strangers who took most of our food."

Henry sounded angry as he said this and then continued sadly, "My oldest son, Alan, tried to stop them and one of them killed him before they took off."

The man had tears in his eyes as he said this last part. He then broke down crying. The other two men looked uncomfortable and shuffled their feet. Jack saw Joshua sniffle and wipe his nose.

Henry finally continued, angry again, "We're decent, God-fearing men, but we went to the county sheriff's office and they were too busy trying to stop the chaos going on in Poplar Bluff. I figured we're on our own. So, we got together with our neighbors and decided to get organized. It brings a whole new meaning to neighborhood watch. No mercy. When it comes to our families, we're going to do what we have to in order to survive."

Jack almost stepped back when Henry said this last part. His jaw was set and there was pure determination in the man's eyes.

He glanced at Jason and saw the man was also surprised.

Jack regained his composure and asked, "Who are those two?" He nodded his head in Ray's direction.

Henry looked over at the two and answered, "That's the Lees. They're a married young couple with no children. They just moved into the old Sanford place a few months ago. The thieves hit them too. Since they're new, they wanted to go with us." The man shrugged at this last part.

Jack nodded. That made sense.

Jack stood with his hands on his hips, thinking. What were they going to do with the group? They weren't starving, and they had guns, so they could get their own food. Since this was a protected area, game should be abundant. The problem was what to do with them tonight. They couldn't just let them go. They might be desperate enough to think they could overcome Jack and his crew.

Jack made a decision, "Alright. This is what we're going to do."

He felt everyone's eyes on him, "Because you attacked us, we can't trust you."

The men started to protest and Jack held up his hand, "I won't put my group in danger because I let my guard down. Jason, please go help Ray bring the other two people over there to that tree. Greg, take these three over there too. I'll be there in a minute. Cat, please keep a lookout for anybody else out there." Jack saw Cat quickly and stealthily move off through the trees.

He turned on his heel and ran right into Chris.

"Sorry," the young man mumbled as he stepped out of Jack's way but fell in beside him.

Annoyed, Jack looked at Chris as he walked and asked, "Why are you under my feet?"

Chris was trying to keep up as Jack headed to the back of the trailer, "I don't know, man! I just happen to be at the wrong place at the wrong time."

They reached the back of the trailer and Jack opened the door, "Well, make yourself useful and take this." He handed Chris some rope as Jack grabbed some other things.

Chris looked down at the rope in his hand then looked back up at Jack in surprise, "You're not going to hang them, are you?"

Jack stopped and looked at the young man in confusion, then he seemed to understand and started to chuckle.

After a few minutes, he became serious and said, "No, I'm not a killer. I'm going to feed them, then tie them up and set a guard on them for the night. It's going to be a pain in the ass to watch them, but I'd rather do that then send them away not knowing if they'll come back to surprise us in our sleep."

He finished grabbing some MRE's and closed the trailer door.

Jack paused for a moment and looked at Chris. "I'm not a bad guy, Chris, but I have something important to do and I can't let anything stop me."

For a brief second, Chris saw sadness in Jack's eyes and then it was gone.

Jack motioned the young man to follow him and they carried the things to the tree. Jack saw the strangers blanch as they saw the rope and he rolled his eyes as he started to hand out the meals.

"Have a seat and eat some food. The rope is not to hang you, it's to tie you up. You'll be tied up overnight with a guard watching you at all times. In the morning, we'll take you away from our camp, give your weapons back, and see you on your way."

They all looked relieved, and Henry spoke up for the group and thanked Jack.

As the strangers sat and tore into their food, Jason came up to Jack and whispered, "We can't feed everyone, Jack!"

Jack looked at his old boss and said, "Then you go take their food away."

Jason looked back at the hungry group and then threw his hands up and walked away.

Jack smiled for a moment, then turned serious again. He was so tired. He rubbed his face, then looked off at the sky to the north. The green sky was still ablaze with lightning, but it didn't seem to be drawing any closer. At least that was something.

Ray was standing near, keeping watch over the strangers.

Jack stepped up to him and said, "When they get done eating, please tie them up and we'll all take turns guarding them and taking sentry duty."

Ray nodded and said, "Sure thing, Jack."

Jack thanked the big man and looked around. He was looking for Kuan. For a moment he was stressed and didn't see the man. Then he noticed the man was standing about fifteen feet away and was calmly holding the reins of the strangers' horses.

Jack was puzzled. The man had to have quietly snuck off and gathered them all up. He was definitely an enigma.

Jack blew out his cheeks and walked over to Kuan. "I see you got the horses. Thank you. It sure saves us time hunting them down."

Kuan just smiled slightly and handed the reins to Jack. *Such a strange bird,* Jack thought to himself.

He would get the horses tied up, then find Jason and start planning the guard shifts. It was going to be a long night.

8

Sheriff Frank Green sat in his office in Pigeon Forge tapping the eraser of his pencil on the desk. He was very annoyed.

Before the blast, Frank had been enjoying an extremely lucrative side business. As sheriff, one of Frank's duties was to keep the county free of drugs.

Over the past few years, the demand for marijuana had increased dramatically, and his position afforded him the opportunity to turn a blind eye to hidden growers who paid him a monthly bribe. The ones who didn't were raided and shut down. It was a beautiful operation that was booming once he had the mayor and Judge Washington on board.

When the bomb went off, he wasn't sure what was going on, and thought it would just be temporary. His office was in Sevierville then, and he had assumed the position of concerned government authority figure. He'd sent his deputies to the governor's office in Nashville to try to find out what was going on and when the lights would come back on. At the very least, he wanted to see when the feds would be coming to help. His deputies had returned with the surprising news that it was an EMP blast. Not only that, but that Frank was pretty much on his own indefinitely.

At first, Frank had cursed his luck. Then, the more he

thought about it, the more a new plan formed in the back of his mind. This could be a very good thing.

Frank continued to mull over his plan as the light from the hurricane lamp flickered. He had a feeling it was going to take a long time, if ever, to turn the lights back on. Frank knew exactly how to seem like the good guy, survive, and make a profit all at the same time.

He had already implemented the first part of his plan. People were going to want food, water, medicine and other necessities. He had confiscated the Dollywood Park and had some of his men out there right now setting up a trading post in the huge parking lot.

Another group of laborers were out at the Three Bears Gem Mine, getting it ready to store perishable foods, much like a cellar.

He planned to use the locals for labor in exchange for things they needed, and in fact had already got some takers. He had already removed all the medicines from the local pharmacies and had it all locked up in several storage units at the edge of town. Frank was happy he had found a pharmacist to work for him in exchange for food. The man was at the storage units doing inventory right now. Frank made sure he had plenty of guards.

What had happened to the looters had been unfortunate, but he couldn't very well have let them just walk in and take what they wanted. That wouldn't have been good for his plans. They would need to barter if they wanted something. Either with valuables, sweat or labor. One way or another, they would have to pay for things they wanted.

Now he needed to begin the second part of his plan. He would call a town meeting and tell everyone what would be expected of them as a community. If they didn't like it, then they would be cast out and on their own.

It was a brilliant plan. Even if the electricity came back on tomorrow, he could just say he was doing what was best for the people in his county.

Yet, the sheriff was annoyed. He had known that outsiders would show up. What he hadn't expected was for Jack Denton to come strolling back to town. Now, after years of his absence, if the woman and her friends didn't leave town, Jack would come looking for them. He did not want that to happen.

Frank and Jack were bitter enemies now, when once they had been friends.

Frank saw motion outside his office and turned toward it. It was Tony walking in the front door. Frank was surprised. Tony was supposed to be watching that woman Emma and her friends. What was he doing back here? He glanced at his watch and saw it was almost eleven in the morning.

He stood up and walked out to Tony. "What happened? What are you doing here?"

He kept his voice low so the other men in the room didn't hear him.

Tony shook the empty coffee tin on the makeshift fireplace. "Who drank the last of the coffee?" he demanded.

The other men just waved him off or jeered at him.

He slammed the coffee pot down and grumbled.

Frank clapped his hand down forcefully on the deputy's shoulder to get his attention and Tony jerked his head up.

"Follow me," Frank told him in a low, but stern, voice.

Tony blanched, but did as he was told.

As Frank walked back to his office, he considered whether he should get rid of Tony. The man wasn't very smart and sometimes he caused Frank unimaginable complications. The thing was, though, Tony was loyal. When the sheriff asked him to do something, he did it. No questions. It was hard to find someone like that.

Frank had reached his office and closed the door. He then closed the shades. The other men would know not to bother them until this meeting was finished.

Turning to Tony, Frank asked again in a deceptively quiet voice, "Why are you here? I specifically told you to *watch* the woman and her friends!"

Tony shifted his feet and said, "They're leaving. They had their bags packed and were on their horses ready to go."

He shrugged and looked at Frank.

Frank asked, "You're sure?"

"Yeah, Frank. Besides, why would they stay here? They're not even from here."

Frank thought about this for a minute, then nodded to Tony that he could go. The sheriff was still uneasy about the strangers, but he'd just have to follow up and check out the cabin. Maybe tomorrow.

He watched as Tony breathed a sigh of relief and left Frank's office.

Frank had something else to attend to. He blew out the lamp and left the office.

9

Emma was chewing on some beef jerky as they rode. She was thinking about all that had happened since the blast. It was so surreal. She could hear her friends behind her talking low to each other and then Lori laughed. She smiled to herself and, absentmindedly, reached down and touched her holstered gun. It was sad that in such a relaxing background, they still had to be so vigilant.

They had left Larry's cabin and ridden northwest, in the direction someone would go if they were riding toward Wyoming. When they had reached a creek, they had turned back south and ridden downstream for a mile or two. As soon as they found some rocky ground on shore, they left the creek and were now about a mile down the road that Matt had described.

As Emma put the last of the jerky in her mouth, she felt movement in her backpack, and Bella scrambled out and jumped off the horse. Startled, Emma pulled the reins short to stop Leroy. She watched as Bella dashed off through the trees. She didn't even have time to call to her. She shook her head at the crazy feline when a thought occurred to her.

Emma was sitting idle on the horse as her friends came up alongside of her and stopped too.

"What's up with her?" Lori asked.

Emma quietly shushed her as she looked around. She was listening to the wildlife and noticed that, although there were sounds a little ways away, it was quiet close to her and her friends. This could mean one of two things. Either she was being paranoid and Emma and her friends were causing the silence nearby, or someone with very good woodcraft was watching them. She tended to think the latter, since she always trusted her instincts. Besides, she'd rather err on the side of caution. She also had to factor in Bella's strange behavior. It had only taken a few seconds for Emma to come to this conclusion, so she bent down as though she was checking the tack on Leroy. After a couple of seconds, she straightened up as though satisfied and, at the same time, slipped the Glock out of its new position across her zipper.

She smiled at her friends and said, loud enough for anyone watching to hear, "I thought something was rubbing against Leroy's shoulder. He was walking funny."

Her friends seemed to accept this and went back to talking together.

She gently kicked her horse to go ahead of Lori and Bryan and they didn't seem to care. Emma was in a higher state of awareness now, and could feel someone was watching the group. She kept her handgun ready. After a few minutes of riding, Emma let herself relax, somewhat. If the people watching them were going to attack, they already would have.

A little while later, the trio came to the Carrolls' mailbox and started to turn down the drive.

They had gone about ten feet when a voice came out of

the trees on their right, "Halt right there!"

Emma had expected this, but Lori and Bryan were surprised.

Emma ignored her friends and, faster than seemed possible, she zeroed in on the voice and pointed her Glock directly between the eyes she saw there in the bushes. The owner of the eyes suddenly looked surprised and Emma stated in a low voice, "You've been following us for the past ten minutes. I am an expert marksman and if you don't want to be dead in the next ten seconds, you'll step out and tell us what you want. That goes for anyone else with you. They may shoot at me but I guarantee I'll kill you before I die!"

Her hand held steady and there was not a sound to be heard. Emma saw determination in the eyes as the one they belonged to carefully pushed out into the open.

As the man emerged, Emma saw he had a sawed off shotgun leveled on her at his hip. At that moment, she knew they were in a standoff. She could shoot him between the eyes and hope that his knee-jerk reaction wouldn't be to blow her head off before he died. On the other hand, the stranger could shoot her and hope she didn't get a shot off before she fell. The thing that probably ended up swaying the man's opinion was the pure determination in Emma's eyes and her rock steady gun hand.

The man said, "Well, now. It looks as if someone is going to die if we don't just all calm down and talk to each other."

Emma heard her friends breathing tensely behind her and she knew she was covering them from this man. At least they would have a chance. She jerked her thoughts back and quickly analyzed why this man had waited until now to confront them, and then Emma said, "Matt Carroll came to our cabin and offered us an invitation to come visit. We've decided to take the young man up on his offer."

Emma let the last sentence stand on its own, hoping she was right.

The stranger seemed to relax a little, after hearing Matt's name, but then asked, "What cabin?"

Emma kept the gun pointed at the man's head and replied softly, "Larry Campbell's cabin."

This seemed to be what the man was waiting for and he smiled and pointed the shotgun down, "Well, why didn't you say so!"

Emma heard her two friends let their breath out and she pointed her gun away too.

She felt shaky, but had the presence of mind to smile back at the man.

He looked serious again as he said, "I'm sorry about following you, but we have to be careful now."

Emma nodded and replied, "I understand."

She wanted to say more, but was drained of energy.

Emma had enough manners left to reach down to shake the man's hand, "My name is Emma Hudson." Pointing her finger back at her two friends who were still white with shock, she said, "The two guppies back there are my friends, Bryan and Lori."

They recovered slightly and smiled crookedly at the man.

"Hawk Carroll's my name. I'm Matt's uncle." And he touched the brim of his hat as a kind of salute.

The man continued, "Since Matt invited you up, let's go see what's for lunch."

Emma murmured her thanks and followed the man on up the driveway.

Hawk was leading the way and as they reached the front yard, they came to a halt.

All of a sudden, around the corner of the house, two dogs came running, barking and growling. The two horses became nervous. Emma and Bryan tried to calm the horses down as Hawk yelled at the two canines. The two dogs looked like bird dogs, and they listened to Hawk and backed off a ways still growling. Emma noticed the hackles were still raised on their backs and kept an eye on them as Hawk stepped up on the porch.

He turned to the friends and said, "Their bark is worse than their bite. I'll just go in and tell everybody what's going on." He winked after saying this and Emma had the impression that Hawk was something of a jokester.

As Hawk went into the house, Bryan nudged Scooter up beside Emma. "Were you really going to shoot that man?" Bryan whispered to Emma.

Calmly, Emma replied, "Absolutely. You forget where I come from. If someone threatens my life, or my friend's lives, I will not hesitate to kill that person. Period."

After she said this, her friends were quiet and she could feel their eyes on her, appraising her.

She turned her attention to the porch as Hawk walked back out the door. The dogs had gotten bored and wandered off a ways. They appeared well trained and Emma was thankful for that. Matt was with his uncle and was smiling. "So you decided to come see us. You're welcome to put the horses in the barn." He pointed over to the structure and continued, "There are brushes, feed, and water. When you're done, come on back to the house and we'll get you something to eat. Don't worry about the dogs. I'll keep them up here."

Emma smiled back at the man and thanked him.

The friends reached the barn and Emma jumped down to slide the door back.

After getting the horses settled in, they slid the door shut and headed back to the porch.

Emma appraised the homestead as they walked. The house sat on a slope about thirty yards in front of a low mountain. Trees had been cleared away from the house years ago. Emma approved of this, since that would give an unobstructed view in all directions. As they approached the porch, the front screen opened and Matt reappeared.

Holding the door open he said, "Welcome! Come in and meet the family." He smiled and they entered the home.

As their eyes adjusted, they could see the house was spacious and open. Light was provided by some candles and there were several people of various ages doing different things throughout the house.

Matt led them around and started the introductions.

"You've already met Hawk, my uncle." The man had a cup in his hand and just nodded.

Matt continued, "This is my dad, Jeb." The older man was in the process of setting down a plate of fresh grilled meat. Emma's stomach growled automatically as the smell of grilled hamburgers caressed her nose.

The older man smiled and shook their hands, "Nice to meet you folks. Matt's told us a little about you. We'll talk more after you meet everyone and fill your bellies." Jeb headed back outside and Matt led them on to the kitchen.

There were two adult women, a boy about ten years old, and a teenage girl all working on different projects. To Emma's eyes it looked like the kitchen had been originally designed for the large cast iron wood stove that stood against the wall. She also noticed that even with the windows open, it was hot in the kitchen area. She sure did miss air conditioning.

Matt stopped just short of the kitchen island and introduced everyone. The two older women were his aunt and mother. The teenage girl was Matt's younger sister and the young boy peeling potatoes was Matt's little brother. The young boy was huffing and was obviously not happy with what he was doing.

Matt saw this also and said, "Sheesh, Pete! You sound like a little girl!"

Pete immediately stopped what he was doing and said, "Matt! I should be out there with pa, hunting and grilling!"

He was so serious, Matt didn't say anything for a moment. Then he smiled and said quietly, "If you go out hunting and can't find any game, when you come back home and your belly is empty, will you turn down those green beans or that corn on the cob? Maybe you'll stick your nose up at that homemade cornbread with butter that was made by your mama while you were out looking for game?"

The young boy got the point but then shrugged in irritation.

Matt said, "Think about that, big hunter. Everyone contributes where they can."

Emma was impressed by Matt's logic and the young boy seemed to listen to the older man. She realized that in the world before the blast, young children were not usually taught such important lessons since food came from the grocery store.

As they met everyone, Emma could tell Bryan and Lori were starting to fan themselves and were as hot as she was. Emma placed her hand on Matt's arm and asked, "Can I take my two friends outside and get some air? It's a little warm in here."

Matt nodded yes and Emma could see that he understood.

Emma nodded back at the young man and then eased her friends toward the front door.

"We'll be right back."

Emma flashed a genuine smile as she guided her friends outside.

When the trio made it outside, Emma let go of the two friends and flapped the front tail of her t-shirt, "Jeez! It is so hot!"

Bryan ran his hand through his blond hair to lift it to the breeze, "I need to cut this all off. No sense trying to be cute anymore." He said this in an offhand manner.

Lori spoke then. "I would give anything for an ice cube right about now!"

Matt's uncle, Hawk, walked past them and headed out to sentry duty. The two dogs happily trailed after him.

Everyone was quiet and after the uncle had gotten out of earshot, Emma spoke up, "I am dying to get clean. After we eat, I'm going to ask Matt if there is somewhere to take a bath. The nearest creek is even sounding good about now!" Bryan and Lori heartily agreed.

They were about to go back in when there was shouting out toward the road and the dogs started barking.

Emma and her two friends rushed back into the house.

She took a knee and whipped out the Glock. Bryan quickly whipped the crossbow off his back.

There were a tense few minutes and then Hawk yelled out, "Gatlinburg police chief coming in!"

There was a rustling near the bushes at the edge of the yard. A man came out, in uniform, and slowly walked his horse toward the cabin.

Matt, who was right next to Emma, relaxed and yelled, "Come on up, Len!"

The police chief waved and eased his horse up to the porch.

Emma realized that Matt and his family knew this man and put her gun away. She noticed that Bryan slung his weapon back over his shoulder.

As the man reached the porch, he took his hat off and wiped his brow, "Good lord it's hot!"

Matt stepped out and greeted the man as he dismounted, "You need to dress a little more casual. That polyester isn't very practical."

The lawman chuckled at Matt's ribbing, then was about to step into the house.

He stopped short as he saw the three friends.

Matt stepped up to the man and made the introductions.

Emma smiled and nodded as she was introduced and studied the man carefully. He was about Bryan's height, dark hair, dark eyes, and clean cut. He seemed very watchful and his gun was a classic six-shooter.

Leonard Brantley was his name and he went by Len.

Matt's dad, Jeb, stepped out and clapped the man on the shoulder, "So what are you doing out this way?"

Everyone went into the house and Jeb gestured to the couch where there was a cross breeze and he sat.

"I can't stay long, but I had to come over and talk to you, Jeb. I've been getting quite a few families coming into Gatlinburg. I guess you could call them refugees. I expected a few families that were from other places that happened to be vacationing when the blast happened. But the families that I'm getting are from around Pigeon Forge. The rumors that these people are telling us are pretty shocking."

Here, the police chief looked up at Matt, "A couple of times Matt's name came up as having been there."

Jeb didn't look up at his son before he answered, "I know exactly what you're talking about and yes, Matt was there. I think you mean the Kroger shooting?"

Len sighed heavily and nodded, "Yeah, I was hoping they were wrong."

He looked over at Matt and said, "Tell me what happened."

Before Matt could answer, Emma interrupted, "Excuse me. If you don't mind, we would like to take a bath. Could someone point us to the nearest creek?"

Jeb chuckled, "I'm sorry and yes, the creek is the nearest bath tub but at least it's clean. Pete!" he said loudly, "Can you show these folks down to the creek?"

The young boy lit up and dropped the potato he was peeling, "Yes, sir!"

He dashed up to Emma and said, "Follow me!"

Before he could run off, Emma grabbed his sleeve and said, "Slow down, Tom Sawyer, we need to get our bags out of the barn."

She let the boy go and turned to wink at Jeb. The man smiled back, and then turned to Len.

Emma pushed the screen door open and followed the boy out to the barn.

Her friends were walking beside her and Lori asked, "Where's Bella?"

Emma looked around and shrugged, "I don't know. She should have showed up by now."

Emma dismissed the thought as they reached the barn. Pete was tugging heartily on the gate and Bryan reached out to help the boy.

As the gate slid back, Emma heard a horse whinny its welcome and she smiled as she saw it was Leroy.

Her smile faded as she thought about something and she turned to Pete. "How far is the creek?"

The boy looked up at her and said, "Not too far. I can usually get there and back by lunch if I hurry."

Bryan snorted and mumbled, "That's helpful. Oof!"

This last part was in response to Lori's elbow in his ribs.

He raised his eyebrows at Lori who glared back at him.

"What?"

Lori just sighed and asked Emma, "Are you thinking of taking Leroy and Scooter?"

"Yes. I know these are some good people, but I hate being away from the horses for any length of time. Let's saddle up. It'd just make me feel better."

Her friends didn't complain, they just followed her

example and soon they were ready to go.

By the time they were ready to ride, the friends were sweating freely in the still barn. Emma wiped her face with the front of her shirt and looked around. Pete was entertaining himself with a bug he was following over by one of the stall doors and there, sitting on one of the saddle stands, was Bella. She was watching the boy intently.

Emma walked over to the cat, scooped her up, and tried to put her in the bag. For the first time ever, the cat jumped onto her shoulder and then to Leroy's saddle, for all the world like she had done it a million times.

Emma waited for Leroy to react, but all he did was turn his head, look at Bella, and snort.

Bryan and Lori had watched what happened and now stood with their mouths open in complete surprise.

Emma just tilted her head to the side, briefly, then pushed Bella to the cantle and mounted.

Her friends followed suit and Emma got Pete's attention.

The boy quickly abandoned the bug and led them out of the barn. Bryan jumped down to slide the gate shut and then remounted Scooter.

Pete had already dashed ahead around the corner of the house and the trio hurried to follow.

Emma nervously looked around for the dogs but assumed they were with Hawk on patrol.

She looked ahead to the tree line up against the mountain with longing. She couldn't wait to get out of the green-tinged, hazy heat.

Pete was waiting as the friends gratefully reached the shade.

He motioned to them and quickly walked along the base of the mountain.

They weaved through the trees and Emma thought about Jack and wondered how close he was. She also worried about him being able to find her. She briefly had butterflies in her stomach as she thought about seeing him again. First though, she and her friends would need to keep safe until he got here. Emma hoped they could stay at the Carrolls until he made it.

They had been riding a while when she saw Pete stop ahead and look back at them. She realized she had been hearing a murmuring noise for a while and now, as they rode up beside the boy, it became much louder.

As the trio dismounted and stood beside Pete, they quietly looked on at the site in awe.

The source of the sound was an amazing plunge waterfall with a pool at the bottom. The pool was clear and rainbows glittered where the water splashed down from above.

The boy beside them seemed unfazed by the beautiful sight and broke the silence by stating, "I gotta go now. Pa will be wondering where I'm at."

Without another word, he turned and disappeared back the way they had come.

The friends watched him, then looked at each other and grinned.

"You two go first," Bryan said gallantly.

Emma and Lori asked if he was sure.

He nodded and said, "I'll keep watch. When you ladies are done, we'll switch." He said this last with a wink.

Lori lowered her brows and said, "You better not peek!"

Bryan took on a serious expression and held up three fingers, "Scout's honor."

Emma and Lori squealed like little girls and scrambled down to the pool.

As they reached the edge, the sound of an animal dashing away through the brush made them pause for a second, but then they both dropped down and quickly unlaced their shoes. Kicking them off, they checked and saw that Bryan had his back turned before stripping down.

Hesitating for another moment, the two women gazed at the pool and then holding hands, they jumped in.

As the cold water closed over her head, Emma's eyes popped open at the sheer, silky, luxurious feeling as the water engulfed her.

She pushed off the bottom and shot back to the surface.

As Emma emerged, she glanced around for Lori and saw her bob up about ten feet away. She smiled over at her little friend who giggled and floated serenely on her back.

Emma looked up at where Bryan was and, making sure he still had his back turned, she got out to get the soap from her bag. Easing back into the water, she quickly lathered up her hair and body. The clean smell of the soap made her smile. It was funny how smells triggered memories of better times. She thought about her little townhouse and how easy life had been then.

She dismissed the memories as Lori swam up and reached her hand out for the soap "Oh, dear Jesus, this water feels delicious!"

Emma laughed outright and handed her the soap after lathering up her shirt. She had drifted over to an eddy to scrub out her clothes. She rinsed them out and laid them on a warm boulder to dry.

Reaching into her bag, Emma dried off with the hand towel she found there. She noticed Bella was sitting in the shade on another rock and was twitching her tail.

Lori had just finished washing her own clothes and Emma tossed her the hand towel.

"Do you think we'll be able to stay here for a while?" Lori asked.

Emma shrugged and replied, "We haven't even asked Jeb if we can stay at all. I was thinking about asking if we can stay in their barn, but I think I'd like to use our tents in that little clearing we saw on our way here."

Lori looked puzzled, "Why there?"

Emma examined her thoughts before telling her friend, "I think the sheriff is bad news, and I have a feeling that Matt's family is about to put themselves square in the man's sights. If they do that, I don't want to be in the middle of it."

They had finished dressing into their extra set of clothes. Leaving their old clothes to dry, they started back up the slope.

Lori seemed puzzled and said, "You don't seem to be the type to shy away from a fight."

Emma nodded and said, "You're right. If it involves self-defense of myself or you two, I'm right there. With the sheriff and the Carrolls, it just seems like there is something more going on here. I don't want to get involved in something we can't get ourselves out of. I want to have a safe place to wait for Jack to get here, but I just don't think this is our fight, you know?"

They had reached the hill where Bryan was standing guard and Lori nodded and said, "I think I get it. If the Carrolls were your family or close friends you would be right there in the middle of it."

"In the middle of what?" Bryan asked, catching only the end of the conversation.

"Go take a bath, stinky. I'll tell you later," Emma teased.

Genuine surprise lit Bryan's face. "Stinky?"

Lori waved him off. "She was just kidding. Go enjoy yourself. It feels so good!" This last part Lori said with relish.

Bryan shook his head and rolled his eyes then grabbed his own bag and started to walk away.

"You have some soap?" Emma asked.

He stopped and said sheepishly, "No."

Emma smiled kindly and handed her friend the soap.

"Thanks." Bryan grinned and, shrugging the crossbow and rifle off his shoulders, he walked on down the slope.

Emma turned to the horses and looped the strap of her bag over the pommel.

She removed the Glock and checked the magazine. As she did, Lori watched and said, "When we get to a stopping point, I'd like you to show me how to shoot."

Emma didn't expect this and said so to her little friend.

Lori looked resigned and told Emma, "It doesn't look like this is all going away anytime soon, and I need to learn so you two don't have to protect me all the time."

Emma smiled. "I would be more than happy to teach you."

Lori replied, "Thanks. Bryan has already agreed to show me how to use the crossbow."

Emma replaced the Glock. "I'm going to take a look around. Can you watch the horses?"

Lori agreed and Emma hugged her friend, "We're going to be okay." She said this with more conviction than she felt.

Lori nodded and Emma turned away. Emma hoped she had told her friend the truth.

Before she walked away, she listened to her surroundings. She was starting to do this automatically and it just made her feel safer. She heard the birds chirping in the trees around her. She also recognized squirrels, cicadas and even tree frogs. The sounds comforted her, as she knew it probably meant there were no strangers nearby. As she was listening, she smiled. Emma could hear Bryan whistling happily back at the plunge pool.

She started off down the trail they had emerged from. It had been many years since she had truly exercised her skills in the woods. Even so, it had come back to her quickly.

Instead of just pushing through branches, an experienced woodsman eases around them where possible so as not to break the branches. When one did not want to be followed by another with his skills, this was absolutely necessary.

The placement of your feet was also important. She made sure not to step in soft mud or on bare dirt so as not to leave an imprint.

There were many other tricks, and all of these had to be thought about subconsciously as you kept intently aware of your surroundings.

Emma had done it so often, however, that her body just did it automatically.

She kept an eye out and an ear out for movement as she walked.

Completing the arc from mountainside to creek, she emerged silently about fifteen feet behind Lori and the horses.

Lori was facing away from her and Emma stood quietly waiting for Bryan to top the rise. She had heard him climbing the slope as he returned from his bath.

As Bryan joined Lori, Emma walked up as well and was

about to say something when there were several pops like firecrackers in the distance.

Emma determined it was in the direction of the Carrolls' house and she was instantly on alert.

"Is that what I think it is?" Bryan asked.

Emma nodded and Lori asked, "What do we do?"

For a moment, Emma went blank. She was conflicted. They could ride to the Carrolls' help and possibly get shot in the process. Or, they could hide out here and hope the Carrolls wouldn't tell the attackers about the trio.

As the pops raged on with an occasional shotgun blast, Emma rubbed her temple and thought logically.

If they rushed to the aid of the Carrolls, they had no idea what they would be getting into, not to mention the fact that they were a long ways away. If they did get there in time to help, they might just be shot in the process and they wouldn't do anyone any good if they were dead.

On the other hand, if they just stayed here, they might be safe, but she would have to fight feelings of guilt and cowardice and would have no idea who had attacked the Carrolls.

All of this she processed in seconds and made up her mind. "We're too far away to get there in time to save them, but we can be witnesses."

Her friends looked at her in confusion.

She quickly told them, "I can move faster by myself. I'll jog up to where I can see what's going on while staying hidden. I want you two to stay here and out of sight until I get back."

Bryan was already vigorously shaking his head. "No! Emma, you can't go by yourself, I won't let you!"

Emma pulled up short and cocked an eyebrow at the man. "You won't *let* me?"

Lori quit looking afraid long enough to look at Bryan in amusement.

Backpedalling, Bryan stammered, "I mean, uh, are you sure you don't want any help?"

Lori snickered and Emma lowered her eyebrow. "I'm positive. Please keep an eye on the horses. I'll be back as quick as I can."

Emma could see that Bryan didn't want to let her go, but he nodded.

Lori grabbed Emma and hugged her. "If you die, I'll kill you!" she whispered to Emma and Emma smiled at her friend.

Emma grabbed her belt knife, an extra magazine for her gun, and a canteen.

Looking back at her friends, she smiled encouragingly. "I'll be right back."

She turned and quickly dashed back toward the shots. As she jogged, she made sure to be as quiet as possible. She had the Glock out and carried it low, in front of her. She made sure to stay aware of her surroundings and noticed now that the gunshots had ceased. She slowed her pace since the attackers would be more aware of their surroundings now that they had quit shooting.

A few minutes later, she stopped behind a thick oak tree and caught her breath. She didn't want to give herself away by breathing hard.

As her breathing slowed, Emma studied her surroundings. She was far enough into the trees behind the Carroll home that nobody could see her. Yet she was close enough to hear loud voices.

Now that her breathing was under control, she slipped quietly closer to the edge of the trees. She found a vantage point that had a clear view of the back, side, and part of the front yard.

As the scene came into focus, her mind, at first, wouldn't process what she was seeing. Then it all became horribly clear.

The first thing she noticed were the bodies of the two dogs, lying still, out by where the driveway opened to the front yard. They must have come running at the first shots and were killed for their loyalty.

The next thing she noticed were the men with rifles and handguns walking around. Men in uniforms that matched the uniform that Sheriff Green had on the day she met him.

Emma watched as one of the men came out the back door of the house with his hand clamped around the back of a young boy's neck.

Emma's eyes flew open and her breath caught. It was Pete, their young guide. The boy was yelling and struggling against his captor. The deputy was cursing at the boy and shaking him like a dog shakes a rabbit. They got to the side of the house when the feisty boy bit the deputy and tried to get away.

The deputy howled but didn't let go. Instead, he kicked the boy's legs out from under him and, unceremoniously, slammed the boy to the ground.

Emma dragged her eyes away from the duo and looked to see if anyone else was in sight. When she saw there wasn't, she judged her chances of darting out, knocking the deputy on the head, and dragging the boy back into the trees with her. Desperate to save the youngster, she hadn't thought the plan completely through and started to move toward the man who had his back to her.

Before she took one step, a powerful hand clamped over her mouth from behind and a body pinned her to the oak trunk.

Startled badly, Emma began an all-out struggle against her captor.

Before she could really strike out and thrash around, a voice near her ear whispered, "Sh! It's Hawk. You can't help them! Stop struggling and I'll let you go."

Emma was so relieved that it was Hawk that she went limp immediately and tears welled up in her eyes. He felt the tension go out of her body and slowly released her.

It was at that exact moment that Emma saw the sheriff and two other of his deputies walk around from the front of the house. They stopped next to the deputy who was struggling with Pete.

Emma realized that Hawk had saved her from certain capture, or worse. She looked over at the man and nodded her thanks and then turned back to the sheriff.

The sheriff had his hands on his hips and spoke loudly, "Clem! What in the hell are you doing?"

The deputy finally had the boy under control and had slapped a zip tie on him. The boy was still struggling in the dirt and Emma could hear him crying and yelling, "You killed my mama! You killed her!"

The boy's cries tugged at Emma's heart and they would forever haunt her dreams.

Forcing herself to listen to the exchange, she was also aware of Hawk, beside her, mumbling, darkly, under his breath.

Clem now answered the sheriff, "Frank, I'm trying to calm the boy down!"

Emma thought the sheriff was trying to help the boy, but his next words belied that. "You should have just shot him! Now I have to figure out what to do with him."

He cursed, then turned to one of his other men and said, "Take him on your horse over to the mine and put him with the others. We're going to need all the laborers we can get."

The man nodded and went to get his horse.

Sheriff Green turned back and started to scan the tree line. Emma and Hawk instinctively eased behind the oak to stay concealed.

They heard his next sentence and became alarmed.

"Clem, I need you to get a couple of the other men and find Hawk. I know he was here. He doesn't go anywhere without his wife, and she was in the kitchen."

When Emma and Hawk heard this, they stared at each other and understood they were in danger. Hawk tilted his head toward the waterfall and Emma understood. It was time to leave. Sadly, Emma nodded. They could do no more here.

Hawk stood up and stealthily eased back away from the oak, keeping the trunk between him and the group of men. Emma gave him time to move away, then she followed suit. They were careful to watch where they stepped so as not to make any noise.

Emma didn't realize she was holding her breath until she had put about twenty yards between her and the men. She started feeling a burning in her chest and slowly let her breath out.

She glanced ahead at Hawk and realized they were making good time.

Hawk stopped and waited for her to catch up and, even though they were far enough away to go unheard, he still whispered, "I take it your friends are down by the waterfall?"

Emma didn't risk vocalizing and just nodded.

Hawk just turned toward the falls and rushed off, trusting Emma to keep up.

She did, easily, and soon they were nearing the falls.

When they arrived at the top of the slope, there was

nobody there and Emma started to panic.

Before she could get too worried, Bryan stepped out where she could see him. They had been concealed in some bushes and Emma sighed with relief.

Bryan walked over and Lori followed him.

"What happened?" Lori asked anxiously.

Emma felt tears start to fill her eyes again but forced them back. Before she could say anything, Hawk spoke up gruffly, "We gotta go. We don't have time to talk about it now! Do you still have both of your horses?"

Bryan looked alarmed at the man's tone and glanced at Emma before nodding.

Hawk looked relieved, "Good. Let's get them and get a head start. We'll head to Gatlinburg and tell them what happened. Len was a good man and hired good deputies."

Bryan caught the past tense and asked, "Was?"

Emma nodded, "Get the horses, Bryan, please."

Bryan hurried then and had just reached the bushes when they heard voices and bodies crashing through the trees back the way they had just run.

Hawk spoke, "Dammit! Out of time. Grab the horses and follow me single file. Don't say a word! Emma, I can tell you understand tracking. Bring up the rear and use a branch to cover our trail. We have just a few minutes. Let's move!"

Hawk reached out and grabbed Leroy's reins from Bryan and started off down the slope toward the plunge pool.

Bryan started to follow then hesitated.

Emma didn't wait. She grabbed a small leafy branch off a nearby tree and started to brush the group's tracks away.

Bryan decided that Hawk must know what he was doing and started after him. Lori followed with Scooter, and Emma quickly brushed the tracks away as she walked backward.

As the group reached the plunge pool, Emma backed into Lori and turned to look at what the holdup was.

She saw Bryan gaping as he watched Hawk push through some high grass up against the cliff face and disappear through the waterfall.

The voices were getting closer and Emma hissed, "Just follow him, Bryan! Hurry!"

Bryan snapped out of it and quickly followed the man. Lori was right on his heels and Emma continued to wipe away all traces of their presence.

As she backed toward the secret entrance she saw her and Lori's drying clothes and quickly gathered them up in one arm as she brushed with the other.

She had just reached the high grass and jumped through the waterfall when she heard the voices reach the slope they had just left.

Emma had no idea what to expect on the other side of the waterfall. For all she knew, she would slam into the side of a granite wall. Surprisingly, she fell into Lori's body. Her friend had seen her coming and grabbed Emma to keep her from falling.

Emma whispered her thanks and looked around.

Everybody, including the horses, was soaked. They were in a cave and Emma shivered in the chilly air. The cave roof started at the water and sloped back from about ten feet high, and then disappeared back in the darkness. It stretched about twenty-five feet across and had plenty of space for the group to huddle in.

Voices and shouting on the other side of the water brought everyone's attention back to the searchers.

Bryan and Hawk were soothing the horses to keep them quiet. As loud as the waterfall was, it still wouldn't cover the sound of a loud whinny if one of the horses got agitated.

Emma wiped the water from her face and silently slid the Glock out and let it point downward. She was ready if the men on the other side found their hiding place. The handgun held seventeen rounds, and she had an extra magazine. Her eyebrows lowered as she thought about the atrocities these men had committed. She would not go down without taking some of those assholes with her!

Shifting slightly, Emma made sure that she would be the first person they saw if they came through the water.

Time seemed to crawl by as Emma watched the vague shapes through the water. The men were searching everywhere and Emma sent up a prayer of thanks that the men didn't have dogs.

After what felt like hours, but was really only about twenty minutes, the sounds dwindled away and Emma stopped seeing shapes moving on the other side. She felt her shoulders relax and became aware that Lori was shaking and had goose bumps on her arms.

She eased over to her bag that was still hanging from her horse saddle. Reaching in with her left hand, she brought out her tightly rolled blanket and handed it to her friend.

Lori smiled gratefully and shrugged the small blanket onto her shoulders.

Hawk handed Leroy's reins to Emma and put a finger to his lips in a shushing motion. Emma nodded and repeated the gesture to her friends.

After waiting for Emma to let her friends know to stay quiet, Hawk leaned over and whispered in her ear, "We'll have to stay here for a while. Frank is sly. He'll leave at least one man nearby to make sure I don't come back here."

It made sense and Emma nodded. As she whispered this to Lori, Hawk moved deeper into the cave. Emma stayed where she was and kept watch through the water. Still no motion out there.

Lori had just finished whispering the message to Bryan when Hawk returned.

He had a big rock in his hand and taking the horses' reins from the friends he set the rock down, pinning the reins to the floor. The horses seemed to be half asleep, but he obviously didn't want to take any chances.

Motioning to the friends, he led them to the back of the cave.

Emma noticed that the roof of the cave sloped gently and

went back about thirty feet before ending at a granite wall. She also noticed shapes in the gloom and saw Hawk digging in one of his pockets. Holding an item in one hand, he covered it partially with the other and put his body between the item and the waterfall.

Suddenly there was a murky light and Emma realized he held a small flashlight. She looked at the shapes against the back wall and realized they were supplies. There were crates of canned food, and bags of vegetables. There were several stacked plastic containers. Some held ammo, according to the writing on the outside, and another large container said it held medical supplies.

Hawk was searching the containers for something and when he found it, he turned off the flashlight. Pocketing the light, Hawk reached out and grabbed the container and lifted it away from the others. He lifted the top off and started grabbing something from the container and handing it to Emma and her friends. It was ripped up rags and Emma knew what he wanted them to do.

She shared the rags around and everybody started using them to dry off. She watched Hawk as he finished drying himself. The man reached out and scooted another container toward him. He opened it and handed each person a scratchy blanket. Emma realized they had to be Army surplus blankets and she quickly put it around her shoulders. Instantly, she felt warmer. Lori already had Emma's blanket, so she declined Hawk's offer when he got to her.

After everyone settled on the floor, Hawk spoke up in a low voice, "Jeb and I were the only ones who knew about this hidey hole."

He was quiet for a few moments and Emma didn't say anything. She knew he was grieving for his family.

After a minute, he went on, "We kept the canned food in here already, but after the blast we started putting more things in here to be better prepared. We always thought we might use the supplies as a backup if we started running out of things at the house. Now…"

He just shook his head and couldn't go on.

The three friends felt heartsick for the man, but had no idea what to say to him. No words could help the man through his suffering, so Emma gently squeezed his shoulder instead.

Without looking at her, Hawk patted her hand then stood up and walked away. Emma knew he was trying to compose himself and she let him go.

Turning to her friends, Emma asked, "Are you guys okay?"

Both nodded and Bryan asked, "What happened? Where are the others?"

Emma sighed, "It was Sheriff Green and his men. When I got to the edge of the clearing it was all over and I hid to watch. I saw one of the men chase Pete and hogtie him and I started to rescue him when Hawk grabbed me and, very probably, saved my life. At the very least, he kept me from being captured."

Lori spoke up, "Did they arrest them?"

Emma slowly shook her head as she looked at her friends,

"No, just Pete. I heard the boy yell at them about killing his mother."

Lori sucked in her breath at the same time that Bryan hissed, "Are you serious? You must be joking! This is America, you can't just go around killing people!"

Emma sadly looked at her two friends but could find no words to say.

She didn't realize that Hawk had returned until he spoke. "Yes, when there is no longer a justice system in place to keep evil people from doing evil things, anybody can kill anybody else."

Lori was shaking again but not from the cold this time.

Emma let her friends think about what they had just learned and turned to Hawk. "Tell me how it happened."

Hawk closed his eyes for a moment, and then began, "I had taken the dogs with me, mistakenly thinking that anybody who came to the house would use Little Cove road."

They had all sat again and Hawk went on, "They must have come up through the valley to the south. I underestimated them and it cost my family their lives." He dipped his head.

Bryan asked, "What do you mean? Out of all the people here, why did they come after your family?"

Hawk looked back up and Emma could see the rugged features in the gloomy light and absently thought, *This man has had a hard life.*

Hawk took a deep breath and slowly removed his hat before answering, "We have some time so I'll tell you. Before all this happened, we knew about Frank's activities." He said this last word with bitterness.

"He and his department are corrupt. We didn't know how long he had been taking bribes and such, but Jeb found out a few months ago from a good friend.

"When the financial crash came a few years ago, a lot of people lost their jobs or businesses. They looked for other jobs, but there were none to be had. Somehow, Frank knew the people who were desperate to feed their families and keep their homes. He approached these people and made a proposition. He would put them in touch with someone who would lay out the plan. This person told the people that if they let them use part of their farms and turn a blind eye, the people would get money at the first of each month."

Here Hawk smiled sadly. "When your children have no food, or you have letters from the bank threatening eviction, it's hard to turn down any money. Jeb's friend had fallen on hard times about a year ago. His children were going hungry *and* he was behind on his mortgage. The sheriff approached him, offered him this opportunity, and threatened him if he told anyone. Jeb's friend was desperate. He agreed and never told a soul. That was until Jeb confronted him as to where he was getting all his money.

"Jeb had become suspicious, and when he asked, the man broke down. He told Jeb everything and begged Jeb not to tell anyone.

"Jeb agreed, as long as the man would tell him everything and keep him informed. Jeb knew he couldn't do anything to the sheriff until he had enough evidence against him."

Hawk paused and angrily rubbed the back of his neck before continuing, "To make a long story short, the police chief of Pigeon Forge was on Frank's payroll. When Jeb went to him with the knowledge of what was going on, the police chief told Frank, and the sheriff subtly threatened Jeb.

"This all came about just two weeks before the blast. Jeb was planning to go to the FBI and put an end to Frank's business. He never got a chance." Hawk bit the last sentence off in anger and Emma could see Hawk was replaying everything in his mind.

Emma reached out, sympathetically, and patted the man's forearm, "There's nothing you could have done. Frank is clearly nuts."

Hawk nodded but Emma could see he didn't believe her. He would just have to find his own way through this.

Emma looked at her friends and suddenly realized they hadn't eaten anything and she was starving. She shrugged off the blanket and walked over to the horses. Rummaging in her bag, she felt around for some food packs and walked back to the group.

"Looks like we're going to be here a while," she stated and handed out the food.

As Emma sat back down and enjoyed the food, her mind wandered back to Jack and she hoped he was safe and getting closer.

10

Jack had been the next to last person to guard the prisoners and that had worked out perfectly. Now that his turn was finished, Cat had taken over and he was headed down to the lake to bathe. It was still somewhat dark so he carried his flashlight, towel, clothes, and soap. He was getting used to cold baths and as hot as it had been yesterday, he would welcome the refreshing water.

There was a pier and Jack gratefully walked out until it was deep enough for him to jump in. Jack made sure there was a ladder to get back up. He then switched off his flashlight and waited for his night vision to return. As it did, he carefully looked around to make sure he was alone. When he was sure, he set his things down and quickly undressed. Steeling his nerves, he jumped into the water.

The cold water wasn't as much of a shock as he thought it would be, and he quickly bathed and pulled himself back on the pier. He briskly toweled dry and dressed, listening to the birds starting to chirp as he did.

Grabbing his dirty clothes, he walked back down the pier and saw that the sky had lightened considerably. He could now see the red sprites that Ray had told him about.

During the night, the strange storm had completely disappeared. He thought about what route they would take as he walked.

He hoped they could avoid most people as they went. He kicked a rock as he realized they probably wouldn't be able to avoid everyone. They would just have to deal with it as it happened.

Jack came out of the trees and saw that everyone was stirring.

Ray walked up to him and asked, "Did you just come back from bathing?"

Jack nodded. "Yeah, there's a pier that you can use. If you don't have soap, I have some."

Ray's face lit up, but instead of heading toward the pier, he headed to the other side of the truck where Cat was guarding the five strangers.

Jack was puzzled until he saw Ray talk to Cat and point excitedly toward the pier.

Suddenly, Jack understood. The way they were looking at each other now, he was surprised he hadn't seen it before.

There was something going on between them.

Jack realized he was standing there gawking like an idiot so he ducked his head and hid a smile. It was good to see some things on earth went on as usual.

He peeked and saw Ray asking Greg to take Cat's place while she went to bathe.

Greg started to say something and Ray just glared at him and he shrugged and nodded.

Grinning, Cat grabbed her bag. Ray stood at the head of the path while she went down to the pier.

Jack just grinned and shook his head as he turned back to the truck.

He saw Jason was gingerly stretching his left arm out and looking at the bullet wound in his upper arm. Jack had forgotten about it, but now was concerned as he saw Jason wince. Jack changed his course and walked to the trailer. He grabbed the first aid kit and a bottle of water.

Walking over to Jason he said, "How's the arm?"

Jason tried to blow it off. "It's fine. I just need to stretch it."

Jack shook his head. "Now's not the time to be stubborn. Let me clean it and put some antibiotic ointment on it. You'd be doing me a favor since I really don't want to saw your arm off if it gets gangrenous."

Jason blanched but then nodded and held out his arm.

As Jack was finishing with the dressing, he saw Dai Ji Kuan off to one side practicing what he assumed was Tai Chi. The man was so calm about everything. Jack couldn't understand what the Chinese man was thinking. He shook off the frustration as he put the first aid kit away.

He noticed Cat was back and was smiling, looking refreshed.

Jack turned his attention to the five strangers and walked over to them. They were all awake and looked sullen.

"I'm sorry I can't offer you anything to eat, we can't spare anything," Jack said, then continued. "After we leave, your guns and knives will be left close enough to use on the ropes. Your horses will be tied up over there." He pointed over to the area where Ray and Cat caught the couple last night.

"We'll be long gone and I encourage you to go back to your families. Don't follow us." He said this last part with a touch of menace in his voice and he saw they were suitably alarmed.

When nobody said anything, Jack nodded curtly and turned to Greg, "I'll watch them, if you want to go bathe."

Greg thanked Jack and he joined Ray on the way to the lake. Jason had heard what Jack said and took the group's horses over to where Jack said they would be and tied them up.

Jack glanced over at the truck and saw Cat and Chris putting things away and getting ready to go.

Kuan was finished with his exercises and calmly went over to help the two pack.

Soon the two agents were back from the lake, and Jason and Chris took their turn.

Henry, the apparent leader of the five, asked Jack, "Who are you people? Are you with the government?"

Jack looked over at the older man and said, "You don't need to know that. All you need to know is that we're the good guys."

After a few seconds of silence, Jack went on, "When you leave here, go home and get organized. Gather your closest neighbors and form a neighborhood watch. Not a tame neighborhood watch, but a watch on steroids.

"Make sure everyone has a weapon to defend their homes and families and be sure they know how to use those weapons. Nobody knows if this is the way things are going to be from now on, but prepare as if it will be. I think it will get worse before it gets better."

As he finished talking, Jack could see the group was thinking about what he'd said. He took the opportunity to look over at the truck and saw everything was ready.

Jack placed the group's confiscated items about ten feet away from them. He then took an open pocketknife out of the bag and stuck it in the ground just far enough away that it would take some time to get it with their feet and cut the ropes.

He looked at Henry and said simply, "I wish you luck."

Jack turned quickly and walked to the truck where everyone else was loaded up, waiting. Sliding into the driver's seat, Jack inserted the truck key and they were off.

As the truck neared the main road, Jack put the brakes on and asked Jason to make sure nobody was on the road.

Jason nodded and stealthily jogged up to the turnoff.

After looking carefully both ways, he jogged back and said, "All clear."

Jack nodded and turned east onto the road and accelerated.

It was mid-morning and already starting to get warm. Jack was glad he had a light t-shirt on, but he was still starting to sweat. With the windows down, it was a little better, but not much.

Jason asked, "Which way are we going? I know you looked at the map."

Jack replied, "There are going to be more people out walking. As the event lasts, more people will get desperate. I'm going to cut through more back roads and try to get to Nashville. Once we get close, I'm going around it and reconnect to I-40. Beyond that, we'll just have to wing it. I know we can't travel after dark unless we find something to make the headlights less noticeable. Otherwise, we're just going to attract everyone's attention to ourselves."

Jason nodded thoughtfully. "Maybe some red plastic. At least it won't be so glaringly obvious."

They both fell silent for a bit then Jack changed the subject. "Why don't you tell me about this device that we're supposed to use to knock out the EMP's effects?"

Jack had been waiting for the right time to ask Jason about this mysterious device and now, with a long drive looming ahead of them, seemed to be the perfect time. Jack waited expectantly for his old boss's response.

Time dragged on as Jason looked away and appeared to gather his thoughts. Jack sat patiently waiting.

After a while, Jason sighed and then spoke, "We found out about the bombs a few years ago. Once we knew the details about how advanced their plot was, a committee was formed to find a way to either stop it or defend against it. I was named one of three committee advisors and was given top clearance. Secrets that for decades were only known by a few, were now completely revealed to me in the hope that we could use any means possible to stop the event."

As the sun continued to rise and the miles rolled by, Jack sat quietly listening to Jason's revelations. Several times, they had to stop and move stalled automobiles off the road, but most cars were already near the side of the road. It was to Jack's advantage that when cars stall, people instinctively angled them to the side of the road.

Jason continued his story. "Our government has been on damage control mode since Roswell. Things you heard on the Internet and whispers attributed to conspiracy theorists are mostly true."

Jack whipped his head around and stared at Jason. The man's face was calm but drained of all color. Jack let his old friend continue. "Groom Lake." Here, Jason paused, and for a few minutes, Jack didn't think he would continue. He waited and then Jason went on, "The things they have there are…it's…"

Jason's voice had gotten more quiet and somber, which wasn't like the old Jason.

Jack gently prodded him, "Groom Lake? Isn't that—?"

Jason cut him off, "Yeah, Area 51. The UFO place. The Administration did a really good job making everyone think that anyone who even *says* the word UFO is a crackpot." He was slowly shaking his head as he looked out the front windshield.

Jack wanted to ask him some questions, but he stayed

quiet, waiting for Jason to continue.

Jason looked over at Jack and he saw his friend's face had aged just in the small time since they broached this subject. Jack felt bad but he needed information.

"What did you see, Jason? Tell me what to expect." He gently prodded Jason and it worked.

"There are things, Jack, which I couldn't explain to you. Even if I could describe it, there is no way for you to understand the strangeness of the material used in these devices."

Jason looked over at Jack with questioning eyes to see if Jack understood.

"When you look at chrome, you know it's chrome. When you look at gold, you know it's gold, and so on."

Out of the corner of his eye, Jack saw Jason's left hand tremor ever so slightly and for some reason that unnerved Jack more than anything Jason had said. He waited.

Jason took a breath and went on, "There were so many devices and angled metal that had an appearance to them." He stopped and had no words for a few seconds. Jason composed himself and shifted in his seat to face Jack more squarely. "When I was allowed in, I was almost smug. I had been briefed on what to expect. I found out later that my briefing omitted a lot of important details."

Jason's eyes were wide and Jack, again, waited.

"I touched some of the items they had and they felt like silk and water combined into a solid object."

Jack glanced at Jason and said, "Are you sure? That can't be possible!"

Jason came back to himself and looked sternly back at Jack, "I know what I saw! I also know what I felt."

Jack was a little rattled. He believed Jason; it was just a lot to take in.

They fell quiet for a while. Each mulling over all the shared information.

Before they could go on, they saw the truss part of the bridge spanning the Mississippi River. They had come to Caruthersville, Missouri, the only bridge over the massive river for sixty miles in either direction.

Suddenly, Jack pulled to the side of the road behind some bushes.

There was a two-mile flat straightaway that gently sloped up to the large cantilever bridge. Something had caught Jack's eye and his instincts saved the day.

Jason looked at him. "What is it?"

Jack shook his head, distracted, as he switched off the truck.

Jason sighed and got out of the truck to quietly talk to the other passengers.

Jack squinted as he focused on the road ahead and searched the scene to identify the source of his alarm.

Then, he spotted it. He reached to the floorboard and grabbed the binoculars.

Before raising them to his eyes, he slid out and just listened. He heard sporadic gunfire.

Jack placed the field glasses to his eyes just as he saw a bloom of orange fire erupt from the sides of the bridge.

At first, Jack thought the group of cars that were arranged at the entrance to the bridge had exploded for some reason. Then, he realized that an explosion had occurred on the bridge itself.

A second later he saw the top of the bridge disappear. As the boom of the explosion reached the group, they jumped.

Jason had come around to Jack's side and he muttered, "Jesus…"

Jack swept his fingers through his hair in agitation. "Christ! Are you kidding me?" he asked in exasperation.

Turning to Jason, he said, "We can't go this way. We'll have to go downstream about sixty miles and hope that bridge is crossable. We need to find out what's happening though. Do you think Ray's group can do some recon?"

Jason was nodding before Jack finished his last sentence. Turning away, Jason spoke with the three agents.

Jack looked back at the bridge and realized he was hearing a firefight. A battle. He never thought he would hear that noise on American soil.

Jack turned back to the truck. He saw that everyone had gotten out, and he looked around to find a place to hide the truck and trailer.

Jack grabbed a pair of pliers and cut the barbed wire fence on the south side of the road. The bushes were a perfect camouflage, and he drove the truck through the break in the fence. Kuan and Chris trailed the truck as Jack eased the rig to a stop.

Jack walked over to the opening and started cutting branches to cover the breach. He was surprised to see Chris grabbing branches and lining the opening.

Kuan had smoothly joined Chris and this surprised Jack even more.

As he finished the cover, Jack overheard Jason giving the last instructions to Ray, "Just find out what's going on and get your asses back here!"

Ray was in the zone, and when in the zone, it was a whole new world. The air seemed electrified and his senses were acute.

He looked at his team and saw they were the same.

Looking up under his brows, he told Jason, "We'll be back in an hour. Tell me where you'll be, just in case we're late."

Jason understood, and pointed. "We'll be right over there. I'll expect a full report."

Ray nodded and walked off. Cat grinned crookedly at Jason then strode off behind Ray. Greg watched the whole thing and rolled his eyes.

Ray called to Greg and he followed.

* * *

Ray decided to lead the way on the left.

He signaled Cat and Greg to fall in behind him and watch his back. From what he had seen, Ray thought the two teams of engaged combatants were fighting over the bridge. If that were true, they would be focused on each other.

As they neared the bridge, Ray put up a fist to stop his two other team members. Everyone stopped and assessed the situation.

Ray watched as the two groups exchanged fire. The groups seemed to be evenly matched and both had good cover. He quietly eased through the bushes and finally came within forty yards of the group on this side.

He saw several people yelling back and forth at each other and looking for ammo.

Ray looked up where the missing section of bridge had been and saw a group of people who were clearly military. They had camo outfits on and AR-15s. They were moving from cover to cover on the far side of the hole in the bridge and they seemed to be arguing.

Just ahead of him, Ray heard this group of militants were arguing as well. Some were saying to save their ammo.

Ray had heard enough and had just decided to leave when he heard a commotion behind him. He spun on his knee and saw Cat about five feet from where Greg had just taken someone down. Ray rushed back to the two and reached them just as Greg stood up. Ray saw there was an unconscious teenage male lying on his back. He was African-American and had a shiny new AR-15 lying next to him.

"What happened?" Ray hissed at Greg.

Greg shrugged as he looked at the youth. "He must have been a sentry. He didn't see us as he tried to sneak up on you." He scratched the back of his head and continued, "I jumped him and knocked him out."

Cat raised an eyebrow and Ray sighed. Now they were going to have to take the guy with them. On second thought, this might even be better. They'd take the kid back and let Jack and Jason question him. They'd find out from him what was going on.

"Alright. Cat, you watch our back and Greg and I will carry him." Ray eyed his two teammates. "No more surprises. Okay?"

Greg replied, "It's not my fault, Ray! Honest! He…"

Ray didn't let Greg finish. He held his hand up. "Not now, Greg."

Greg sighed grumpily but helped Ray lift the boy.

As Ray and Greg swiftly retraced their route, Cat picked up the rifle and followed them.

Arriving back at the truck, the two agents dropped the boy on the ground and caught their breath.

Jason and Jack walked up and stared at the youth like he had two heads.

"What's he doing here?" Jason asked.

Greg piped up, "We didn't think we had enough people in the truck and figured we'd bring him along."

Cat snorted a bark of laughter before containing it, but Ray shot Greg a withering glare. Greg looked back at Ray with a look of mock surprise.

Jason's face turned dark and he snarled at Greg, "Okay, smartass! That's enough! What happened?"

Greg seemed unperturbed and answered, "He was sneaking up on Ray and I had to do something, so, I hit him in the jaw. He should be coming around any minute."

As Greg finished, there was a groan from the boy and everybody looked at him.

Jack retrieved some duct tape before the boy became fully conscious, and taped his mouth, hands, and feet. Then they sat him up against the front bumper of the truck.

His head started to slump to the side and then his eyes jerked open wide.

He looked up at them all and started to speak. When he realized his mouth was taped, he started breathing hard and struggling. That was when the boy realized his hands and feet were tied and he really started to struggle.

Jack felt sorry for the young man and squatted next to him. Placing a calming hand on the boy's shoulder, Jack gently said, "We're not going to hurt you. We just want a few answers."

The youth had calmed as Jack spoke and his eyes darted to the others. When they got to Greg, the boy's brows lowered angrily.

Jack saw this and told Greg, "I don't think he likes you

much. Why don't you go see about Kuan?"

Greg sighed and walked away.

Turning back to the young man, Jack said, "I'm going to remove the tape from your mouth. When I do, I want you to keep quiet and answer our questions. If you yell, I'll knock you back out. If you answer my questions, I'll let you go and we'll leave. Is it a deal?"

The boy looked around, then slowly nodded.

Jack hoped the boy was telling the truth and he reached up and quickly snatched the tape off. It was the less painful way.

The young man hissed, but didn't yell.

"Who are you people?" the youth asked.

Jack said, "We'll get to that, but right now I want to know your name."

The boy looked at Jack and seemed to relax. "My name's Simon. Simon Fell."

"Nice to meet you, Simon. My name's Jack. What's going on at the bridge?"

Simon's eyes narrowed and he asked, "Why do you want to know?"

Jack sighed inwardly at Simon's suspicion. *He probably thinks we want to hurt his friends at the bridge.* Jack needed to reassure Simon that they weren't going to do that.

Jack shifted and said, "Listen. We don't want to hurt anyone. We just wanted to cross the bridge. Now that your friends blew it up, we're going to find a new place to cross.

However, it's important that we understand what the fight's about so we know what to expect down the road. I'm pretty sure that this same thing is happening everywhere. Now, please tell me what's going on here."

While Jack was talking to Simon, Ray and Cat decided to give them some time and wandered off to keep watch.

As Jack waited for Simon to answer, he saw Chris a few feet away, listening intently. He still didn't know what to make of Chris. By his actions, Jack would usually think of him as a spy. That was impossible, though, since nobody could have timed Chris's appearance so perfectly.

He returned his attention to Simon as the boy spoke. "You promise to let me go if I tell you?"

Jack nodded, "I give you my word."

Something in Jack's demeanor convinced the boy and his shoulders slumped. He realized he didn't have a choice anyway and he began, "We live here in Caruthersville. We were getting used to life after the blast and had a nice routine going. Everybody had something to trade or could work for food or things we needed. Then, a few days ago, an organized group of guardsmen from Dyersburg came over the bridge and said they were setting up martial law in the region. They have set up FEMA camps over on the Tennessee side and were going from town to town to gather up refugees to go to these camps.

"They said that the refugees would be given food, shelter, water, and protection in exchange for labor. After they left, my pa said that we had all that now and he wasn't about to leave. Dad's a member of the city council and they all agreed with him. The council sent Mr. Jeffers over to tell the Guard thank you but we didn't need any help. Mr. Jeffers came back with a message from the leader of the Guard saying that we didn't have a choice."

Simon spat the last few words out in anger but went on, "He said he was acting on the authority of the government and they would be coming to 'evacuate' everyone, and we were told to make preparations."

He angrily shook his head as he had a far-off look in his eyes. Coming back to himself, Simon spoke a little louder, "Ain't nobody going to tell us where to go and what to do, mister!" He aimed this last rant viciously at Jack.

Jack understood Simon's frustration. The American people weren't accustomed to having their freedom taken away and they would fight to the death over it.

He sighed as he recognized the growing unrest they had witnessed over the last couple of days. Another civil war loomed on the horizon if something wasn't done. Even then, it may be too late to stop it.

He looked back at Simon as the boy went on, "That made my pa and the rest of the council angry and they held a town hall meeting. A vote was called for and most of the people wanted to stay. The ones who voted to go were just lazy and thought they could get free food and shelter."

He stopped and looked angrily at Jack. "We let 'em go and good riddance! We told them to tell the leader of the Guard not to come across the bridge. We knew he would anyway, so we rigged some fertilizer bombs to the middle of the bridge and waited for them to come over."

Simon spat and then finished his story. "Right after the sun came up, we saw them starting over on the far side, and we lit the fuse. That happened just before I spotted the big guy. Then that asshole hit me!"

Jack apologized for Greg and then asked Simon if he wanted some water.

The young man nodded and Jack told him he'd be right back.

He asked Chris to keep an eye on Simon and then beckoned Jason to follow him to the trailer.

He kept an eye on Chris as he talked to Jason. "We're running out of time. As this situation drags on, there are going to be more and more skirmishes. We've got to get going. You round everyone up and we'll check the fluids in the truck. As soon as we're ready we'll head south. I'm going to check the map and see what route to take."

Jason asked, "How are we going to keep Simon from giving the alarm?"

Jack replied, "The same way we left the last group."

Jason sighed, then turned away.

Jack got some water and walked back over to Simon.

After he held the bottle for the boy to drink, Simon swallowed and then said, "You guys better hurry if you're going to cross the river downstream."

Jack's ears perked up and he asked, "Why's that?"

Simon wiped his mouth on his shoulder and said, "Because the river's rising. Pretty fast, too. Must have been a crapload of rain up river, and with the springtime runoff, it's going to be a heck of a flood."

It dawned on Jack what the boy was saying and he blanched.

He quickly stood up and instinctively looked toward the river. Of course, he was too far away, but he could only imagine the rising waters.

He turned to Chris and said, "Go find everyone and tell them to get their asses back here! Hurry!"

Chris didn't look surprised and this briefly nagged at Jack, but then he forgot about it.

He reached in the truck for the map and spread it on the truck hood. Tracing his finger across the potential routes, he memorized the best roads to take and then folded it up and tossed it on the dash.

Looking around, he saw word was spreading like wildfire to the rest of the group about the impending flood and everybody was moving with a purpose.

He took his knife out and cut halfway through the tape on Simon's hands but put the piece of tape back across his mouth.

Looking into the young man's eyes, he said, "I gave you my word to not hurt you. Now, I need your word to not tell anyone about us until we're on down the road. Do you promise?"

The boy seemed to come to a decision and nodded. As Jack stared back at Simon, he felt in his soul that the boy would honor his word.

He smiled at Simon and then got Chris to help him drag the youth away from the truck. When they had him a safe distance away, they all loaded up and Jack started the engine. He saw shock in Simon's eyes as he did a U-turn and drove back down the road away from the river.

Before they got back on the interstate, Jack pulled to the side and got out.

Everybody was watching him, but Jack ignored them. He had taken Simon's AR-15 and extra cartridges.

He now handed them to Ray and said, "We're going to be using the main road, so we'll be coming across more people. I don't want to hurt anybody, but this is just in case."

Ray understood and took the weapon.

Jack then went to the back of the trailer and opening the door, he removed a Mossberg twelve-gauge riot gun with a box of shells. He also withdrew a Winchester .30-.30 rifle with ammo. He took the two weapons back to Greg and Cat. "Same for you two. You can figure out which one you want."

He paused as the remaining agents took the high-powered weapons and smoothly loaded them.

When they were ready, he said, "I don't want to hurt anyone, but things are getting serious now. We have to hurry to make it across the Mississippi before it floods. Unfortunately, the only place to cross is in Memphis. That was a dangerous city even before the blast. I'm not taking any chances. If anyone seems a threat, rack that Mossberg, or cock the rifle and point it at them. If they still don't back off, wound them and let them know you mean business."

Ray was impressed. He heard a steely tone in Jack's voice that he always had suspected was there, but had not heard up to this point. He had a hunch now that they'd make it.

Jack had pulled over next to two stalled vehicles, one in front of the other. He now turned back to the trailer and removed a siphoning tube and a gas can.

As he walked over to the first car, he said over his shoulder, "This is the last pit stop for a while. If you need to go to the powder room, better do it now."

This lit a fire under everyone and they took turns in the bushes and keeping watch.

Jack finished siphoning the gas and had gotten a full five gallons. They still had quite a bit of gas in the trailer, but he was taking every opportunity to scavenge more. He checked the inside of the two cars for anything they might use.

All he found were empty fast food bags and other trash.

Looking around to make sure everyone was back, he took his turn.

Arriving back at the truck, Jack slid into the driver's seat and started the engine.

As he sat and listened to the rumble of the powerful engine, he said, "They'll be desperate now, Jason."

Jason looked confused. "Who, Jack?"

Looking over at his friend, Jack replied, "The people. Everyone. They know the power isn't coming back on. They'll do what they have to in order to feed their families. And themselves. Very dangerous."

He looked over at Jason to drive his point home. "I grew up in Tennessee. Memphis is part of my old stomping grounds. I can only imagine what this event has done to stir that hornet's nest. We have to make it across the river in Memphis. If we can't, we'll have to waste more time and go down to Helena two hours farther. That is not an option."

Jason nodded. "I understand."

Jack looked at Jason a moment longer, then put the truck in gear.

11

Emma sat up with a start. She was breathing hard and looked around to see what woke her. Seeing the cave, it all came back to her and she became sad as she remembered the massacred family. She reminded herself that this was the sheriff's fault, and silently vowed to rescue Pete and bring Frank Green down in the process.

She shook off the poisonous thoughts and sensed the horses moving restlessly in the dark. They must be tired of being in the cave. Emma felt around for the flashlight and woke Lori up in the process.

"What is it?" Her friend whispered sleepily.

"I'm looking for the flashlight," Emma whispered back. She kept feeling around, and finally found it just as she heard Bryan stirring.

She cupped her hand around the end of the light so that just a tiny pinpoint of light would show. She switched it on and checked her watch. Seven fifteen. They'd been asleep for several hours. Emma felt refreshed and ready to get out of this cave. She looked over to where Hawk should be and saw he was gone. She quickly glanced around in the weak light and confirmed he was no longer in the cave.

She saw Lori and Bryan stretching and rubbing their eyes.

As she stood up to get some water, Hawk splashed through the curtain of water.

It scared Emma badly enough that she had her Glock out and pointed at Hawk before she knew who he was.

Once she realized it, she relaxed and bowed her head.

"I almost shot you!" Emma stammered.

Lori and Bryan sat stunned.

Hawk had been looking wide eyed at Emma, but now he said quietly, "I'm sorry, girl. I didn't mean to startle you. By the way, do you own a cat?"

It was such an unexpected question that Emma blinked twice before answering, "Yes! Why? Did you see her?"

Before her last question, Hawk was nodding and now answered, "She's right outside the cave on a low branch waiting for you."

Emma noticed that he seemed sad and was still grieving for his family. Her heart went out to him but she had no idea what to say.

"Well, that's good to know. She'll still be there in a bit. What did you find out?"

Hawk replied, "It looks like they've moved on to look for me somewhere else. I don't think they realize that you all are with me."

He looked over at Emma. "You're free to leave. Get far away from here and keep your head down."

He stepped over to get his bag and Emma looked at her

friends. She shot them a questioning look and they both raised their eyebrows and shrugged.

Emma thought quickly as Hawk put supplies in his bag. She was determined to help him, but she didn't want to put her friends in danger.

As he continued to go through the supplies, Emma walked over to Lori and Bryan. "I'm going to help Hawk." Her friends started to whisper protests but she cut them off.

"You two don't need to be put in danger. I'll go back with you to Larry and Rita's. I'm sure they will let you stay there."

Emma was thinking, with her hands on her hips, and didn't see the look that passed between her two friends.

Before she could say anything else, Lori reached out and clutched Emma's forearm. "If you think we're going to sit around while you go have all the fun, then you must be crazy!"

Emma looked up at her friends and saw Lori had a scared, but determined, look on her face. Glancing at Bryan, she saw he looked the same.

Emma started to shake her head, but Bryan spoke over her. "You're not going to change our minds, Em. It's all for one, remember?"

Emma closed her eyes and sighed in exasperation, then opened them and smiled sadly at her two friends, "You know we could be killed doing this?"

Bryan and Lori returned the sad smile and nodded together.

Bryan said quietly, "I couldn't live with myself if I didn't help do something. Besides, what else do we have to do while we wait on your 'hero'?" He said the last part with a jaunty little wink.

Lori jabbed him with a sharp elbow then said to Emma, "He's right, you know. The sheriff and his men need to be stopped. I can't do a lot, but I can be a lookout or cook or do something!"

Emma's eyes watered as she looked at these two people and realized she loved them like siblings. With a lump in her throat, she hugged them without saying a word. She then turned quickly toward Hawk.

"We're going to help you."

He dismissed Emma. "No, you're not. It's too dangerous."

Emma's brows lowered as she set her feet and she answered back, "Yes, we are! We're aware of the danger. You have no idea the shit we went through to get away from Atlanta. If anybody is aware of the danger, it's us! I am sure you could probably do this yourself, but wouldn't it be nice to have people watching your back? It's obvious that Frank is capable of murder, and he has threatened all three of us too. If we don't help you and you don't stop him, he'll come after us next!"

As she finished, there was a deafening silence in the cave. Everyone was staring at each other as they thought about what had just been said. Emma held her breath as she awaited Hawk's reply.

After he pondered the possibilities, he relented. "Okay. I understand. But you three will listen to me and do *exactly* as I say. If you do, we might just make it out of this in one piece."

He looked at the floor of the cave and shook his head. "I must be crazy," he mumbled before turning back to the supplies.

Emma grimaced at her two friends before retrieving their own bags to put supplies in.

Bryan and Lori quickly joined her, and they all made preparations.

* * *

Sometime later they were ready and Hawk told them to wait as he went out to make sure it was clear.

As the friends waited, they watered the two horses and made sure the tack was tight.

Soon, Hawk was back and gave the all-clear. They walked through the falls in single file with Bryan bringing up the rear.

As soon as she cleared the water, Emma was watching her footing when she heard a distinct, almost angry, 'Meow!'

She smiled, even before looking up at Bella.

The feline was sitting up on the branch with her tail wrapped around her paws and seemed to have a disapproving look on her face as she gazed down at them.

After they all took a moment to get most of the water off, Emma handed the reins to Lori and walked over to the branch. "Hey there, fur ball! You didn't want to come in to see us? Oh, I get it. You didn't want to get your fur wet."

Hawk was watching all this with amazement. As Emma scooped the cat into her bag and put it over her shoulder, the man looked even more surprised.

Bryan had watched his reaction and as he led his horse past the man, he laughingly said, "You'll get used to it. I did."

Hawk closed his mouth and shook his head. "I've not seen anything like that."

"Yeah. Me either. Until now."

Emma brought up the rear and took Leroy's reins from Lori.

Emma asked, "We need to feed the horses?"

She left the statement hanging, since she was afraid to mention Hawk's brother Jeb's house.

Hawk hesitated at the lead position and then stopped.

Squaring his shoulders, he turned to the friends. "Jeb had horse feed in the barn. I have to go there anyway. To bury my family." He almost got this last part out before he hitched a sob.

He bit it off and went on, "You're welcome to it, if there's any left."

Emma immediately felt bad and said, "Thank you, Hawk. We'll help you and keep watch."

She didn't know what else to say, so stayed silent. It was slow going in the dark. It took a while to get back to the spot that Hawk and Emma were at earlier.

They all kneeled in the shelter of the trees as they scanned the clearing. Hawk kept them there for what must have been thirty minutes. Emma was about to say something to Hawk when he grabbed her hand hard and she winced.

Looking up in his face, she could barely make out his eyes and he shot a look across the yard to the other tree line. As she watched, she saw a small flame appear and then go out. A cigarette. She watched as the red spot flared as the smoker inhaled. She couldn't see the owner of the cigarette, nor how many others there were. She felt bad for Hawk. It didn't look like he'd be able to bury his family. He must have thought of this too. His grip on Emma's hand increased, painfully! She gently twisted her hand free and subconsciously rubbed her fingers.

Hawk appeared not to notice as he watched the glow for another minute. Then he held out a hand in front of the friends, palm down. Hawk waved the hand toward his chest in a gesture for them to follow him.

Emma looked at Bryan and Lori to make sure they understood. She nodded to Hawk to lead on.

He turned and stayed hunched over as they eased the horses through the trees as quietly as possible.

When they reached an embankment and moved silently to the other side, Hawk called a stop. They were far enough away from the watchers to risk talking.

Hawk breathed out a sigh. "I'm going to have to do something about them."

Emma knew he was talking about the smoker and nodded. "One of us can cause a diversion and the other can sneak up behind him."

Hawk was already shaking his head. "It's too dangerous. I'll take care of him. You three wait for me here."

Emma was getting tired of Hawk's macho crap. "Dammit! We're here to help you! Can't you get it in your thick Southern skull?" She spat this out quietly, but he got the point.

Tilting his head back for a moment, he mumbled something that Emma couldn't hear, but was sure wasn't flattering.

When he looked directly back at Emma, she could see the set of his face in the pale light. There was a smoldering anger, but she didn't think it was aimed at her.

He spoke and she knew she was right. "If you want to help me, then all I can say is thank you. Tell me what you have in mind."

She was relieved the man was going to let them help. "I say we give you time to get over near them. Once you're there, you'll need time to make sure there's just one person. After about twenty minutes, get a tree between them and you. Cover the flashlight end until just a pinpoint of light shows and flash it for each person you see. That'll let us know how many to expect. Once we know that, Bryan and I will leave the horses with Lori and walk up to knock on the door. That'll get their attention. As they watch us, you take them out. Do you have a watch?"

He looked thoughtful at her plan, then nodded.

Emma continued, "How long will it take you to get in position?"

"About twenty minutes. I'll have to go slow so they don't hear me. I'm thinking there's only one, but I'll need to stay still and watch just to make sure. Say another ten minutes. Give me thirty minutes before you get worried."

Emma nodded and stuck her watch out. Flicking on the covered flashlight she said, "Stick your watch out here so we can make sure they coincide."

They got the watches squared away and Emma switched off the flashlight. They were on the bank of a little creek and Hawk eased down to the creek bed. Removing his hat and laying it aside, Hawk reached down and grabbed some black mud. He proceeded to cover every inch of his skin that wasn't covered in clothes.

Picking up his mountain hat, he put it on the pommel of Leroy's saddle. "I'll be wanting that back when I'm done."

Emma nodded and watched the man slip away. He didn't make a sound and she mentally wished him luck.

Turning back to her friends, she told Bryan, "Make sure that crossbow's ready." She said this as she checked the Glock. When she looked at Lori, she saw her feisty little friend holding her knife in a ready position. She smiled, sadly, that life had come to this.

"Lori, we need you to stay here and watch the horses. We may need a quick getaway."

She waited for an argument from her friend, but it didn't

come, "I'll be right here, you guys. You better not leave me hanging!"

Emma was close enough to see the tears in Lori's eyes and she chuckled as she gave Lori a bear hug. "Do you really think we could be that rude?"

As Emma released her friend and stepped back, she saw that Lori was already looking for Bryan. Emma understood and walked over to Leroy to give the two a few minutes together. She checked her watch and then removed the bag from her shoulder. She hooked the strap over the pommel next to Hawk's hat. As she released the strap, Bella's head popped up and she looked inquiringly at Emma.

"Oh no, little girl! Don't even try it! You need to keep your furry butt right here!"

She could hear Bella purring and she smiled sadly as she rubbed the cat's ears. This seemed to calm Bella and Emma kept petting her until she heard Bryan moving behind her.

"You ready?" he asked as she turned toward them.

She saw that Lori was trying to hold back tears, and Bryan had a determined gleam in his eye.

"I'm ready. Lori, I know Bella's going to follow us. Don't try to stop her. It'll be more trouble than it's worth. We'll all be fine and be back here before you know it!" She said that last sentence with more conviction than she felt. It seemed to help Lori, though, and that's what counted.

Lori seemed to have renewed energy and stood taller as she grabbed the horses' reins. "I know. Please be careful and kick their asses!'"

This briefly surprised Emma but then she saw Bryan's crooked grin and snorted a laugh.

Emma checked her watch again and saw it was nearing time. "Let's go."

Emma and Bryan climbed silently back up the slope. As they reached the top, they stopped for a moment to make sure there was no one around. When they were sure, they quietly made their way back to the edge of the yard. They kneeled behind an oak and, shading the light, Emma flicked it on to check the time. Five minutes until show time.

She could feel her adrenaline flowing, and she took this moment to slow her heart rate.

As she did this, she listened closely to her surroundings. She heard crickets and frogs, but that didn't help much because they were croaking near her and Bryan too. She stared across the clearing, waiting for the signal. She felt Bryan shift next to her as the time dragged on.

There it was! Emma held her breath as she saw one flash of light. She waited to see if there were more. After only the one flash of light, Emma let out her breath and glanced at Bryan. He looked back at her and nodded.

She checked to make sure her gun was loose in its holster. She liked where it was, across her zipper. She found that it was easier to get to and the movement was less noticeable to other people.

Bryan and Emma stepped out of the tree line walking side

by side. There was no reason to be deceptive, so they casually walked around the back of the house to the porch.

She expected to be shot at any moment. As a result, every muscle in her body was tense.

When they got twenty feet away from the steps, she started to gradually slow her steps. She hissed at Bryan to let him know.

He understood and followed Emma's lead. She started to worry. Hawk should have been finished by now and should have called out to them. She quashed her misgivings and kept moving forward.

Suddenly, there was a gunshot and Emma screamed before she could help herself. She felt Bryan flinch and fall into her. After checking herself for a gunshot wound, she immediately thought of Bryan and swung around. She was expecting him to be on the ground and blood to be blossoming from his chest.

When she saw he was okay too, her eyes went round at the possibilities, "Oh, Jesus!" Emma barked, "Hawk!"

She said this as she grabbed on to the front of Bryan's shirt.

They both realized they needed to find shelter at the same time.

Since they were only ten feet away from the porch, they turned together and sprinted to safety.

Reaching the porch, they were breathing hard as they heard another shot from the woods.

She was confused as to what was going on. She hovered behind one of the columns trying to think it through. It sure was quiet now.

After waiting for more gun shots and not hearing any, she started to breathe a little easier.

She had been watching the trees in the direction the shots had come from, and had seen no movement.

Now she drew her brows down in puzzlement. Someone should have come out of the woods, shouldn't they?

Bryan hissed at her from the other column, "What the hell happened?"

Emma hissed back, "I don't know!"

She thought furiously. "Maybe they didn't see us and they shot Hawk twice. To make sure!"

Bryan looked out from behind his cover and searched the tree line. She could tell he was as confused as she was.

A movement caught her eye and she zeroed in on it.

It was small, about a foot away from where the trees started, just below where Hawk had signaled them.

The movement stopped, and as she concentrated, it dawned on her what it was. Bella.

Her jaw dropped open, and she heard Bryan exclaim, indicating he'd seen it too.

She looked over at Bryan, who angled a cocked eyebrow back at her.

She closed her mouth and waved him off.

Emma decided to take a chance and stepped down off the porch. Bryan gasped and whispered, "Emma!"

She ignored him and started walking toward the cat. When she realized she wasn't going to be shot, she started walking faster and then ran. She heard Bryan's footsteps as he ran down the steps after her.

Bryan caught up to her and they were out of breath as they reached Bella. Before entering the trees, Emma whispered, "Hawk!"

She wondered why she was whispering and then shouted, "Hawk! Where are you?"

Bryan had his crossbow up and was trying to look in every direction at once.

The animals in the immediate area were quiet. She heard a noise straight in front of them and she didn't hesitate. She pulled her Glock and ran directly toward the noise.

She was beyond angry now. If that noise was someone who'd hurt Hawk, they would pay. She didn't realize, that to Bryan, who was following her, she looked like a wild stallion. She was running full-tilt through the trees with her black hair streaming behind her.

Emma knew in the back of her mind that Bryan was trying to keep up with her, but she didn't care. At this point, she could only see red.

She realized she was gritting her teeth as she came around a tree and saw the leaves and dirt thrown around.

Emma stopped abruptly and Bryan almost ran into her. He dodged to the side as she slowly looked around.

Bryan's gaze followed hers and they saw three bodies on the ground. One of them was Hawk.

Emma's medical training kicked in and she ran to him. Hawk was lying on his back and his left hand lay on his belly. His right arm was flung up by his head, and his eyes were closed. Emma fell to her knees beside him and sent up a prayer as she felt for a heartbeat.

There was a pulse! The pulse was weak, so she knew he must be injured. Her hands shook with excitement as she began to check him over.

When she reached his left hand her breath hitched as she felt wetness, and Emma knew she'd found it.

"Bryan, he's been shot! Keep an eye out and..."

"Girl." It was Hawk, and he was whispering.

Emma leaned over so she could hear him, "Hawk, you've been shot. I'm a nurse. Keep quiet and let me check your wound."

He had turned his head and now shook it, slightly, as he spoke again. "No, Emma, you can't help me. I need you to listen."

Tears started in Emma's eyes as she slowly nodded.

"Good," Hawk said with a little grimace.

Emma hadn't noticed all the blood under Hawk until now and she knew he was right. He had little time left.

Emma was aware of Bryan going over to check the body deeper in the woods.

She returned her attention to Hawk. He was clearly in pain and she tried to calm him.

He grabbed her hand and pulled her closer. "That one is alive!" he said between clenched teeth. He pointed with his chin at the body that Bryan hadn't checked yet.

Emma abruptly looked at the man that Hawk indicated.

"Bryan! That guy's alive! Cover him!"

Bryan hurried to the unconscious man and pointed his weapon between the man's eyes.

Hawk was saying something else, so Emma leaned closer.

"You're a good person, girl. I knocked him out so you can question him." Hawk was slipping away.

She thought he was gone, but he gathered his strength to spit out two more things. "The cave holds more! Use it to find out where Pete is, please!" He was squeezing her hand almost to the point of breaking it as he started to say something else. Before he could, he passed away. Emma was staring into the man's eyes as she watched the life flow out of him. It always broke her heart when she witnessed it, but this was the first time she had really known the person. And it hurt.

She took a moment to get her feelings under control. Then, she placed both of Hawk's hands gently across his stomach.

Leaning down and staring into the dead man's eyes, she whispered where Bryan couldn't hear her, "I swear to you that I will do my best to find Pete. I also promise to make Frank Green's life a living hell, if I don't kill him outright."

Emma, very briefly, thought about the change that had come over her since the blast. Then she dismissed the thought and stood up.

She walked over to Bryan and asked, "Did you make sure the other piece of shit is dead?"

Bryan looked a little startled at her tone, but then answered, "Dead as a doornail."

Nodding to Bryan, Emma reached down and felt for the unconscious man's pulse. Slow but steady. Perfectly healthy, but out cold.

She shook herself and stood back up. "If he comes to, hit him here or here." She pointed on either side of the front of her jaw.

Before Bryan could ask, she said, "There are nerves that come through holes in the jawbone on each side. Trust me, he'll go down."

Before Bryan could say anything, Emma turned away and walked back to Hawk. She knew he wouldn't mind her borrowing his shoelaces.

It took her a minute to get them unlaced. Walking back to Bryan and the man, she got down and roughly jerked his hands together.

She was tying the last knot when the man started to moan and come around. She shoved his tied hands away and held her palm out to stop Bryan from conking the man on the jaw.

Bryan hesitated and then relaxed.

As the man became conscious, he realized where he was and that he was tied up.

Emma waited patiently until he said something.

Soon, he did.

"Hey!" he said, jerking his hands around, "this hurts!"

She studied the man before she spoke. He had stringy brown hair, dirty t-shirt and jeans, second hand boots and the smell of old body odor.

She was disgusted as she asked him in a quiet, authoritative voice, "What's your name?"

Bryan stood beside her with the crossbow bolt trained on the stranger's throat.

The man was in his mid-thirties and knew enough to sense he was in trouble.

"Jarvis," he replied sullenly.

That's all he said, and Emma knew she would have to 'encourage' him to tell them more. She was tired and didn't want to deal with him here. She hoped they had a few hours before these two would be missed.

She turned to Bryan and handed him her Glock. "Don't let him move. If he does, kill him like his friend killed Hawk."

Emma said this in a flat tone and she meant it.

Bryan saw this and hardened his heart. After taking her gun and nodding, he looked at Jarvis and sneered. He pointed both weapons point-blank at the man's chest, and the man quailed.

Emma took her knife and cut the laces from his boots. Jarvis started to kick, and Bryan showed he meant business by squatting and pressing the barrel of the Glock to the man's temple. Something in Bryan's eyes convinced Jarvis that this stranger would kill him. He stopped struggling.

Emma finished and removed his shoes. Once she'd done that, she threw them as far away as she could and Jarvis said, "Hey! What'd you do that for! I paid good money for those!"

Emma ignored him and told Bryan, "Give me a minute."

She walked back to Hawk and gathered up his gun and ammo and went through his pockets for anything they could use. When she was done, Emma walked over to the other dead man and realized it was a short-haired woman. She shook her head and searched the woman's body also. Not finding anything useful except the woman's .38 pistol, Emma stuck the pistol in her waistband and walked back to Bryan and the prisoner.

"Let's go." She reached down and grabbed the man under the arm. The grip that Emma had on him forced him to either get up or face a painful twisting of the arm.

At this point, Emma didn't care. She had tried to stay out of this fight, but Sheriff Green and his men chose to involve her and her friends. So be it.

Jarvis whined but struggled to get up, which he finally did. "Jesus, lady! You're hurting my arm!"

That did it!

Emma gritted her teeth and jerked up on the man's elbow and he scrambled to follow her lead. Listening to him squawk and protest, she finally got him over to Hawk's body and unceremoniously shoved him onto Hawk. She apologized, mentally, to Hawk.

"What the hell, lady!" Jarvis mewled.

Emma had *no* sympathy. "Look at him." She spoke under her breath, but loud enough for him to hear.

"What?" the dirty stranger asked.

Emma put her shoe on the man's shoulder and shoved him face to face with her dead friend. "Look at him!" she seethed.

Jarvis looked scared at Emma's voice and then looked at Hawk. He pushed himself away.

In a cold controlled voice, Emma said, "You killed this man. You might not have pulled the trigger, but you may as well have. He was a good man with a wonderful family who loved him and only wanted the best out of life. You helped take all of that away. You were here, weren't you?"

Jarvis was definitely scared now. He heard something in Emma's voice that frightened him badly. He physically tried to distance himself from the dead man.

Emma let him squirm a few feet away. After letting him think about what she had said, she squatted next to him, despite his smell.

"You will tell me everything." She spoke in a demanding

voice that gave no room for denial.

She went on, "I am a nurse. I am so close to being a doctor that you should really be frightened. Do you know why?"

She waited to let the idiot think. After a moment he shook his head.

"Because I know ninety percent of what doctors know about the human body, and yet, I did not take the oath to do no harm."

The man's eyes widened and he gaped like a fish.

Emma had ended the statement with a wide, crazy looking smile.

Jarvis leaned away from her in real fear.

Emma took the Glock from Bryan and barely touched the man's nose. She got the best angle for him to look down the barrel.

She waited for him to get nervous, and he did.

"Do you see that big bore hole? That is what's waiting for your miserable life if you give me any, and I mean *any*, problems."

Jarvis was sweating and afraid. He nodded, hesitantly. He was scared Emma would shoot him. She tapped him, playfully, on the nose with the gun barrel and then stood up.

"Bryan, would you please grab this piece of crap? We're going to the barn. I think I saw an engine hoist in there." She saw Jarvis's eyes get bigger, if that was possible.

Bryan didn't know what Emma was up to, but he saw

terror in the man's eyes, so he followed her lead.

"Get the hell up!" Bryan demanded as he grabbed the man's elbow in the same grip that Emma had used.

Amazingly, it worked! Jarvis whined and jumped up.

"Where are my shoes? I need my...!"

Emma rounded on him and snarled. "You don't get to have your shoes! You'll think twice about trying to run without them." She spat out this last sentence and then continued leading them back to the barn.

As she walked, Emma examined this side of her that had come out unexpectedly. She was basically a good person. She followed most of the rules and tried to help people anytime she could. There came a time, however, when enough is enough. She hated lazy people who fed off the goodness of others. Bullies, she despised a bully, and that is what Frank Green and his cohorts were. Bullies.

They arrived at the barn door and Emma jerked it open. With the flashlight now unshielded, she flashed it around the interior of the structure. She saw the horse stalls were now empty, thanks to the sheriff. There were the rafters and on the walls were various tools that Jeb had used to keep his farm running.

She looked at Bryan. "Take him over there and sit him on that bale of hay."

Bryan nodded and Emma retrieved a coil of rope. Walking back to Jarvis, she could tell he was frightened. For a split second she felt pity. But then, like a movie projector, images of the murdered family flashed across her mind and shut that pity down.

She reached across and tied one end of the rope around the shoestrings binding his hands. Stepping back, she looked up, and in the glow of the flashlight, she picked out the rafter she wanted. After two tries, she had just managed to get the end of the rope over the rafter when it dawned on Jarvis what she was planning.

He jumped up and was running for the barn door, when Emma snapped the end of the rope she was holding.

He must have thought he could break her hold or else had forgotten that he was tied to the other end.

Almost in slow motion, Bryan and Emma saw Jarvis come to the end of the rope. His hands whipped back over his left shoulder and his feet shot out from under him. There was a sickening snap, as one of his shoulders dislocated. He howled in pain just as the full force of his body slammed to the barn floor. He curled up in the fetal position as he favored his left shoulder. Emma could see his left arm had an unnatural twist to it.

This may have been the best thing to happen. As a nurse, she knew he would be in constant pain until the shoulder could be reduced. She would fix his shoulder, but not before he answered her questions.

He was still howling in pain. Emma pulled the rope tight and tied it off in a knot. Before walking over to the man, she looked at Bryan. "Please go get Lori. She probably heard the shots and is worried to death."

Bryan asked, "What about him?"

She smiled sadly and said, "He's not going anywhere."

Bryan looked back at the prisoner and nodded.

He covered his own flashlight and switched it on. He looked at Emma one last time and then was gone. She briefly examined that look and realized Bryan had looked at her with respect and a little fear. That was the first time he had looked at her like that. It hurt a little, but she knew he'd get over it. As soon as they were done here, he'd see she was the same old Emma. She hoped.

Jarvis's howls had degenerated into loud whimpers now that he wasn't moving around. Emma knew the shoulder still hurt him, but the nerves weren't being stretched if he laid still.

Walking over to the man, she bent down and rolled him onto his back. He was in so much pain that he didn't fight her.

She wanted to hurry, before her friends got back.

Emma looked him in the eye and said, "Tell me where they took the boy, Pete."

Jarvis looked at her out of pain-filled eyes. She could see that he feared her. That would make this easier for her to do.

"I'm not telling you nothing!" the man spat out. Emma saw flecks of spittle fall out over his lower lip onto his shirt.

She sighed heavily and said, "You know, in a way, I was kind of hoping that would be your answer. Remember when I told you I'm a nurse? That means that I know how to fix your shoulder." She hesitated and let that little tidbit of information sink in.

She saw hope dawn in his eyes, then she went on, "I also know exactly what to do to your arm to cause the maximum amount of pain. After I saw what you people did to this family, I WANT you to give me a reason to hurt you. Do you understand?"

He didn't answer, but Emma saw absolute terror in his eyes and knew that he did.

"I'm going to ask you one more time. Tell me where they took Pete."

She narrowed her eyes, gripped her gun, and waited.

Jarvis was breathing heavily between clenched teeth. As Emma waited, she soon realized he wasn't going to speak.

She didn't want to do this, but knew she had to.

Steeling her stomach, she found a rag and tied it over his mouth. Emma then gripped his elbow almost gently. She saw his eyes go round and his breathing increased. Sweat popped out on his forehead.

She still paused. She felt like this was a point of no return and she hesitated to cross that line.

But then, she knew she had to. She had to do this in order to do the right thing and save the boy.

With renewed conviction, Emma slowly and steadily pushed upward on Jarvis's arm. He started to scream again and clamped his eyes closed. The rag muffled the screams, somewhat, but the sound still tore at her. She blocked it out and continued to strain the arm against the already stretched tendons. She knew it was excruciating. Suddenly, Jarvis went limp and quit screaming.

Emma relaxed on the elbow. She knew he had passed out from the pain and she would have to wait. When the pain of an injury became too great, the brain protected itself and shut down.

When he came around, he would remember how excruciating the pain was and would be more likely to talk. It was a necessary step.

She didn't have long to wait. Jarvis moaned after a minute, then his eyes shot open. He whimpered behind the rag and cut his eyes at Emma in a begging expression.

Emma still gripped his elbow and now she twisted it, ever so slightly.

It was enough. He screamed against the rag and she heard him say, "Okay! Okay! Okay! I'll tell you!"

Emma immediately let up on his elbow and pulled the rag down. He was sweating freely now. Emma smelled urine and looked down at his pants. There was a wet stain where he had peed himself and that told her how much pain he had really gone through.

Emma's stomach rolled and she knew from that reaction that she retained her humanity and was glad. You never knew what might happen when you took this dark path.

She returned her attention to Jarvis. "Tell me."

He was still breathing heavily as he spoke. "If I tell you,

will you fix my arm?"

Emma nodded. "Absolutely."

He sensed that she was telling the truth and relented. "They took him to the gem mine."

Emma waited for more but he was quiet.

"What gem mine? Where is it?"

Jarvis hesitated and Emma encouraged him by softly squeezing his arm.

He inhaled sharply then nodded, "It's on the east side of the main road. About a mile south of Wears Valley Road."

He finished, exhausted.

She was just about to ask him another question when Bryan returned with Lori and the horses. She gave Jarvis a breather and walked to her friends.

"Emma?" Lori asked, "What's going on? Bryan wouldn't tell me."

She looked past Emma at the prisoner, "Who is that?"

Emma stepped back and looked at Jarvis as she said, "That would be Jarvis. One of the sheriff's men. He was left here to take Hawk prisoner. Instead, Hawk knocked him out but was killed by a woman. She was another of the sheriff's people and must have surprised him. He managed to kill her before he died."

Lori sucked in her breath, "Those were the two shots I heard! Oh, Emma! Hawk's dead?"

Lori had a stricken look on her face as Emma nodded sadly.

Lori recovered somewhat and looked closer at Jarvis. "What are you doing with him?"

Emma didn't hide anything from Lori. "Hawk knocked him out so he could question him about Pete's whereabouts and the sheriff's operations. I'm filling in for Hawk since he can't do it."

Emma said this grimly and Lori heard her tone. "What do you mean?"

Emma sighed, "I'm questioning him by using the injury to his shoulder. He tried to run away and dislocated it. I'm taking advantage of his pain."

She said nothing further and watched her friend as Lori quickly mulled this over.

"Has he told you anything?" Lori asked.

Nodding, Emma answered, "Yeah. He told me where they took Pete. I'm still waiting for him to tell me everything else about Sheriff Green."

Lori scratched the pink scar on her cheek then said, "Well, what are you waiting for? Finish making him talk."

A dark cloud had formed over her face and Emma saw that her friend was thinking not only about Hawk and his family, but the incident that occurred back in Kennesaw.

Emma was a little surprised and didn't move for a moment.

Lori saw her hesitate and asked, "What's wrong? Do you

need me to hold his legs or something?"

Emma heard Bryan snort a short laugh and she relaxed. "No. I got it. I need you and Bryan to keep a look out while he finishes telling me everything. I'll come get you when I put his shoulder back in. I'll need someone to help hold him down."

Lori nodded curtly and turned to Bryan. "Let's go, big guy. Emma's got work to do."

Emma saw the knife in Lori's hand as she turned away, and knew her friend was okay.

Bryan mock-saluted Lori as she passed him, and she slapped his chest. "Stop it."

After they left, Emma turned, walked back to Jarvis, and said, "You were telling me about Frank and what he's up to."

He was holding his arm next to his body in a less painful pose. This made him braver. "I've told you enough!" he said with defiance.

Emma shook her head in amazement. "You really are stupid, aren't you?"

Jarvis glanced uncertainly at Emma as she moved closer to the man.

Squatting down, she reasserted her grip on the injured elbow and Jarvis started to whimper.

"Really?" Emma whispered softly.

She increased pressure and he caved.

"No! No! Shit, lady! Okay." He tried to scoot away.

"Tell me," Emma said softly.

After a pause, Jarvis started talking. He rambled on for about an hour, and it dawned on Emma that even though this man might look like nothing, his powers of observation were good. He told her things about Frank that Hawk and his family probably weren't aware of. She dismissed a lot of the petty stuff, but then he hit on something that caught her attention.

"He's never been married," Jarvis said. He was starting to sound like he was glad to get things off his chest.

"When Frank was in high school, he was one of two great players on the football team and they were best friends. Frank was a star offensive lineman. The other guy was named Jack. Jack Dennison or something like that. He was the quarterback."

He started to move, then winced and held still for a moment.

Emma's mouth was dry. She licked her lips and said, "Was his name Jack Denton?"

Jarvis thought for a second and said, "Yeah! Yeah, that was him."

He looked at her, "How'd you know?"

Emma shook her head, "It doesn't matter. Tell me about Frank and this other guy."

Jarvis hesitated as he sensed this information was important to her. "I-I don't know."

Emma was impatient now. She remembered how Frank

had reacted to Jack's name, and she knew she needed to find out what happened between the two men. She also felt they were running out of time.

She gripped his elbow hard and slowly pushed up. She knew this was grinding the head of the upper arm bone against the already inflamed nerves of the socket.

Jarvis didn't expect this and squealed like a girl.

"I don't have time to play with you, Jarvis! If you don't finish telling me about Frank and Jack, I will twist your wrist behind your back!"

She had her teeth clenched together and there was fire in her eyes. The man had no doubt that she would do this. He had already told her everything else; he might as well finish.

When he spoke, his voice trembled and he said, "Uh, well, the story I got was that they were friends growing up. In high school, they weren't as close and then something happened their senior year that made them enemies."

He stopped to catch his breath and whimpered.

Emma forced herself to be patient. After a moment, when it was clear that Jarvis wasn't going to continue, Emma started to grab the man's elbow again.

Jarvis saw this and said, in a high-pitched voice, "Wait! I was just thinking. I'll finish telling you."

Emma saw he was resigned and waited while he gathered his strength. Soon he continued, "No one knows what happened that night. All we know for sure is that there was some confrontation one night on a road outside of town.

It was their prom night and there was a woman involved." Jarvis shrugged before he thought about it, then yelped at the pain.

When he went on, he was grimacing. "Soon after that, the other guy joined the military and didn't come back to town except to visit his parents before they died."

Emma was beginning to understand Frank's reaction to her mentioning Jack's name. She looked back at Jarvis and asked, "What happened that night?"

The man was clearly exhausted as he shook his head and said, "I don't know. Nobody does. I'm Frank's cousin and drinking buddy, and he would never talk about it. In fact, he almost beat the shit out of me one time when I asked him about it."

Jarvis quit talking and Emma realized he had told her all he knew. It was time to finish up here and get going. She stood up and walked to the barn door. While she and Jarvis "spoke", Emma had noticed that her friends had looked in on her from time to time. She knew they had been checking on her and letting her know they were okay.

Sliding back the door, she saw Lori had found a chair to sit in and had it tilted back against the barn wall.

She saw Emma and sprang to her side. "What did he say?"

Emma stretched her arms above her head as she saw Bryan walking up to them.

As he reached them she answered, "He confirmed everything that Hawk had told us about Frank's operations.

The sheriff has changed it up a little bit since the blast. Now, he's using prisoners, or people he's arrested, to work at his different projects. The sheriff is saying that since this is a time of emergency, he, the mayor, and the judge are the law until the government gets organized.

"He told me a lot of other things, but nothing else really relevant to this. The main thing is that the sheriff is holding Pete at the gem mine. He also told me where it is. I need to reduce the man's shoulder and then we need to figure out what to do with him."

Lori stared at her friend. "You don't mean to kill him, do you, Em?"

Emma could see that her friends had seen such a change in her that they truly believed she might kill the man.

She smiled sadly at her friends and replied, "No, I haven't gone that far over the edge." The smile left her face as she became serious again. "We can't let Jarvis go, however. He'll run back to the sheriff and tell him all about us. As far as Frank is concerned, we've left the area. I want to keep it that way." Emma decided to wait to tell her friends what she had learned about Frank and Jack.

Her friends looked relieved that Emma wasn't going to kill Jarvis.

Bryan then said, "They're going to come looking for him and the dead woman. We need to make a plan and get out of here."

Emma sighed and nodded. "I know. I say we bury Hawk, then make it look like he got away with Jarvis. That'll worry the shit out of the sheriff and they'll be looking for Hawk and Jarvis. Meanwhile, we'll take Jarvis and tie him up somewhere. I haven't figured out where. Any suggestions?" She raised her eyebrows at her friends and waited.

Bryan and Lori looked at each other as they thought. Emma was searching her own mind for any place that might work. She paced back and forth as she thought.

Lori said, "What about Larry and Rita? There's a basement in their cabin."

Emma shook her head, "No, I don't want to involve them. Did you see how freaked out they were about everything?"

Her friends went back to thinking. It was then that it dawned on Emma.

She raised her hands and said, "Hey! What about the cave! Frank doesn't know anything about it, and we can tie Jarvis up well enough that he can't escape. After we get Pete, we'll let him go!"

Bryan was looking at her, but started shaking his head as she finished. "If we're able to get Pete, we'll need the cave to hide in so they can't find us. If Jarvis knows about it, he'll lead them straight to us. We can't give away our only hideout."

Emma was frustrated, but knew Bryan was right. They would just have to think of something else. Meanwhile, she had to fix his shoulder.

"We'll think of something. Bryan, you keep watch while Lori and I put his shoulder back in. Are you up to it?" She asked Lori, gently.

Lori squared her shoulders and said, "You bet!"

Emma smiled as she squeezed Lori's hand and they turned back to go in the barn.

Stepping up next to Jarvis, Emma could see he was semi-conscious. The man was curled in a ball, protecting his left shoulder and whimpering.

Emma spoke softly to Lori, "We're going to turn him on his back. While I do this, I'll need you to keep him on his back, okay?"

Lori seemed calm and determined as she nodded.

Emma moved next to Jarvis and said, "I'm going to put your shoulder back in. I won't lie to you. This is going to hurt like hell, but you'll feel better once I'm done. Do you hear me?"

The man's eyes were closed but he nodded curtly, so she knew he had heard.

She stood up and grabbed the flashlight. Lori had her own flashlight on.

"I'm going to look for something. I'll be right back."

Lori nodded and Emma moved away. She needed some kind of cushion to put in his armpit as she pulled on the arm. She searched the barn and finally decided a rolled up saddle blanket would do. She grabbed it and walked back to Jarvis. She asked Lori for her knife and cut the strings tying his hands.

Rolling up the blanket, she explained to the man what she would be doing. She nodded to Lori as she rolled him onto his back and Lori positioned herself on her knees next to his right shoulder. Jarvis squealed just as his shoulders touched the floor but then stopped and panted.

Emma told the man, "You need to slow down your breathing. I want you to concentrate and breathe in through your nose and out through your mouth. While you do that, I'm going to put this cushion under your left arm. Then, I've got to put my left foot in your armpit, grab your wrist, and slowly pull down on it. It's going to be almost unbearable for a moment, but don't tense up or it will take longer to pop back in. Got it?"

He was sweating freely now, but his pain-glazed eyes were open and looking right at Emma with a pleading look. He nodded again.

Emma hesitated as she thought of something, then held her finger up for Lori. Standing back up, she went over to the barn wall where she had seen a riding crop and grabbed it from the wall.

She took it over to Jarvis and said, "Bite down on this when the pain starts. It'll help."

He opened his mouth and she placed the crop between his teeth.

She positioned herself next to the man's left hip. She looked at Lori, who nodded back at her. Wiping her hands on her shirt, Emma placed her left foot in Jarvis's armpit, grabbed his wrist with both hands and leaned back slowly and steadily. She could feel the muscles and tendons working against her and she pulled harder.

Jarvis was grinding his teeth against the crop and started screaming. His eyes were squeezed tightly shut and his neck was arched back.

Emma knew she was close to popping it back in, and she gave the arm just one final tug, and then it happened. Emma felt the head of the humerus slide over the socket and seat itself right into the joint. Jarvis quit screaming immediately but was still panting. His entire body went limp and Emma let go of his arm.

Jarvis spit out the riding crop and Emma stood up. She felt drained. Lori had pushed herself back from Jarvis and stood up unsteadily. She looked over at Emma and smiled hesitantly.

Emma nodded slowly at her friend and then looked back down at Jarvis. It always amazed her how quickly the pain subsided when a patient's dislocated limb was reduced.

Emma was about to walk outside and get some air when Jarvis said quietly, "I'll help you get Jeb and his family out."

He stopped and panted some more.

Emma wasn't sure she heard correctly. "What did you say?" she asked breathlessly.

Jarvis gathered his strength and said a little louder, "I'll help you get them all out. Jeb, Pete, the whole family."

Stunned, Emma looked over at Lori. Maybe it was the pain talking.

Emma crouched next to Jarvis and asked, "What do you mean? The sheriff had everyone but Pete killed. I heard the gunshots!"

Jarvis still had his eyes closed, but slowly shook his head. "No...he didn't shoot them. He tranquilized them."

This confession shocked Emma and she stood up.

Still processing this information, she asked, "Why would he do that?"

Jarvis had a puzzled look on his face as he opened his eyes and looked at Emma. "They knew about his operation and he needed to do something about them. No matter what happened at the Kroger parking lot, Frank's not a killer. At least, I never heard of him outright murdering anyone. The Kroger shooting was an accident. Those deputies were scared and didn't think.

"Frank is taking advantage of the blast by declaring martial law so he can find a reason to put Jeb and his family in jail. Whoever is in jail will be used as free labor for the good of the community."

He stopped to catch his breath. Emma looked over at Lori and saw tears of relief brimming in her eyes. She looked back down at Jarvis as he went on, "He's also sending a message to everyone who lives in Pigeon Forge. He's letting everyone know that as long as this *emergency* is here, he is in charge and there ain't anybody else they can run to. He's gambling everything on the power not being restored, and it's working. Just about everyone has turned in their horses and handguns. Newcomers have been turned in by the locals, and Frank's registered their names and where they are staying."

Again, Jarvis rested. Emma could tell he was feeling

better, so she took the opportunity to ask, "What did you mean when you said you would help us?"

Jarvis shifted a little and tried to sit up. Emma reached over to his good arm and helped him.

His head hung for a minute and then he looked up at her. Emma believed he was sad as he replied, "I'm not a bad guy, and I've been tired of Frank's shit for a while. I was more afraid of him than anything else. Everybody was in his pocket and nobody would go up against him until Jeb found out. You probably won't believe this, but I actually volunteered to sit out here and wait for Hawk. I was going to tell him that I would help him get his family away from Frank, if he would let me stay with his family for a while. Janine, the woman who Frank had picked to keep watch with me, had just gone into the trees to use the bathroom when Hawk jumped me. Next thing I knew, you were there tying me up."

Emma chewed the inside of her lip as she thought. She and Lori needed to talk to Bryan about this. Alone.

She decided to tie Jarvis back up until they made a decision.

She got the rope and told Jarvis, "I need to talk to my friends about this. I'm sorry, but I'm going to have to tie you back up."

She expected the man to fight her, but to her surprise he just winced as he held up his hands for her to tie.

After she was finished, she motioned Lori to follow her outside and they found Bryan.

"Jeb and his family are not dead," she told Bryan.

"What?!" Bryan demanded. "We heard the—"

Emma cut him off, "I know. Jarvis said it was tranquilizers and that they were taken away, with Pete, to the gem mine."

The friends just looked at each other for a moment.

Something dawned on Lori and her hands flew up to her face. "Oh no! Hawk thought his whole family had been murdered! He died not knowing!"

Emma sadly nodded and said, "I thought of that too. We need to bury him before we do anything else. Right now we need to decide if we can trust Jarvis."

Bryan shook his head, confused. "Trust Jarvis? What did I miss?"

Emma filled him in and by the time she got to the end, Bryan was angry. "You want to trust this guy? After all he admits that he's been a part of? I don't trust him a bit! I think he'll give us up the minute he gets a chance! Why are you even thinking about this?"

"Because, if he is telling the truth, we can use him!" Emma hissed urgently.

Bryan paced and listened as Emma continued, "He is the sheriff's cousin and knows a lot about Frank Green and his operations. He knows the layout of the mine and the habits and routines of the deputies."

Bryan seemed to be conflicted as he asked, "What if he's lying? We could get over there and Jarvis could just turn us over to the sheriff!"

Emma walked over to Bryan and rested her hands on his

forearms as she looked up into his eyes. "Bryan, if we don't let him help us, we have to keep him prisoner somewhere. We'll also have to figure out exactly where Jeb and his family are and how to go about freeing them. Sometimes you have to take a leap of faith, and this is one of those times."

Bryan still seemed hesitant, so Emma added, "If you want, you keep a close eye on him and put a bolt in his back the minute you think he is lying."

She quirked the corner of her mouth to let him know she believed it would be okay.

Bryan rolled his eyes and his shoulders relaxed.

Emma released his arms as he replied, "I will, you know. I'll be watching him!"

Emma nodded as she started back into the barn. "I'm counting on it. Now, let's go see how much time we have to bury Hawk and get ready to move."

Emma wore a determined look as she led her friends back in to question Jarvis further.

12

They had made relatively good time, and were just outside of Memphis. Jack had decided to pull off the main road until dark. It was almost dark now, and he was itching to go. The gravel road they had pulled off on followed the Mississippi. This allowed him to find a scarcely populated area to hide in the brush.

The river was about a hundred yards away and they were high enough above it for Jack to see the rising waters. It was a race between darkness to conceal them, and the rapidly rising waters of the mighty river.

As Jack organized his thoughts, he turned his attention toward the I-40 bridge and saw bonfires and heard gunshots. He guessed this was activity from the gangs and other unsavory people taking advantage of the main bridge over the river in Memphis. There was another, smaller highway that crossed about two miles away. Jack had been thinking about the best place to get across as he drove. The moment anyone figured out that they had a working truck, they would be the most wanted people in the area. They would have to sneak across.

He had another idea. There was a railroad bridge that crossed the river less than two hundred yards north of the smaller road crossing called the Harahan Bridge.

The last he heard, Memphis was trying to turn it into a walking path. It had been a long time since he had kept up with the happenings in Memphis, but it was worth a try to see if they could sneak across there. Once they made it across, they could bull their way onto I-55 less than a mile from the railroad bridge and leave the city behind.

Now that it was dark, Jack was going to get them close to the Harahan and then send a team to scout it out. Jason had walked up and was wiping his brow.

"Jesus, how'd you live down here? It is hot."

Jack looked at Jason with a grin, "Some of us had air conditioning. But, I know what you mean."

Jason took a swig of water and handed it to Jack. "You about ready to go?"

Jack nodded as he handed the bottle back and asked, "Did you talk to Ray and the others?"

Jason squinted over at the gunshots. "Yeah. They're ready."

Jack didn't reply as he folded up the maps and made sure everyone was ready.

He checked the headlamps to make sure the thin red plastic that covered the lights was still well attached. It should allow them to see ahead of the truck without the glare being seen from far off. It would have to do.

Before he got into the truck, he turned to the group in the back and said, "We'll be going under the interstate to the railroad bridge. Keep it quiet and be watchful. Don't use your guns unless absolutely necessary. We don't want to draw attention to ourselves. Use your hands and knives if possible."

They all murmured agreement and got into position. Jack could see Dai Ji Kuan in the corner with his staff. It was eerie how little he talked.

Jack shook his head and got behind the wheel. It was hard to see in the gloom, and he held his breath and switched on the headlights. The darkness pushed back a bit and he could see ahead about fifteen feet. He quickly got out to check for glare and saw there wasn't any. Satisfied, he got back in and shifted into drive. They would have to go slow, which grated on his nerves. He would just have to be patient.

Jack eased the truck down the gravel road at about ten miles an hour. He had the windows down and was glad to hear the engine barely purring. He forced his shoulders to relax and glanced at every shadow.

Two miles later, they pulled up under I-40. Jack immediately turned off the truck and sat quietly.

After a moment, Jack released his breath and opened the door. He got out, eased the door shut quietly, and looked around. They were sheltered from the open and Jack waited as everyone else got out.

Jason spoke up in a soft voice, "Ray, you and Cat go up onto the bridge and scout the way. As soon as you see what's going on up there, get back here and let us know."

The two agents checked their weapons and eased off into the gloom.

Jason turned to Greg. "I need you to go back down the way we came. Keep an eye behind us. We need to make sure no one sneaks up on us. We'll be going slowly so cover us."

The usual jokester attitude was gone and now, Greg was all business. He nodded as he disappeared like a ninja.

Jack had been only half listening. He had been feeling a building anxiety that had only now become overwhelming. As Jason had been instructing the agents on what to do, Jack tried to focus on his inner feelings. Chris came up to him and asked, "Hey man, are you okay?"

Jack was staring in the direction of the river. He ignored the young man's question and held up his hand in a halting gesture. He needed to concentrate.

He walked away a few feet toward the river and cocked his head to the side. He wasn't listening to the river so much as he was listening to something inside himself.

The mild anxiety that had been building was now the familiar buzzing at the base of his skull.

Jack felt like this only when something big was about to happen. He needed to figure out what it was.

As he stood facing the river, it came to him. He remembered all the pouring rain the day before and the rising waters of the Mississippi.

His eyes flew open wide as he realized what was about to happen.

Whirling around, he pushed past Chris and ran to Jason and called, "Go get Greg!"

He turned back to Chris. "Get in! We have to get across the river!"

Turning back to Jason, Jack saw the man running back with Greg.

He jumped in the truck and started it. By the time he slammed it in gear, Jason and Greg had scrambled in.

"What about Ray and Cat?" Jason asked.

"We'll grab them on the way," Jack muttered.

But Jason wanted answers. "Jack," he said, "what's happening?"

Jack was going as fast as he could without swerving off the road.

Absently, he replied to his friend, "I've got a feeling that the rain yesterday has flooded the river upstream and it's heading this way. I'm trusting my instincts." He glanced over at Jason with a deadly expression and continued, "It's big, Jason."

Jason was familiar with Jack's uncanny ability, and he blanched.

He turned back to look through the windshield about the time Jack saw Ray and Cat and stepped on the brakes.

Ray had a puzzled look on his face and opened his mouth to ask something, but Jack spoke urgently, "Get in! There's a wall of water coming!"

Ray snapped his mouth closed and he and Cat dove into the bed of the truck.

Jack gave them just enough time to get in and then he hit the accelerator.

Thirty seconds later, they reached the turn onto the Harahan Bridge.

Jack eyed the two railroad tracks and quickly figured out he would have to straddle the rails. He didn't take the time to worry as he jammed the truck into gear and let up on the brake. The truck bumped up over the first rail and settled between them. It was going to be a little bumpy, but Jack couldn't worry about that.

He glanced over his shoulder to make sure everyone was still there, then turned back to the front. The anxiety was back and tingled right at the base of his neck.

It grated on Jack's nerves as they moved. They were going faster than he thought, but it still *felt* slow. He kept looking out the driver's side window to keep an eye on the water level upstream.

They had almost reached the midway point and Jack had just started to relax, when a slow roaring caught his attention. It was coming from upstream and Jack whipped his head in that direction.

"Holy shit!" Jason said as he saw the same thing Jack was seeing. The green glow illuminated the river just enough for everyone to see a huge wave coming toward them.

Jack recognized the wall of water and knew they still had about half a mile to go. Jack gritted his teeth and yelled, "Hang on!"

He pressed harder on the accelerator and the truck surged ahead. The jarring increased, but Jack didn't care. They had to get across!

Jason was on the edge of his seat looking toward the oncoming water and saying, "Go, Jack, go!"

Jack couldn't go any faster without losing the trailer, and he yelled this back at Jason.

They still had about a hundred yards to go when the water hit. Jack made it another fifty yards when the first big tanker was swept into the pilings. Jack and the others felt the jarring as the bridge shuddered then snapped sideways.

The truck and trailer slid sideways as the bridge tilted toward the north.

Jack had no choice but to pour on the speed and hoped his passengers held on.

He gunned it and the engine roared as the truck battled up the rapidly tilting bridge. He could feel the trailer pulling down on the truck and slammed the transmission into low. The wheels spun and then caught at the last minute. The truck popped up onto the unaffected part of the bridge and had almost dragged the trailer with it when the entire section under the trailer gave out and fell away.

Jack slammed the accelerator down and heard the wheels spinning as the trailer dangled off the hitch. It only stayed that way for two heartbeats and then the sound of screeching metal announced the bumper tearing away from the truck. Jack knew when it happened because the truck jumped forward before he could slam on the brakes. Jason looked at the people in the truck bed and made sure they were there as they raced the last few yards to safety.

As they came off the bridge, Jack pumped the brake and the truck slewed sideways into a huge bonfire that had been placed at the entrance to the bridge. The burning wood went flying everywhere as the truck skidded to a halt.

Out of the corner of his eye, Jack saw people jumping out of the way of the truck, and he knew they were sentries posted to stop people from coming this way.

He had no intention of stopping.

Before the sentries could recover, he lowered his eyebrows and released the brake, stomping on the accelerator and spinning the wheel to the right all at the same time. He could only hope that his passengers were hanging on.

Jason gurgled something unintelligible but Jack dismissed him. He was not about to lose the truck too. Emma was within reach, but without the truck, it could take weeks.

With this thought pushing him on, he mentally willed his way down the rails. There were shopping carts, metal barrels, and other trash that he had to skirt or run over, but the old Dodge made a path.

He had no idea how much time passed, but it couldn't have been more than two or three minutes when he felt Jason's hand on his arm and realized his friend was yelling at him.

"We're clear! Shut it down! Jack! Jack!" Jason was trying to reach the wheel.

Jack shrugged him off as he let up on the gas.

As the old truck shuddered to a stop, Jack realized they were both breathing heavy.

He didn't waste any time. He put it in park, but left it running as he jumped out.

Facing the truck bed, he quickly counted and saw that, miraculously, they were all there. He looked back down the tracks and saw, about seventy five yards back, people were coming.

He didn't wait for niceties, he just jumped back in and Jason scrambled to follow. Jack had put the truck into gear and had just started to release the brake when Jason shut the door.

"Are you trying to kill us?!?" his friend asked.

Jack glanced dismissively at the man, and then sped on down the rails.

A few minutes later, he found a turnoff and took it. There were some token concrete barricades, but he went in the ditch around them. Jack was happy to be off the rails.

He had not allowed himself to think how hard the rails were on the truck and he wouldn't now, either.

They came to the next intersection and Jack swung to the right. He didn't even hesitate. He knew that people were checking out the spectacle of the flood and he took full advantage of that. He sped off down toward the interstate and had to wend his way around abandoned cars. Once, he cut it too close and heard the squeal of metal against metal and knew he'd have to explain to old Jim what happened to his truck.

They almost made it to the interstate when he saw people with flashlights trying to flag them down. But they could not stop. Good people or bad people, he wouldn't take the chance.

Jack could see that the group was still thinking as though driving rules still applied. They were spread out blocking the on-ramp to the right and the road ahead. They were not blocking the off-ramp to the left.

He gunned the engine and the faithful truck shot up the left exit ramp onto I-55 south. If he had been in a humorous mood, he would have found their facial expressions comical. As he passed the group, they started firing their weapons on the truck, which answered the question whether they were good guys or bad.

The strangers were too late and the truck too fast. They made it.

As the truck roared onto the interstate, Jack saw right away he needed to slow down. There were a lot more cars left just sitting everywhere.

After several miles, Jack began to calm down. They had only encountered a few smatterings of people who simply watched, in surprise, as they passed.

Soon, they would need to get off the interstate, and he looked for a turnoff.

He saw the exit for Collierville and took it. Looking down at the fuel gauge, he knew they would have to find gas in the next fifty miles or so.

Easing onto 385, Jack saw they were in a less populated part of town.

As he sped up, Jason asked, "So. What's your plan, Jack?"

Jack thought, then said, "I'm going to head this way for a bit and then I'm going to pull over and check the map. How does everybody look?"

Jason looked back at the others. "Hanging on for dear life."

Jack nodded, "Good."

After another few minutes he saw what he was looking for. Making sure no one was around, he turned off the road at a deserted oil change shop. He figured there wouldn't be anyone around and he was right.

Switching off the lights, Jack eased the truck behind the shop and turned the engine off. The silence was overwhelming.

Jack opened his door and got out. He rubbed his hands up his face and back through his hair.

By the dim green light, he saw the rest of the group climbing out and walked toward the back of the truck.

Greg landed on the ground and said, "You sure do know how to throw a party, Jack!"

Jack ignored the man and bent down to see where the bumper used to be.

Jason was directing Ray and his team to secure the area. They eased off into the gloom and Jason joined Jack.

"Any other damage?"

Jack shook his head. "Not that I can tell. We're lucky the bumper just tore right off. I hate losing all the supplies, but it could have been worse."

Chris had joined them and asked, "What are we going to do now?"

Jack looked at him and answered, "The only thing we can. We'll take what we need as we go. There's no other way."

He saw Chris nod and turned away toward the building. Striding toward it, Jack could tell the building had been looted.

The front glass door was smashed out and he bent over to step inside. It was dark so he felt his way to the cash register.

He knocked his shin on an overturned chair and cursed. Apparently, Chris had followed him in and now he ran into Jack's back.

Jack didn't realize how tense he was until he turned and snapped at Chris, "Why are you following me?"

This stunned Chris, and Jack was close enough to Chris that he could see the surprised look on his face, causing him to feel bad about yelling.

"Listen. I'm sorry, Chris. I guess I'm just a little more stressed than I thought. Come on. Help me look around and get a few things. First, we need a flashlight. See if there are any left down the aisles. I'm going to check up by the register."

Chris nodded and grinned. "Okay! I'm sorry for following you, Jack. I just wanted to help."

Jack smiled at Chris and said, "I know. Find a flashlight."

The young man moved off, feeling his way down the first aisle.

Jack sighed and turned back toward the register. When he reached it, he felt his way around the counter. There was debris everywhere, and he was careful to move his hands slowly in case there was glass.

His hand touched something and he smiled in recognition.

He rolled his thumb across it and struck the lighter.

Light flickered out from the little Bic and Jack quickly shielded it and looked around. With the help of the lighter, Jack hastily searched and found a flashlight. He saw where the batteries were and stuck the lighter in his pocket.

He had almost gotten the batteries in when Jason stuck his head in and said, "We've got headlights coming!"

Jack heard the surprise in Jason's voice as he finished screwing the top on and hissed, "Chris! Come on, we've got company!"

Chris said, "What?"

Jack didn't answer. There were windows still intact on the side of the store closest to the highway. He pulled his revolver and peeked around the corner of the closest one and waited. He could see a glow approaching from the southeast out on the highway. He could also hear a low, powerful growl in the background.

Chris was beside him now and asked, "A vehicle? Who is it?"

"Shh!" Jack hissed, "I don't know. Just watch!"

Jack turned back to the road and watched as the vehicle crossed over the road they were on and showed no sign of slowing down.

There was enough of a glow for Jack to see it looked like a Humvee. Before he could move, there was another vehicle just behind the first and then two more.

Jack stood still making sure they went on and didn't stop.

As soon as he was sure, he covered the flashlight and went back to looking for anything they could use on their trip. There wasn't a whole lot left, but he managed to find some bottles of water and beef jerky. He grabbed a plastic bag and started loading things up. All the leftover lighters, a small tool kit, and a first aid kit from behind the checkout counter.

Chris asked Jack, "What do you want me to grab?"

Jack replied, "Get some quarts of oil and some antifreeze."

Chris nodded and hurried away. Jack was still looking for stuff when Jason came in. "Ray's back. They were hidden near the overpass and said the vehicles were military."

Jack nodded absently. "Figures. They're getting organized."

Jason took the things Jack handed him out to the truck.

Jack made one more pass. He was looking for something specific.

He'd just about given up when he found it: tubing for siphoning gas and gas containers.

There were several abandoned cars in the parking lot. As

long as they were here, he was going to take the gas.

He reached the truck and asked Chris and Jason to go get more tubing and gas containers. They nodded and jogged off.

Jack hurried to the closest car and was screwing the gas cap off when Ray walked up. "What can I do, Jack?"

Jack was starting to sweat. "I need you, Cat, and Greg to get back up on that overpass and watch for those hummers. They'll be coming to look for us if someone reports seeing us. Let me know the minute you see lights! Hopefully it will take them awhile, and by then we'll be gone."

Ray caught Jack's anxiety and he nodded tersely before turning and running for his team.

Jack went on with siphoning the gas, and in two minutes he had both small containers full. He jerked the tubing out and quickly carried the containers over and filled the truck. Jason had filled one large container and just as Jack had emptied his last container, Jason handed him his. Jack totaled the amount and figured they had put about five gallons in the truck.

Jack was itching to go but knew he had to check the oil and radiator fluid. He could skip it now, but that wouldn't be good if the truck messed up just when they needed it most.

He raced around to the hood and yelled, "Chris! I need you now!"

Jack turned back to the hood and jumped back as Chris was standing right there.

"Jesus! You scared the shit out of me!" Jack took a split

second to wonder how he had gotten there so fast, but then dismissed it for more important things.

"I need you to hold the hood up while I check the fluids. Jason, I need you to check the tires and undercarriage. Hurry!"

Jack saw that the radiator fluid was low but the oil was good. After refilling the antifreeze, Jack slammed the hood down and saw Jason coming back to the front of the truck.

"Go get Ray! We need to leave!"

Jack looked to see where Kuan was. He was in the bed of the truck and seemed to be meditating. Good enough.

Jack saw Jason coming back with the agents and said, "Load up!"

Ray said, "I think they were turning around. We need to go!"

Jack agreed and after seeing that everyone was in, he got in and swung the door closed. He turned the key, but nothing happened. Jason was breathing hard, and saw that the truck hadn't started.

"What?" Jason asked.

Jack didn't want to believe it, so he tried again. He said a prayer as he tried again. There was just a click.

"*Shit!*" Jack yelled.

He opened the door and jumped out, "Chris! I need the flashlight!" Chris was there instantly. Jack opened the hood. He must have knocked something off when he was adding the fluids. Jack willed himself to shut everything out and think.

After a second, he opened his eyes and said, "Distributor."

He reached across and adjusted the distributor cap where he had knocked it off and then quickly said a prayer.

He said, "Get in." And slammed the hood. Everybody jumped into the bed. He hesitated for a second and then, forcefully, turned the key. With a roar, the engine turned over and Jack was calm again.

He didn't even look to see if everyone was there. They knew the train was leaving. He turned on the lights, roared out of the parking lot, and raced toward the highway. He had a general idea of where he needed to go.

As they sped onto the road, Jack could see a glow coming up over the overpass. He made a decision.

He spun the wheel and crossed the median. There was a batch of trees on the other side of the highway and Jack headed straight for them.

Just before he reached the trees he turned off the lights and coasted in under them.

Jack had just made it when the hummers topped the overpass. They slowed and then stopped. Disabling the interior light, Jack reached for his revolver and eased out of the truck cab.

Not closing the door, Jack watched. Everyone was quiet as they observed the people in the hummers stop and shine flashlights all over the area they were just at.

Jason stood next to Jack and held up a fist. Everyone held their ground.

It took a full five minutes and then the hummers were off. They headed the direction Jack had been going and probably would have overtaken them.

Jack breathed a little easier and put his gun back in the holster.

Jason rested his hand on Jack's shoulder and said, "We need to find a place to rest."

Jack agreed and said, "We need to find the back roads. They can't cover everything. We'll need to get out of town, and then we'll pull off and take turns sleeping. I'm exhausted."

Wearily, Jason nodded agreement and they returned to the truck cab. Reaching in the glove compartment, Jack retrieved the map and was about to call Chris when he showed up with the flashlight and handed it to Jack. Jack took it and covered the lens before switching it on. He heard Jason quietly asking Ray and his team to spread out and keep watch. Jack checked the map and found where they needed to go.

Shutting off the light, he said, "Get them back. We need to go."

Jason rounded everyone up and jumped in. Jack turned the key and put the truck in gear. He turned the truck around and headed in the same direction the other vehicles had gone. The next exit was a smaller road cutting directly north to I-40. Once they reached it, the interstate would take them straight to Nashville. From there, it was just a short way to Knoxville and Pigeon Forge.

Jack saw the on-ramp to the left and drove down it the wrong way. At the bottom of the ramp, there was a car blocking the way. Jack quickly put on the brakes and stopped about thirty yards away.

He called out the window, "Ray! I need you to go check out that car. Be careful."

Ray jumped out and Greg followed.

While they were waiting for the two agents to return, Jack turned to Jason and said, "Those were military hummers, but those weren't military personnel. Where did they get military hummers that run?"

Jason replied, "A couple of months before this happened, a memo was sent out to all the National Guard units. It instructed them to store at least two vehicles underground and to harden them against an EMP blast. Most of them probably didn't have time to do it, but it appears the one here in Memphis followed orders."

Jack rubbed his temple. "You waited until now to tell me this?"

Jason shrugged. "After the blast we didn't see any other vehicles. I just thought there hadn't been time to do it."

Jack stared ahead at the two agents and watched as they shoved the car in the ditch.

"They were up to no good," Jack mumbled.

Jason asked, "Who?"

Jack went on, "The guys in the hummers. If they had been the good guys, they would have stayed at the river to help the people on the other bridge. They didn't. They heard there was another vehicle running around and they wanted to get their hands on it."

Ray and Greg had made enough room for the truck. Jack pulled to the bottom of the ramp so they could jump in the back.

After turning north, Jack went on, "All the big cities are going to be like this. This is the last time we go through a major city. All back roads from here."

Jason replied, "That's going to take longer."

Jack shook his head. "Maybe not. It takes time on the main roads to dodge and move cars. I would think there'd be fewer obstacles. Either way, we have to do it."

Jack had just seen the first sign pointing to I-40 when a group of people surged out from the side of a building and started shooting. Jack had just enough time to swerve and punch the accelerator. Jason had pulled his gun and had his head level with the bottom of the window shooting sideways. Jack spun the wheel to straighten the truck up and heard several bullets strike the metal on the passenger side.

Jack didn't stop and before long, he saw the exit. Stomping the brake at the same time he spun the wheel, Jack sent the truck fishtailing up the ramp. The adrenaline was still pumping and his thoughts were bouncing from one thing to another. Briefly, he thought how good he was getting at driving crazy. He supposed it was like anything else. Practice makes perfect.

He dismissed the thought and refocused on the road. They were headed out of town now and he looked for somewhere to pull over so he could make sure everyone was okay and to check the truck.

He couldn't make himself pull over for more than an hour. Finally, he saw a slight embankment open up on both sides that ran back about fifty yards before trees sprang up. This was where they'd stop for the night.

Jack let off the gas and let the truck slow before angling the truck up the embankment. He drove right up to the tree line before turning the lights and engine off.

He sat for a moment listening to the tick of the engine while he felt the last of the adrenaline seep from his body.

For a full five seconds, nobody moved. Then Jack took a breath and opened the door. Chris was sitting with his back up against the cab of the truck behind the driver. As Jack started walking to the back of the Dodge, Chris's arm flipped out to hand the flashlight to Jack before he asked for it.

Jack took it with a smile and hooding it, he switched it on and began a systematic search of the truck to make sure the bullets didn't hit anything important or cause any leaks.

Jack could hear Jason in the background trying to find some food. Luckily, some of the bags were in the truck bed, not the trailer.

Finishing his inspection, Jack stretched his neck muscles as he joined the others.

He saw that Ray and the other two agents had spread out to secure the perimeter.

Kuan had also gotten out and was at the front of the truck looking up at the green sky. Jack dismissed the man and turned back to Jason and Chris.

They had the tailgate down and were going through the bags.

Jack left them to it and got the map out of the glove compartment. Spreading it out next to the bags, Jack pointed the flashlight at it and studied the roads.

They would be coming to Jackson, Tennessee, in about five miles. They would need to skirt it and there was only one road they could take that would bypass Jackson. That's what they would do.

Jason said, "Looks like crackers and water for supper tonight. We'll need to find some food tomorrow. Shit! I sure wish we hadn't lost the damn trailer."

He had a forlorn look on his face.

Jack said, "I'm just glad we didn't go with it."

Chris grabbed his bag that had been sitting next to him and shook it happily. "I've got some canned chicken!"

Jason and Jack looked at the man and Jack asked, "You would be willing to share with us?"

Chris handed over two large cans of chicken and a sleeve of crackers. "Of course. You guys are helping me out. It's the least I could do."

Jack thanked the young man and set the food with the other items on the tailgate.

Turning to Jason, Jack said, "I need to talk to you. We'll be right back, Chris."

Chris waved a dismissive hand and the two friends walked a short distance away.

Jack started, "With any luck, we should be in Knoxville sometime tomorrow. I'm going to drop you and the others off at the site. What did you call it? Atlas?"

Jason said, "Atlas Research and Development."

Jack said, "Yeah. Anyway, I'm going to drop you all off at the site and then I'm going on to Pigeon Forge to get Emma."

Jason nodded. "How long will it take you to get back to Knoxville?"

Jack said, "Normally it only takes about an hour to get there. I'm not even sure where Emma will be. I'll have to look for her. Best case scenario, she'll be right where I asked her to go."

Before going on, he placed his hands on his hips and sighed, "Worse case, I'll have to look for her for a while."

Jason looked like he was waiting for something more and Jack asked, "What?"

Jason shuffled his feet around and looked back at Jack. "What if she didn't make it to Pigeon Forge?"

Jack looked straight at Jason and didn't hesitate. "She made it." He said this softly with a little smile.

They stared at each other for a few seconds and then Jason smiled back. "Alright, friend. So, if she's not where she's supposed to be, how long will it take you to find her?"

Jack replied, "It's a small town. A day or two tops."

Jason nodded. "Okay. I'll get Kuan started on the project. I'll post Ray and his team outside the site to guard it, and we'll hopefully get it going before you get back."

Jack asked, "You never told me exactly what this thing is. Where'd you get it?"

Jack could tell Jason hadn't expected this question. After a few moments of silence, he turned to Jack. "The short version is, it's a reverse-engineered device found in a crash in New Mexico. It wasn't the Roswell crash though. It was the Aztec, New Mexico, crash of 1948 that had a whole, intact UFO that gave us all the information we are still trying to decipher.

"The UFO devices are made of material not of this planet. That means the materials have different properties from the materials of Earth. It has taken years for our scientists to understand, study, and comprehend the reactions and properties of these materials and then apply that in the small section of each machine. I had no idea until I was made to understand. It's the same as if we dropped a computer in the middle of a group of monkeys. That's without including non-terrestrial material making up the computer."

As Jack listened, he was at first skeptical. The more Jason spoke, however, the more Jack could see that Jason was scared. He realized that his friend had seen some incredible things and really believed what he was telling Jack.

Jason continued, "I don't know how our device is supposed to work, I'm no scientist." Agitated, Jason began pacing back and forth while rubbing the back of his neck.

"Top scientists have been working on it for years. Ever since you told us about the schematics."

Jason stopped pacing and dropped his hand. "Just before the blast, I talked to them. They said the device was ready, that it should work, but that there seemed to be one piece missing."

Jason was looking at Jack with a haunted expression. "A key," Jason said. "There's a piece missing that looks to be a physical key, and we've tried everything. It won't work without it!"

Jack could see that Jason was completely frustrated by the missing key. He tried to calm his friend. "Hold on, Jason. We have the world's most qualified scientist with us. We'll get him to the device and surely he'll be able to bypass any need for a key."

Jason still looked doubtful, but nodded.

Jack knew there was nothing else to say. He laid a hand on Jason's shoulder as a comforting gesture.

"Come on. We need to set the watch schedule and get some sleep."

13

It had taken Bryan and Emma quite a while to bury Hawk and the woman. As Emma finished covering the graves, she thought about what Hawk had said before he died. They needed to go to the cave and see what all was in there. It was important enough for Hawk to say something about it with his dying words. Before they buried him, Emma had gone through his pockets again. It puzzled her that he had a set of keys in his pocket. Since the blast had occurred over a week ago, he hadn't needed car keys for starting a car. She put them in her own pocket and would think about it later.

Bryan snapped his fingers in front of her face and she realized he had been saying something to her.

"You okay?" he asked.

Emma nodded and said, "Yeah, I was just thinking."

Bryan repeated, "I said Lori's coming back with the horses." He pointed toward the barn and Emma saw her friend coming back this way.

She looked over to check on Jarvis and saw that the man had fallen asleep next to a tree trunk.

"We need to go to the cave. Hawk said something about it before he died."

Bryan stared at her. "What are we going to do with Jarvis?

I don't trust him enough to let him know about the cave, do you?"

Emma thought for a moment, then said, "We'll all cut across to the tree line, then you and Lori stay with the horses and Jarvis. It won't take me long to go to the cave and check it out. When I get done, I'll come back and we'll plan our next move. Just keep an eye out. I don't like the sheriff, but he's no idiot and he'll be looking for these two soon."

Lori had heard the last part of this and asked, "When you get back from where?"

"Hawk said there was something in the cave that would help us. I'm going back to take a closer look. You three are going to wait for me over there." Emma pointed across the yard.

Lori hesitated a moment and Emma asked, "What is it?"

Lori looked uncertain about saying anything but then asked, "Don't you think it would be better to rest today and then go tonight?"

Emma quickly looked up and saw that she had been so focused on what she was doing, she hadn't even realized that it was almost dawn.

Looking back at her friends, she couldn't help but feel frustrated that Lori was right. She knew that they needed to rest, and a daylight attack was definitely out of the question.

Emma sighed but nodded. "I guess you're right."

She looked over at Jarvis and realized they would have to tell him about the cave. There was no other choice.

Stepping over to the man, she nudged his leg with her toe. He sprang awake. "What!?"

He had jerked his arm in the sling Emma had made for him, and now he sucked in a breath between gritted teeth. "Damn! Damn! Dammit!"

Emma felt bad for startling the man. "I'm sorry, Jarvis. I didn't mean to scare you, but we need to go."

With his good hand, he rubbed his eyes and asked, "Where are we going?"

She hesitated, then said, "You'll see. We're going to rest today and get ready to hit them later."

She watched his reaction but sensed he was telling the truth when he said, "That's probably best. Frank's deputies are usually drinking on the job at night. Frank's never there."

Rubbing his shoulder, he followed Emma back over to her friends.

Grabbing Leroy's reins, she was about to head off when Bella appeared in her usual fashion.

"AARGG!" Jarvis yelled as Bella leaped from a branch onto Leroy's saddle, right next to Jarvis's head.

Apparently, being scared twice in a row was too much for the man and he pulled his right arm back to hit the cat when Bryan came to Bella's rescue.

Almost too fast for Emma to see, Bryan grabbed the dirty man's wrist with his left hand and stuck the end of the crossbow to the side of the man's throat. He said quietly, "Bella has frightened me a time or two, but she's kind of like family now, and I would like nothing more than to have an excuse to end your miserable little life right now."

He released the man's wrist but kept the crossbow on the side of Jarvis's neck as he continued softly, "Go on and give me an excuse."

Emma stared wide-eyed at Bryan as he said all this, and Lori's jaw dropped. Nobody moved until, finally, Jarvis slowly grinned and eased back away from the horse.

"Hey, that's fine. I didn't know it belonged to you," Jarvis said in a joking manner.

Emma was studying the man. Quickly, she made up her mind.

"Hang on a second, Bryan. I dropped something over by Hawk's grave. I'll be right back."

Bryan was still watching Jarvis, but nodded at her. Jarvis was concentrating on Bryan's crossbow and didn't pay attention as Emma walked past him. He also didn't see it coming when Emma turned abruptly, and in one smooth motion drew her pistol and brought the butt down across the back of his head.

Bryan and Lori watched in astonishment as Jarvis dropped to the forest floor. As one they looked up at her. Lori was in total shock, but Bryan grinned like a fiend.

"When he almost hit Bella, I looked into his eyes. I realized he was lying about helping us. I just can't believe I almost fell for it!" she told her friends.

Lori put her hands on her hips and looked down at the

man. "Well," she said shortly.

Bryan, on the other hand, said, "I am so glad you did that! I didn't like that asshole! Didn't trust him, either."

Emma holstered her gun and reached in her bag for the shoestrings. She had brought them, and the gag, just in case.

Blowing out her breath, she quickly threw the rag at Bryan and asked him to gag the man.

While he did that, she tied his hands together with one of the laces and tied his feet together with the other one.

Standing up, she pushed Bella off the horse and asked her friends, "Do you think we can lift him up on the saddle?"

Bryan and Lori nodded together and they all three hefted the stinky man across the horse's back.

Leroy snorted and sidestepped as the unfamiliar weight was draped across him.

Emma stepped up to Leroy's shoulder and gently rubbed it while softly mumbling soothing words to him. He finally stood still and Emma rewarded him with a soft pat to the side of the jaw.

Turning back to her friends, Emma somberly said, "Well, back to what to do with him."

Bryan spoke up. "If we can get him to the cave before he wakes up, we can make sure he is tied up well and let Lori watch him while you and I go free the prisoners."

Lori lowered her brows and looked at Bryan. "Hey!"

Emma ignored Lori's comment as she said, "That might

work."

Lori squawked, "What? You can't leave me behind! I can help!"

Emma finally heard Lori and sought to soothe her. "I know you want to help, but we need you to keep an eye on Jarvis. If we leave him by himself he might get loose and give us away. If you watch him, Bryan and I will be safe and, hopefully, free Jeb and the rest of them!"

She was pleading now. Emma really needed Lori to watch Jarvis.

Lori seemed to be listening when she replied reluctantly, "Ah, when you put it that way…"

Emma didn't give her friend a chance to back out. She hugged her hard. "Thank you, Lori! We won't be gone long, I promise."

Lori seemed surprised and Emma knew she hadn't really said she would guard Jarvis. She hoped that her overwhelming gratitude would convince her friend the rest of the way.

It worked. Lori hugged her back, but then stepped back at arm's length and angrily said, "I'll wait only twenty-four hours after you both leave. If you're not back by then, I'll tie him to a tree, gag him completely, and come looking for you! So, if you don't want me ruining your fun, you better make it back in time!"

Emma chuckled then said, "Listen. I know I said I was going to teach you to shoot."

Lori waved dismissively, but Emma went on, "You need

to have a gun, so…"

Emma reached over to where she had put Hawk's sawed-off shotgun in Scooter's saddle and pulled it out. Reaching in her pocket, she pulled out four shells.

"Let me show you something," Emma said, standing next to Lori.

Emma saw her friend was now serious and concentrating.

Emma handled the shortened gun expertly. It was a double-barrel shotgun that had to be broken open in order to remove the spent shells. She went slowly and showed her friend the few things Lori would need to know to operate the weapon.

The beauty of Hawk's weapon was the fact that it did not need to be aimed, nor did it take much to unload and reload it.

Finishing the short demonstration, Emma snapped the weapon back together and held it out for Lori.

As her friend, gingerly, took the gun, Emma said, "Don't be afraid of it. It's a tool. An extension of your arm. All you have to do is point and shoot."

Emma smiled at her friend as Lori handled the firearm, getting familiar with it.

After a minute of handling it, Lori realized it wasn't going to bite her and she really started to get a feel for it.

She found the button to break the gun open and did so.

Emma held her hand out with two shells and Lori took

them. Putting the shells in, Lori seemed much more confident as she snapped the gun closed.

As she turned and practiced pointing the gun, Emma stepped up and said, "Here. Hold the gun at your waist and use your other hand to steady it on the stock."

Lori nodded and imitated her.

Emma nodded in approval and added one more bit of advice, "Think of it as a water hose. Once you point that and shoot it, it's going to spray buckshot at anything in front of it."

Lori looked frightened at the description for only a brief moment, but then took on a determined look and nodded at Emma who finished by handing the other two shells to her.

Emma then turned to Bryan and gave him the dead woman's .38 pistol. "Just in case you needed a little more firepower," she said.

He grinned and took the gun from her.

"Now, we need to go before Jarvis wakes up."

The two women led the horses across the clearing and into the trees as Bryan trailed behind and kept watch.

The sun had almost made it over the top of the mountains and Emma glanced at the green sky, wishing the normal blue color would magically reappear.

She shook her head at her own foolishness and after a while they came to the waterfall.

Turning to Leroy, Emma checked to make sure Jarvis was

still unconscious. Seeing that he was, she checked his pulse to make sure she hadn't hit him too hard.

No, he had a steady pulse. She waved Lori to follow her and asked Bryan to keep watch. Before entering the cave, Emma reached up and removed her bag and placed it next to a tree. Bella wouldn't appreciate going through the waterfall. As she turned away, Emma saw the feline pop out of the bag and smiled. She'll keep Bryan company.

Leading the horses, the two women disappeared into the cave.

As they entered, Emma raised the flashlight to turn it on. There was a commotion behind her and before she could flip the switch on, something hit her from behind and knocked her to the floor.

Jarvis must have been pretending to still be knocked out. He had her pinned to the floor and was yelling, "You stupid bitch! Nobody gets the best of Jarvis! Nobody!"

Emma thought quickly as she fended the man off with her forearm. He was trying to beat her with his fists tied together and his smelly breath was all over her face.

Lori must have found her flashlight because a bloom of illumination suddenly lit the interior of the cave.

Emma was staring straight into the bloodshot eyes of her attacker and gritting her teeth. Before she could think to be afraid, a strength of unknown origins gathered in her belly and she felt it spread out to her limbs. She heard an animalistic growl come from somewhere and realized suddenly that it was coming from her throat.

Anger, hatred, frustration, and indignation boiled over. She pulled a foot up and placed it on the wild man's hip and with all the adrenaline-fueled strength, practically threw the man across the floor of the cave.

Emma scrambled to pull her gun with one hand and her knife with the other. As she crouched to face him, she had a sneer on her face and quietly welcomed the man on.

Jarvis howled his anger and was trying to break the ties on his feet and jump at her when a deafening boom erupted to Emma's left.

In slow motion, Emma watched Jarvis's body get lifted by the force of the shotgun blast, before slamming into the wall of the cave. Bryan came flying through the wall of water and almost crashed into Lori. Emma had turned toward Bryan's entrance and saw that Lori had a frightened look on her face and was letting the shotgun dangle by her right leg. The horses had bolted out of the cave the moment the shotgun blast had sounded, and Bryan headed out after them.

Tears had started to roll down Lori's cheeks and she turned to Emma and asked in a broken voice, "Oh, dear God! What have I done?"

Emma heard her friend's voice tremble and her heart went out to this beautiful, kind human being who never asked to be put in this position.

Emma quickly holstered her gun and knife with trembling hands and rushed to her friend's side. Grabbing her in a hug, she squeezed Lori tight and whispered, "You saved my life. Honey, you did what you had to do! It was kill him or he would have tried to kill me. If you hadn't done it, I would have!"

She felt Lori quietly sob against her shoulder and knew that all she could do was to comfort her friend.

After a few minutes, Lori's crying seemed to die down, and Emma relaxed her hug and gently pushed her friend to arm's length. "Are you okay?"

As soon as she finished the question, Emma bit her lip. What a stupid question!

But her friend seemed to gain strength from it and just nodded as she wiped her tears.

Lori glanced hesitantly over at the crumpled body of Jarvis and asked, "Is he…he's dead, isn't he?"

Emma had seen the left side of the man's chest blossom with blood and the left half of his face disappear with the shotgun blast, and she gently nodded as she said, "Yes, Lori. He won't be hurting anyone, ever again."

Lori accepted this better than Emma had hoped. Her little friend just nodded and used her t-shirt to wipe her eyes and nose.

"I'm going over to check him out. Why don't you sit down over there and I'll be right back." Emma pointed in the opposite direction of the body and Lori again nodded and walked away.

Emma could feel the aftereffects of the dwindling adrenaline as her hands and feet tingled, and she took a deep breath to restore calm to her system before heading over to him.

She was just about to walk over to the body when Bryan, thankfully, came back in with both horses. Emma pointed her chin at Lori in a silent signal to Bryan and he nodded. Emma turned back to check the body as she saw Bryan rushing to Lori's side.

Shaking off her concern for Lori, Emma refocused on the task at hand. She reached down and retrieved her dropped flashlight and thanked God when it switched on.

She didn't think she would need it, but she pulled her gun just in case. Better safe than sorry.

As she got closer to the body, she saw that she hadn't needed to worry. He was dead, alright. Blood covered everything. It was just as she had told Lori. Just to be positive, she reached down and felt his right wrist for a few seconds, feeling for a pulse she knew was not there.

She released his wrist and stood up. Before she could stop the thought, she realized they wouldn't have to worry about what to do with him anymore. They also had to get him out of the cave.

Emma looked back at her friends and made a decision.

She had to push the body off the supplies, and she unceremoniously shoved him on to the cave floor. She started going through the containers and finally found what she needed. It was a coiled rope about ten feet long.

She blocked out any feelings as she tied the rope around the body's torso, under the arms. She checked the knot.

When she was done there, she looped the other end of the rope around the saddle horn belonging to Leroy.

Bryan had seen what she was doing and had left Lori to come over. "You need some help?"

Emma shook her head and said softly, "Please stay with her. She needs you right now and Leroy's going to do all the work for me." She smiled gently to let Bryan know she was okay with this.

He looked at her for a moment longer, then knit his brows together in worry.

Emma patted his arm and smiled to reassure him again, and he turned back to Lori.

Emma sighed at the thought of what she had to do, but started leading Leroy out of the cave. The horse balked, but Emma continued to softly speak to him and finally coaxed him into dragging the body outside.

When they were out, Emma wiped the water out of her eyes and led the horse up the slope and along the bluff that followed the creek.

She forced herself not to look back as the body bumped along behind her. After about fifteen minutes she stopped Leroy. Beside her was a natural depression along the bank and above the river.

She bent over to look inside and saw that it was actually a sinkhole where the ground had dropped away, presumably where the water had eaten away the embankment underneath.

There were some small tree roots laced across the hole,

and she pulled her knife to cut them away.

Before bending to the task, she stood still and listened. Looking all around her, she made sure she was alone.

She then crouched and cleared the hole. She saw it was at least four feet deep and three feet across. Perfect.

She tied Leroy's reins to a nearby tree branch and rubbed his forehead. He nuzzled her shoulder and she turned toward the body.

She had one unpleasant job left and then she could bury him.

She took a breath and quickly went through his pockets. She found a pack of generic cigarettes, lighter, two crumpled one-dollar bills and his wallet. She threw the smokes in the hole, pocketed the lighter, and then went through his wallet. She had a brief twinge of guilt, but that quickly passed as the memory of the man's contorted, angry face from the cave passed across her mind.

She found his driver's license and studied it. She memorized the address, just in case, and then put it back. There were some worn business cards for auto shops and auto parts store, which made her guess he had been a mechanic, and she left all those alone. The last thing she found was a dog-eared photo of a sad looking woman and two young children. A boy and a girl.

Emma assumed this was Jarvis's wife and children and she hesitated, thinking.

Making a decision, she pocketed the photo and got the

man's license back out and pocketed that also. She replaced the wallet in the man's jeans and stood up.

She looked around again to make sure she was still alone. Satisfied, she walked back over to her horse, taking up the slack in the rope as she went.

Reaching Leroy's head, she whispered, "I need you to help me with one more thing, boy."

He just blinked at her and she turned to the saddle. As she mounted, she wrapped the loose coil of rope tight around the pommel, then backed the horse away from the body. Leroy bobbed his head as he complied, and soon, the body dropped cleanly into the hole. The only things showing were the man's feet.

She sighed, knowing what she had to do.

Emma dismounted and walked to the hole. Without hesitation, she reached down and stuffed the man's legs into the hole with the rest of his body. She stood back up and looked to make sure all of him was in.

When she was sure, she walked a small ways from the creek into the trees and started gathering rocks, branches and then leaves until the body was completely buried. She added a few more rocks to completely cover it, then strewed some leaves around and brushed away any footprints or drag marks.

When she was completely done, Emma stood for a minute, looking at the makeshift grave.

Emma felt the need to say something, so she did: "Dear

heavenly father, this man tried to hurt me and my friends. Lori was only trying to save my life. Please forgive her. I know she didn't want to kill him. Please forgive Jarvis. I think he just lost his mind."

Emma couldn't think of anything else to say over the man. She gathered the horse's reins and started back to the cave. She walked ahead so she could brush away any footprints, blood, or drag marks.

Before long, she found herself back at the waterfall and looked at her watch. Nine o'clock. If they weren't already, the sheriff would soon have someone out at Jeb's looking for Jarvis and Janine.

She quickly led Leroy back through the waterfall and saw Lori and Bryan still sitting and talking quietly.

They looked up as Emma entered, then stood up and walked to meet her. Bryan handed her a rag to dry off with.

"How did that go? Are you okay?"

Lori had asked this, and Emma could tell by her face and her voice that she would be alright.

Nodding, Emma answered, "Yeah, I'm fine. I buried him and said a prayer."

Bryan hiked an eyebrow at her as she said this and she told him, "Everyone deserves a Christian burial. It's the right thing to do."

He quickly lowered his eyebrow and looked chagrined.

Emma went on, "Since we don't have Jarvis anymore, we need to find a map. We're going to have to stay here until tonight, so this is what I think we should do.

"We need to go through everything in here and see what supplies we have. If we don't find a map, we'll have to wait until later and go through Jeb's house. We're not familiar enough with this town to just ride off and hope we know where we're going."

She slumped to the ground and said, "Right now, though, I need sleep. I don't know about you guys, but I am hungry, thirsty, and exhausted."

Bryan looked at her sympathetically and walked over to a container.

When he came back, he said, "Here. Lori and I found something to eat while you were gone."

He was holding out a gallon container of water, two cans of Vienna sausages, and some crackers.

Emma smiled up at him and said, "Ah. The breakfast of champions!"

The three friends all sat together and Emma opened the sausages.

As she ate, she saw her friends look at each other pointedly, and she slowed her chewing.

"What?" she asked, looking back and forth between the two.

Bryan started, "Well, Em, while you were burying Jarvis, Lori and I were talking and, well, we were just wondering if maybe we're a little out of our depth?"

Emma had completely stopped chewing as she heard Bryan say this. She glanced at Lori to gauge her friend's reaction. When she saw Lori look at the ground and shuffle her feet, Emma knew Lori agreed with Bryan.

She finished swallowing, sat back, and thought about what Bryan had said. Her initial feeling, when he first said it, had been one of betrayal. Her feelings were hurt that her friends didn't want to help her. She quickly dismissed that thought and really considered what he had said. Emma stood up and turned toward the cave opening to give herself time to think.

Behind her, Bryan glanced at Lori, then said hesitantly, "We know you're a badass, no one is denying that. We want Jeb and his family free as much as you do. I just don't know if we're the best ones for the job."

Bryan looked over to Lori and Emma knew he was trying to protect Lori.

Lori spoke then, "I love you, Emma, and you know that. I just want you to think about what we're doing here."

Emma waited for them to say more, but they fell quiet. She had been so bent on justice that Emma hadn't stopped to think about what might happen to her friends.

She took a swig of water as she thought. Her friends watched her as she continued to war within herself about what to do.

Her friends were just following her lead. They had chosen to come with her. She closed her eyes and thought back to when this started, at the Busy Bee Café. They trusted her and Emma knew they would try to follow her through almost anything. She needed to remember that and make better choices.

As much as it irked her, Emma knew they were right. She loved them like family and vowed to do the right thing. She opened her eyes and looked around at Bryan and Lori.

Blowing out her breath, Emma said, "You guys are right. I don't know what got into me, but I needed to step back and look at the whole picture."

Emma stepped over and grabbed them both in a hug. They were obviously relieved and hugged her back.

Emma backed up after a minute and said, "We'll rest for a while, then head to Gatlinburg. What do you think?"

Bryan and Lori started to talk at the same time and then stopped and looked at each other, laughing.

Bryan spoke up and said, "I heard Hawk say that he thought Len was still at the house when the sheriff ambushed them. If so, then he's either dead or Frank's prisoner. Thanks to Jarvis, we don't even know what's true anymore. Either way, I think you're right. We need to get to Gatlinburg and let them know."

Emma agreed as she picked up on his train of thought.

"We need to go through the cave and find out what Hawk was trying to tell me. After that, we'll go to Larry and Rita's and let them know what's happened. The more people who know, the better. As soon as that's done, we'll ride to Gatlinburg. Len was a good man and Hawk said his deputies were good men too. We're just going to have to count on that."

Emma looked at Bryan and Lori and saw they agreed with her.

She smiled at them and said, "Let's go through everything, then rest."

Her friends agreed, and then wearily turned to explore the cave.

14

They had slept for just a few hours. Jack thought he was the only one who had insomnia. When Jason had roused him from dozing for his turn at watch, he'd followed Jack around restlessly.

Jack finally asked him, "Why don't you go get some sleep?"

Before Jack finished talking, Jason quickly shook his head and said, "We're so close, Jack! I'm too wound up."

Jack understood. "Yeah, I'm feeling the same way. Let's go look at the map. You can at least show me where Atlas is."

Jason followed Jack to the truck. Jack grabbed the map and spread it out on the hood. He covered his flashlight until there was just a pinpoint of light and pointed it at the map.

"Show me where the facility is." Jack gestured to the map.

Jason bent over and studied it. "Right here. There are caverns all across Tennessee, so it was just a matter of finding some private property in a remote area and building it how we wanted it. This property was perfect."

Jack looked where Jason had pointed and realized he knew the area. It was actually southeast of Knoxville on a state road. Very near a tourist trap called Tuckaleechee Caverns. But the area Jason was pointing to was isolated. Jason was right. It was perfect.

"How did you pitch it to the locals?" he asked Jason.

Jason shrugged and replied, "Zinc mine. Tennessee is currently the second largest producer of zinc in the nation. We have an actual zinc mine operating there and used the cover to explain away construction of the main chamber."

Jack absently rubbed his jaw and felt the stubble. He briefly wondered how long it would be until he could have a real shower and shave.

Dismissing the thought, he asked, "Is the operation finished?"

Jason sighed. "We finished it a year ago. We constructed a faraday cage to enclose the chamber and protect our components. The scientists assured me that the device would be impervious to EMPs. They've done tests on it with electromagnetic waves with no effect at all. They wrote in a report that the tests showed that the device seemed to be absorbing the waves. Storing them somehow. We ran out of time before figuring out how it worked."

Here, Jason's face twisted and he finished, "Of course, it would have helped to have the key."

Jack saw his friend was distraught and changed the subject. "Looking at the map, Atlas is just south of Maryville. We'll take this back road, here, and avoid Knoxville altogether. When we get to the mine, I'll leave you, the agents, and Kuan."

He traced his finger across the map and finally tapped Pigeon Forge. "I'll take Chris with me. He and I will part ways when I get to Pigeon Forge. He can make it on over to

Asheville on his own."

Jason was nodding and said, "You think it'll take twenty four hours to make it back to the mine?"

Jack put his hands on his hips as he tilted his head up at the green sky. He didn't answer for a moment as he contemplated all that could go wrong.

Finally, he looked at his friend and said, "If all goes well, I'll be back the same day."

Jason was watching Jack and saw the hesitation. "I don't need all three agents. I'm sending Greg with you." He lifted his hand, angrily, as Jack started to protest, "No, Jack! Don't fight me on this! Listen, when you drop us at the mine, we'll be relatively safe inside. You, on the other hand, have further to go and more of the unknown to contend with. You need him, Jack, and he's good. Trust me."

Jack saw that Jason wasn't backing down and sighed, "Alright, Jason. I can use all the help I can get."

Jack looked at his watch and saw that it was four fifteen. He switched the light off and looked back at the sky. There were a lot more red sprites shooting up in the haze and Jack wondered what it meant. It didn't matter, they were moving as fast as they could.

Turning to Jason, he said, "Let's get going. We can all sleep when this is over."

Jason agreed and they began to wake the others.

* * *

They had been driving for about seven hours when Jack slowed and cruised to the side of the road. They had skirted around Nashville in the early morning hours. Jack believed their timing had been crucial in slipping past the city unmolested.

It was mid-morning and Jack knew they needed to take a break. He needed to double check the map and see where they should turn off the interstate. They should top off the gas before getting on a more rural road. They had stopped several times today and siphoned gas along the way. They had also found a half case of bottled water in the back of a SUV. No food, however, and they had just finished the last of the crackers.

Jack had picked this spot because he saw a cluster of cars just ahead.

Jason guessed why Jack had stopped, "Gas?"

Jack nodded and got out. He stretched as he looked around.

There were two passenger cars and a jackknifed tractor trailer about forty yards away.

He was aware that the three agents were getting out of the truck. Chris had stood up and was looking intently over the cab at the eighteen-wheeler.

Jack was still looking at the tractor trailer when Ray and Jason joined him.

The trailer portion was stretched across the opposite lanes. The only writing on it said Wilson Trucking. Jack could see the doors to the trailer were hanging open. Apparently, somebody had already rummaged through it.

Jack knew they should go see if anything might be left in it that they could use, but something was niggling at the back of his mind. Something didn't feel right.

Quietly, he said, "Ray, take Cat and circle around the front of that truck and back into the woods. Be careful, something doesn't feel right."

Ray nodded and went to get Cat.

Jason started to say something, and Jack held up a fist.

Immediately, Jason stopped.

Swiveling his head, Jack looked around at the trees. There wasn't a breath of air, and the humidity was already stifling.

That niggling feeling was starting to intensify. Just when he was about to pull his gun, Chris was right next to him and covered Jack's gun hand with his own. Jack glanced at the young man and saw that he had a frightened look on his face.

Jack started to shake his hand off when Chris whispered where only Jack could hear, "Walk back, casually, and stop Ray and Cat from leaving. Trust me! We have to get in the truck and leave. Now! You're going to be ambushed from people inside that trailer. They want your truck and you can't let them get it!"

Jack was looking in total astonishment at Chris, but quickly recovered. The young man completely believed what he was saying, and given Jack's abilities, who was he to question Chris? Better safe than sorry. He'd question Chris later.

Ray happened to look up as he and Cat were about to take off and saw Jack coming toward him. He waited as Jack came near and listened as Jack told him to get ready to leave instead. Jack had been going over the map in his mind.

Once he got everyone loaded up, they would reverse the truck, turn around, and head back to that last off-ramp. The way he was feeling, he thought it best to avoid this road altogether. It was time to leave the interstate.

Jason had eased over to Greg. Both men had observed the way Jack and Chris had acted and, without being told, backed up and got in the truck.

Everybody was loaded and Jack had just eased the driver's side door open, when men and women started pouring out of the trailer. Jack didn't hesitate. Jumping in, he twisted the key, shifted the truck into reverse, and burned rubber backward as he craned his neck out the driver window.

As soon as the mob from the trailer saw that their prey was getting away, they started firing at the Dodge.

Jack didn't have time to look at them; he was trying to watch where he was driving. He sent up a prayer of thanks when he heard Greg start firing the AR-15. That should make them dive for cover. It must have worked, because the pings from the gunshots quit for a minute. It was just enough of a lull to let Jack slam on the brakes, spin the wheel, and wrench the gearshift into drive. He sure hoped everyone was hanging on!

The Dodge engine howled as Jack pushed the accelerator halfway to the floor. Now that they had almost gotten away, he didn't want to do anything to hurt the engine.

The exit was about a half mile down the road and he slowed as they reached it. After looking around carefully, Jack eased down the ramp and came to a stop. He turned southeast and kept driving. He didn't think that mob was following them; he just wanted to put a little more distance between them and his group.

Jason glanced over at Jack and asked, "What tipped you off? About those people?"

Jack realized that Jason hadn't heard the conversation between him and Chris.

He shrugged and said, "Just a gut feeling." It was only a half lie.

He felt Jason's eyes linger on him, but ignored him. They had finally gone about five miles on the road. Jack had been right about the lack of traffic. They hadn't seen but two cars and a tractor since they'd left the interstate.

Jack looked for another stalled vehicle and soon came upon a ten year old Honda. He had to slow down quickly. The Honda was right in the middle of the road just around a curve.

Jason stuck out his right hand to brace himself against the dash.

Jack had his gun out in a hurry. He'd already put the truck in park, but left it running as he eased open the door.

He heard Jason follow his lead and noticed Ray and Greg had already spread to the sides.

Cat had stayed in the bed, pointing her gun at the Honda.

Greg had his rifle pointing back down the way they had come.

Jack had no feelings about this car, but he wasn't taking chances. He had his pistol held out in front of him as he walked, in a crouch, toward the driver-side door. He knew the others were watching his back.

Reaching the car, Jack pulled his gun arm back and looked in the window. There was nobody in it, and it was the cleanest car Jack had ever seen.

He brushed off the thought and pulled on the door handle. Locked. Jack was surprised. Who would lock their car and leave it in the middle of the road?

He dismissed the thought and tried the other doors.

They were all locked. How bizarre.

Jack finally found a hefty rock and smashed the driver's side window.

Reaching down, he popped the gas lid and loudly said, "Chris! Bring that tube and gas can!"

Chris jumped from the truck, grabbed the stuff and hurried to Jack.

Jack thanked him and started siphoning the gas.

While they waited, Chris looked in the car and whistled, "Man! That's a tidy car!"

Jack knew what he meant. "Yeah, I thought it was weird. Why don't you pop the trunk? I'm curious to see what's in there, now."

Chris headed to the driver's side and popped the trunk.

Jack watched as Chris lifted the trunk lid. He expected the trunk to be as clean as the rest of the car, so he was astonished to see it packed full of stuff.

He saw a lot of clothes and some tools, but there were also plastic grocery bags and several duffel bags.

Jack was so intent that the gas ran over before he noticed. He quickly drew his attention back to the gas can and jerked the tube out. He put the lids on and took them to the truck. He noticed Jason and the agents were still keeping a lookout.

He told Jason, "I'm going to go through the trunk. We'll be back in a minute. Can you fill the tank?"

Jason gave him a curt nod and Jack hurried back to Chris. He saw Chris had waited on him and they looked at each other before sifting through the clothes. Jack was surprised when he realized they were clean. They could use them. Someone had to be able to fit them. He removed them and placed them on the hood.

Returning to the rear of the Honda, Jack saw that Chris was just opening the first plastic bag. He pulled out some shampoo, soap, and toothpaste. Chris lifted the bag out and placed it on the ground. The next bag held two pizzas that were long past their frozen state. Thank goodness they were wrapped in plastic and cardboard. The last two plastic bags held canned food items and Jack grinned. Chris placed those two bags next to the bag with the shampoo. The tools Jack also took. His tools had all been in the lost trailer.

Turning back to the trunk, they saw a duffel bag and a backpack remained.

Jack unzipped the duffel bag and saw there were some items a person would take to the gym. The owner must have been a racquetball fan. Jack decided to take the bag and slung it over his shoulder as he watched Chris go through the backpack.

Chris pulled out some college textbooks, pens, notebooks, and then he pulled out a tightly rolled Ziploc bag.

Jack was perplexed as he watched Chris unroll the bag.

As soon as Chris opened the bag, however, Jack knew what was in it. The smell hit Jack and the distinctive odor told him it was pot.

Chris snorted a laugh and one side of his mouth lifted in a crooked grin as he looked a question at Jack.

Jack gestured for the young man to bring everything with them. You never knew what you could use in future trades.

Chris still had a smirk on his face as he zipped the backpack up and shut the trunk.

Grabbing everything up, Jack and Chris transferred it all to the Dodge.

Jack called over to Jason, "Help us push it out of the way."

Soon, the car was facing off the opposite side of the road and the group loaded up. Jack noticed that Kuan had stayed in the bed of the truck and was chanting softly under his breath with his eyes closed.

He hesitated, and briefly wondered if Kuan was going to be of any help. He banished the negative thoughts and shut the door.

Reaching into the glove compartment, Jack pulled out the map and studied it. Jack saw that they were only about forty miles from Maryville. It would be another twenty miles, after that, to Atlas.

Jason had turned the engine off to fill the tank and Jack restarted the truck. Shifting into gear, Jack glanced and made sure everyone was in.

It was comforting to know that the agents Jason had picked were highly competent. He didn't have to watch his back as much since he trusted their skills.

Jack spoke up, "We'll look for a good place to pull off the road. I know we're all hungry, and Chris and I found some canned food in the trunk."

Jason agreed, "That'd be great. I'm starving."

After driving a while, Jack addressed something that had been bothering him, "When we get to the facility, who will be there?"

Jason shook his head and replied, "I don't know, Jack. When I talked to them last, there were five scientists. They were at a standstill without the key."

He fell quiet and Jack let him think.

Soon, he continued, "All of the men that were at Atlas have families. Add the fact that they're not military, and my guess would be that they won't be there. After the blast, they would have known what happened and would have wanted to get to their families. With the shield completed yet still not working properly? I wouldn't blame them. Why would they stay?"

Jack asked another question. "Do you think Kuan can figure the device out? Maybe bypass the need for a key."

This was the very heart of the problem. Jack could tell by Jason's body language that he had been distressed over this very thing.

Jack tried a different question. "Okay. What about how the device works. If Dai Ji can get the damn thing to work without the key, can you tell me how it's supposed to operate? You called it a shield when I first saw you. Obviously, it's too late to use a shield. But, if it isn't a shield to protect us from EMPs, then what in the hell is it supposed to do?"

Jack realized that this tidbit of information had been bothering him for a while now.

If possible, Jason was even more distraught and Jack glanced at his friend in time to see him visibly try to calm himself and take a deep breath.

"I can only tell you what I've been told. This device was found in the wreckage of a crashed airship years ago. It was mothballed until our technology was up to speed enough to understand some of it. Scientists have been working on it since it was pulled out of storage seven years ago. They finally figured out that it was used to manipulate the earth's electromagnetic field. Once they had it ready to work, I had it moved to Atlas and built the facility around it to the specifications that I was given."

Jason fell silent and Jack mulled over what Jason had told him.

When he was done, he had one vital question. "Who? Who instructed you and gave you the specifications, Jason?"

Jason answered quickly, almost as if he had been waiting for the question, "That's classified, Jack."

Jack was so surprised, he nearly ran off the road. "WHAT?"

He decided this would be where they stopped. He slowed the truck and was glad to see there was a half-mile stretch that seemed completely deserted. He pulled to the side of the road under the branches of a large post oak tree.

He set the brake before turning his full attention to Jason. "Let me get this straight." He rubbed his top lip to give himself time to calm his temper and noticed he was really starting to get a full mustache.

Turning his attention back to Jason, he asked calmly, "You came to me after years of complete silence. I didn't even know if you were still alive, and I sure as hell didn't know you had ever stuck up for me. You came to me to ask my help to risk my life and drive halfway across a continent to save a world that doesn't give a shit about me. I think I deserve— no, I demand a better answer than 'That's classified'!"

Jack was breathing heavily, and his green eyes were on fire. He pushed back against the door with hooded eyes and carefully watched his old friend as he answered.

Jason was clearly uncomfortable and Jack kind of enjoyed

watching his discomfort.

Finally, Jason turned to him and said, "Jack, I thank you for coming with me and helping to 'save the world.' I can't even begin to understand what you've gone through the last ten years. But trust me when I say that I cannot tell you all the particulars about what is going on!"

Jason was clearly upset and troubled about not being able to tell Jack everything. This made Jack pause. He had headed teams where he couldn't tell them all the parts of the mission. For various reasons. He continued to watch Jason, but with a little more understanding.

Jason pulled his hands down his face as he struggled with what to say. He looked resigned as he finally turned to Jack. "Listen. I promise that when we finally get this thing done, you and I will have a drink and I will tell you everything. But not until then." He raised his eyebrows at Jack. "You have to trust me on this, Jack. It's the most important thing you will ever do."

Jason said the last part quietly. Jack heard the sincere pleading in Jason's voice. He had never heard that before with Jason and knew it was true.

He continued to watch Jason for a minute. Seeing that Jason wasn't going to change his mind, Jack reached for the door handle and said, "This isn't over, Jason. You better believe we'll talk again!"

With that, Jack got out of the truck and slammed the door.

The rest of the group had already gotten out and the agents were scouting the area. Even Kuan had left the truck and had walked over to inspect the old oak tree. Chris was going through the food in the plastic bags. He had lowered the tailgate and was lining the cans up.

"You don't happen to have a can opener, do you?" Chris looked hopefully at Jack.

Jack pulled his knife and held it out. Chris glanced at the knife then up at Jack. He sighed and took the knife.

Jack continued away from the truck. He was looking for Ray. He realized that nobody had told the three agents where they were going, exactly, and what they were hoping would happen. Jack remembered how much it had irritated him in the past to be left out of the loop.

He saw Ray was by the side of the road talking closely with Cat.

Jack cleared his throat to announce his arrival. He could tell they had an intimate conversation going and was trying to be polite.

Ray straightened and turned. Jack was surprised to see the big man blushing.

Deliberately making his face blank, Jack said, "Where's Greg? I wanted to let you three know what's happening."

Ray recovered quickly. "Uh, he went to relieve himself. He should be back any minute, Jack."

Just as Ray said this, Greg walked out of the trees. "What's up?" He had heard the last part of the exchange.

Jack said, "I'm guessing we're about two hours from the facility."

Everybody had gathered around to hear what Jack was saying. All except Jason. He saw what Jack was doing and was keeping a lookout. Even Kuan had turned and was paying attention.

Jack continued, "When we reach the cavern, I'm going to drop everybody off except Chris." He looked at the young man and explained, "You can come with me to Pigeon Forge and then continue on, by yourself, to Asheville."

Chris bobbed his head in agreement.

Jack turned to Greg. "Jason wants me to take you with me. I told him there was no need, but he insisted. I'm giving you the chance to decline. In the old America, you wouldn't have gotten that choice. However, things are different. Times have changed and I'm not that kind of person. It's your choice."

Jack waited patiently as Greg looked around in surprise. Jack found it interesting that the agent looked at Ray first, not Jason. Jason was his boss, but it was apparent that Greg held Ray in higher esteem.

Ray just raised his eyebrows at Greg and shrugged. Greg looked back at Jack and said, "Sure, count me in, sounds like fun!"

Jack saw Cat roll her eyes as he went on, "Ray, you and Cat are going to be the security detail while Jason shows Kuan the device. Kuan, I know we're asking a lot, but we need you to try to get it to work." Jack paused here and warred with himself for a moment about how much to divulge. In the end, he decided they were all in this and deserved the truth.

He looked up and saw they were all watching him closely.

Jack knew there was no easy way to put it, so he just told them the truth. "There's something I need to tell you all. This device that we're trying to activate is not a device that we developed."

He looked around to see their reactions. They all looked confused. All but Kuan, but his expressions didn't change much anyway.

He continued, "When I say we didn't develop it, I mean nobody on Earth developed it. According to Jason, this is a device that was recovered in a crash in New Mexico and has been stored away for years."

Everyone now looked intrigued. Jack thought they would be skeptical, but considering the multiple television channels showing reports of reverse engineering, government conspiracies, and such, on second thought, he understood.

"As I was saying, Jason had top scientists working around the clock for years taking this thing apart to figure out how it works. They figured out most of it, and it turns out it may be able to repel or completely dissipate the electromagnetic effects that are up in the atmosphere."

Jack stopped and considered what he was saying.

After a moment he went on in a softer voice, "Look. I'm going to be honest with you." He held his hands out palms up, and then dropped them to his sides. "I don't know if this thing will work, even if we can get it running. If we can get it working, I can't guarantee it will make a difference. What I can promise you is that there is nothing else that even has a chance to change what's happening. Either it works or it doesn't. I'm going to get Emma and come back to the cavern. If you haven't been able to get it to work by then, well, then you are all welcome to come back to my ranch and make a go of it. Or, we'll drop you off anywhere on the way."

He looked around at every face and saw they were now starting to understand what was actually going on.

There was nothing else Jack could say. He left the group and stepped over to the tailgate. Picking up his knife, he started opening the cans. The sooner they ate, the sooner they could be on their way.

15

Frank had left Clem in charge. He had decided to come on this little errand himself. He would check on Jarvis and Janine after he stopped by Larry's cabin. Frank was worried about Emma and her friends. When he looked into her eyes, he'd seen a very intelligent woman. Until he knew for sure that they had left, he couldn't rest easy.

He reined his horse up. Frank had brought Tony with him. As they stopped their horses, Frank gazed out at the cabin from the cover of the trees.

He had wanted to get an earlier start, but had to deal with the complaints of the townspeople.

Frank sneered as he thought about the small group of men whining about his way of doing things. The sheriff thought there would be more people at the town meeting. Apparently, most of the people were not appreciative of how he, the mayor, and the judge were running things.

After ordering his deputies to go out and see why more people weren't at the meeting, they had returned to tell him most of the people were simply gone. Questioning his men closely had revealed that whole families were disappearing. Frank surmised that they were sneaking out under cover of darkness. The sheriff knew it would only be a matter of time before he would get a visit from one of the surrounding authorities based on allegations from the vanishing families.

Frank sighed. He had two choices. He could either stay here or cut his losses, grab his stash of money, and head out to his cabin in Alabama. If he stayed here, he would have to explain why he'd done what he had. He felt fairly sure he could explain away his actions, especially with all the confusion. But, if not, he had made sure he had a way out.

The first thing he had to do, though, was to make sure those three had left. He would never admit it to anyone, but he was afraid of Jack Denton. Not just of the things he knew, but of the man himself. If the woman hadn't left, Jack would be coming for her.

Movement at the cabin interrupted his thoughts and captured his attention.

The back door of the house opened and a man stepped out.

Frank lifted his binoculars and focused on the figure.

His white eyebrows scrunched together for a moment until he realized who it was.

Larry Campbell. Well, well. Frank scrutinized the rest of the place but saw no horses or other signs of the trio.

He looked back at Tony and smirked. "Let's go have a word with him."

Tony chuckled and the sheriff nudged his horse toward the cabin. He angled his horse to cut Larry off. He must be headed to the creek. He was carrying two buckets and appeared to be deep in thought.

Frank was within three feet of Larry before the man realized the sheriff was there. When he figured it out, the man visibly started. Quickly, he caught himself.

Smiling at Frank, Larry said, "Hey, Frank! Long time no see!"

Frank was trying to decide if Larry was acting or not. Undecided, he replied with a smile, "Larry! Imagine that! Now, I was just out here a couple of days ago. There were two young ladies and a man staying at your cabin. Did you see those folks?"

Frank watched Larry closely as he replied, "Two women? And a man, you say?" Larry looked down at his feet, "No… no, there were some things missing when I got here, but no people."

Frank knew the man was lying; he'd been doing police work way too long.

Frank pulled his gun and pointed it at Larry. Larry looked at that gun and flashed back to junior high and high school. Frank was the consummate bully.

Larry lifted his trembling hands and said, "Frank. What do you want? I don't know anything!"

Frank sneered as he dismounted and said, "I think you do. Let's go have a little talk, shall we?"

16

They had been driving the back roads for two hours. Jack thought he would be exhausted by now. Instead, the closer he got to Pigeon Forge, the more alert he became.

They had just turned onto a gravel road and had driven about a half a mile, when Jason reached out and grabbed Jack's forearm.

"There it is!" he said, and Jack put on the brakes.

Jack looked back and saw a break in the trees and a dirt road leading back into the forest.

He looked over at Jason. "Are you sure?"

Jason nodded and asked, "You see that yellow rag? I put that there the last time I was here so I'd know."

Jack looked where Jason pointed and saw a small yellow cloth tied to a branch.

Putting the truck in reverse, he got it pointed in the right direction and headed down the dirt road.

Soon, they arrived in a clearing at the base of a mountain. Jack was perplexed. He expected to see a large door. Instead, all he saw was the sheer granite face of the mountain.

He put the truck in park and had opened his mouth to ask Jason, when his friend opened the door and got out. Jack abruptly closed his mouth and got out too. Ray, Cat, and Kuan were getting their bags. Chris and Greg had already disembarked.

Jack came around the front of the Dodge and followed Jason toward the cliff.

Ahead of him, Jack watched in surprise as Jason walked right up to the cliff face and abruptly disappeared.

Jack didn't stop, but cocked his head as he followed. By the time he reached the cliff, he'd figured out what had happened. It was an optical illusion. There was an opening in the cliff face that ran parallel to the front of the cliff. It was about two maybe three feet wide and ran almost fifteen feet before it ended.

Jack was standing at the opening and inspecting the well-made illusion.

The rest of the group arrived and Greg whistled, "Pretty snazzy!"

Before following Jason, Jack looked back at the truck and felt his pocket for the keys. He figured it would be okay for the short amount of time he'd be gone.

Ducking down the path, he saw Jason drop a log chain off of a door that looked similar to a submarine hatch. Jason pocketed the padlock and strained as he spun the wheel.

With a screech, he jerked it open and they entered. As the last person made it in, Jason flicked on his flashlight, closed the door, and bolted it.

He shone the light around and Jack realized that the

cavern was large. There were all kinds of equipment in the middle of the cavern.

Jason started to walk away and Jack grabbed his friend's sleeve. "Jason, I need to go. I'll see all of this when I get back."

Jason said, "Are you sure? I'm going to get the generators going and in a bit, you can have a hot shower and a bite to eat."

Jack looked surprise and Jason saw this. "I had the entire cavern fortified and insulated against electromagnetic pulses. Being underground helps too."

He smiled as he said this.

Jack shook his head and said, "I'm sorry, Jason, I don't have time. I feel that I need to go. Now. I'll be back soon to enjoy a hot shower." He smiled sadly at his friend and continued, "Work hard to get this damn thing going, and maybe it'll all be fixed when I get back."

Jason nodded in understanding. "I'll go with you and get the rest of my stuff."

He turned back to the door and unbolted it. With a loud squeal, it opened and the green daylight burst in.

Everybody went to the truck except Kuan. He stayed by the cliff, leaning on his staff and watching the sendoff.

When they were ready to go, Jack shook Jason's hand and Jason said, "Be careful, Jack. Don't take any unnecessary chances."

Jack grinned back and said, "I'll do my best."

Ray and Cat had said their goodbyes to Greg, and Chris was off to the side, watching.

When they were ready, they all three loaded up in the cab and waved as they drove off.

Reaching the paved road, Jack turned right to head back down the mountain.

Greg piped up and asked, "So, how long 'til we get to Pigeon Forge?"

Jack said, "Maybe forty-five minutes."

He looked over at the AR-15 that Greg had standing on its stock between his legs.

"Make sure that thing's loaded," Jack said.

Greg replied, "She's loaded. You don't know me well enough yet, but I'm always ready!"

Jack briefly shook his head at the young agent's cockiness and refocused on the road.

After a moment, Chris broke the silence. "You guys are both armed. Would you happen to have an extra weapon?"

Startled, Jack looked at the young man and asked, "Do you know how to shoot?"

Chris looked back at him and grinned. "Yeah, my dad took me out shooting quite a bit. He's a big stickler on being prepared. He's a damn good shot. As a matter of fact, the only one that can outshoot him is my mom."

Jack laughed, then nodded. "Okay. Greg, would you mind lending him your handgun? He'll give it back when we're done. It's a good idea if everyone's armed."

Greg looked the young man over and said, "Sure. Just make sure you do give it back. I'm kind of attached to it." He pulled out the .32 and gave it to Chris along with some ammo from his pocket, "I've got more, but it's in my bag back there."

Chris thanked the agent. Jack glanced over and saw the young man pop open the cylinder, check the bullets, spin it, and snap it back home. It was obvious that Chris knew weapons and Jack was glad. Every extra bit of firepower helped.

Greg had been watching too. "Man! You weren't kidding! He's Billy the Kid!"

Jack chuckled and slowed as they came to a stop sign at the bottom of the mountain. This was the intersection at Wear's Valley Road. He was back on home turf and knew exactly where he was.

Turning right, they headed toward Larry's cabin, and he felt hopeful that Emma would be there waiting for him.

Greg reached over and switched on the radio, and static issued from the speakers. "I sure do miss some jams." He fiddled with the other knob trying to find a station.

Jack reached over after a minute and turned it off. "There's nothing out there," he grumbled, irritably.

Greg held his hands up in mock surrender, then asked, "Okay, Jack, tell us where we're going, exactly, and what to expect."

He hung his elbow out the window and waited for Jack to speak.

Jack sighed and said, "I thought you knew already. I left a voicemail for Emma the night before the blast. I told her that if something happened, to make her way to this cabin that we had gone to years ago. I'm sure she knew which one I meant. It belongs to a good friend of mine and he uses it as a vacation home. Anyway, by my calculation, if everything went as planned, she should be there now. I promised her I would come get her."

Everyone was silent for a minute, then Greg asked, "What if she isn't there?"

Jack gripped the steering wheel harder and said, "She's here, in Pigeon Forge. She may not be at the cabin, but she's in the area."

He glanced at the two men and saw that Chris believed him. Greg, on the other hand, looked doubtful.

Jack said, "Let's just get to the cabin and see what's going on. If she's not there, we'll decide what to do then."

This seemed to satisfy Greg and he nodded.

Jack saw the road he wanted and turned right. He was excited and nervous. Less than a mile away sat Larry's cabin.

17

Frank was pissed. He was sitting in a rocking chair in Jeb's living room.

Back at Larry's place, he'd had trouble getting anyone to talk. He'd finally had to rough up the woman and threaten worse to get Larry to tell him what he knew. As Frank had suspected, Emma and her friends had not left town. In fact, it turned out that they made friends with Matt Carroll. When Frank had gotten the full story, it didn't take him long to piece it all together. He now realized that they must have been somewhere nearby when he and his men raided Jeb's farm. He didn't know what they had seen, and had come here to see if he could find them.

He spun the barrel of his gun as he sat in the gloom and pondered. He'd sent Tony back to town. As loyal as Tony was, Frank didn't want him around if he found Hawk or the three friends. He had looked around the place and couldn't find Jarvis or Janine. The worthless sacks of shit probably left. He would deal with them later, if he decided to stay. That's what he was sitting there trying to figure out. Should he stay, or should he go? He didn't know what he'd expected to find once he got to Jeb's house, but anyway, it was empty.

It had been an hour now and he found himself in the unusual position of not being able to make a decision. That's why he was angry. If Jeb hadn't forced his hand, he wouldn't have had to try to arrest him on sedition.

Frank stood up, restlessly pacing to each window. Sweat was starting to roll down his neck, but he didn't notice. They were starting to whisper to him again. He could just barely hear them, but they had been steadily getting louder. He hadn't taken his medication since the Kroger incident. It made him fuzzy headed, and he needed a clear head now. Besides, shipments hadn't exactly been coming in lately.

His mind was wandering and he squeezed his eyes closed and popped his head hard with the gun to think clearly again.

That helped, and he paced to the windows again. His eyes were darting from side to side and he was just about to leave. Then there was movement that caught his eye, and he squinted as he tried to see what it was.

* * *

Emma felt bad for leaving her friends, but it was for the best. She didn't need to get them involved in this. It wasn't their fight. It wasn't really her fight either, but Frank and Jarvis had made it personal. She couldn't just walk away knowing that she could have done something to save Pete. She despised bullies, and that's exactly what Frank and his deputies were.

She pulled on the reins to guide Leroy up the slope from the waterfall. She'd found Bella right outside the waterfall and the cat had been more than happy to get into her bag.

She topped the rise and hesitated. Looking back at the waterfall, she smiled as she silently wished her friends well.

Turning Leroy's head, she walked him through the trees. She thought about the things they had found in the cave. Shifting her pack, she decided it was too heavy now. She stopped Leroy and looped the bag over the saddle horn. The contents clinked together as Bella shifted in the bag. One of the things they had found was a box full of pipe bombs. She brought some with her, just in case.

Emma took a deep breath, narrowed her eyes in determination, and nudged Leroy in the sides. He stepped off and Emma went back to musing. Bryan and Lori would be fine. When they woke up and she was gone, they would know what she had in mind and would head to Larry's. Or Gatlinburg. Either way, they would be safe.

She remembered the sound of Pete's voice when he yelled that they had shot his mother. Emma could not ignore that. Plus, she had promised Hawk, and she always kept her promises.

She needed to stop by Jeb's house to check if there was a map of the area.

Emma had come to the spot where Hawk had grabbed her. Leroy was just about to step out into the opening when she reined him in. She had heard voices and cocked her head to listen.

From the direction of the driveway she heard people talking and the snort of a horse.

Emma quickly dismounted and led Leroy behind a tree. She patted and soothed him as she watched to see who it was. Her first guess was Frank or his men. They had probably come out to find Jarvis and the woman.

Soon, she saw the first of the riders come from the driveway and enter the front yard. Emma saw that they were wearing the same color uniform as Len had on and realized they were deputies from Gatlinburg.

She smiled with relief and excitement and was about to reveal herself when she noticed movement at the back of the house.

She stopped and her mouth dropped open as she watched Sheriff Green dart out the back door. He was fast. He kept the house between him and the riders, and before Emma could say anything, he was into the woods and gone.

She quickly weighed her options and realized that by the time she told the men from Gatlinburg what had happened, Frank could be long gone. She had the element of surprise and decided to follow Frank. He knew he was being hunted now and would surely run. Emma guessed he would either try to eliminate witnesses or skip town altogether. If Pete and his family were still alive, they might not be for long. She needed to follow Frank and keep him from getting away.

She remounted and saw through the trees that Frank had his horse now and was quickly mounting up.

As she watched, she heard a noise behind her and drew her gun. She saw it was Bryan and Lori and she quickly looked back to watch Frank.

"Hey—"

She cut Bryan off with her hand as he got beside her. She didn't have time to explain. Frank was darting off through the woods and she needed to follow.

She turned to her friends. "Gatlinburg police just got to the front of the house. Frank just snuck out the back and through the woods. I'm going after Frank. You need to tell the police everything that has happened. Tell them what I'm doing. Frank is either going back to the gem mine or to his house to get his things and leave."

Her eyes were blazing as she looked at her surprised friends. "When you finish here, go to Larry and ask him where the sheriff lives. He'll need to get some things before he takes off, and he'll think he has time. I'll cut him off."

Emma started to kick her horse as Bryan said, "Let me go with you!"

Emma hissed back, "You'll just slow me down! I've got to go! Move it and tell the police!"

With that, she was gone. She had kept a visual on Frank and could still see the branches moving in his wake. She quickly left her friends behind and soon came within sight of the sheriff. He glanced back once, but she made sure she was hidden. He wasn't being very careful, which puzzled her.

He crossed several roads and soon came to a valley. There was grass but no trees, and Emma watched as Frank urged his horse into a run. She held Leroy back in the trees and watched as Frank raced across to the back of a small yellow ranch-style house.

Making a run for it, aren't you, asshole? she thought to herself.

She watched him reach the house, jump off his horse, and loop the reins over a bush. He stopped and turned to scan the way he'd just come, and Emma eased behind a tree.

Not seeing anything, he fumbled with the door handle and then stopped and seemed to be arguing with himself.

Emma drew her brows down as she tried to puzzle out who he was talking to. There wasn't anyone else there, so he had to be talking to himself. That changed things a little. Not only was he a bully, now she had reason to believe he was crazy too. Great.

She sighed and pulled her gun. She would race straight across and enter the opposite tree line. She would then sneak up to his house from that side. She still had surprise on her side, and that would just have to do.

18

Jack pulled the truck slowly up to the front of the cabin. As he turned the engine off, he started to worry. If Emma had been in the cabin, she should have come to the door. Maybe she was just being cautious.

He opened the door and stayed sheltered behind it. "*Hello!*" he yelled to the cabin.

Greg had opened his door just as Jack had. He rested the rifle barrel on the open windowsill.

There was no answer, and Jack's anxiety ratcheted up another notch.

The sun was beating down on him through the green haze and he quickly started to sweat again. He watched the windows and thought he saw a slight movement.

This worried him even more. If it had been Emma, she would have recognized him.

He started to ask Greg to cover him when he heard the front door being unlocked, and a woman's face was at the crack.

She said, "What do you want? We only have a little food, but you're welcome to it if you'll just leave us alone."

Jack saw she had a black eye and her face was puffy like she had been crying. He saw she was scared and he surreptitiously motioned for Greg to lower the rifle. Greg shrugged and did so, but kept it ready behind the door.

Jack spoke back to the woman, "I'm looking for Emma Hudson. She was supposed to be here waiting for me. My name is Jack Denton."

The moment he finished speaking, the woman's eyes flew open and she stuttered, "J-Jack? Jack Denton?"

She turned her head as if someone in the house was speaking to her. She then opened the door wide and started sobbing. She motioned them in and Jack could see she was so overwhelmed that she couldn't speak.

Puzzled, he motioned Chris and Greg to follow as he went up the steps into the cabin.

As they entered, Jack saw Larry Campbell was sitting on the couch with a bandage around his right hand. There was blood soaking the bandage and his nose looked broken and bleeding. He was breathing through his mouth, but managed to smile when he saw Jack.

"Better late than never," he wheezed at Jack.

"My God, Larry! What the hell happened to you?" Jack nodded at the woman as she sat down next to Larry.

Larry shifted and gasped in pain before responding, "Pigeon Forge's finest, Frank Green, paid us a little visit." He spat this out and then held up his uninjured hand.

"He's after Emma, and I'm afraid he's going to find her."

Shocked, Jack simply said, "Tell me!"

Larry quickly brought Jack and his friends up to speed on everything that had taken place. After a few minutes, he ended with explaining what Frank had wanted from him and introducing Rita.

Jack nodded to the woman again, but she was crying and ignored him. The more Larry spoke, the angrier Jack became.

He stood and viciously said, "I should have done something about that bastard years ago! How long ago did he leave?"

Larry replied, "At least a couple of hours. You'd better hurry, Jack. He was talking to himself when he left here. I think he's losing it. No telling what he'll do."

Jack was frantic now and could think of only one thing. Emma. He turned to the door and then thought of something and asked Larry, "Where does he live? In case he's not at the Carrolls'."

Larry said, "Last I heard, he had moved into his parent's house after they moved to Florida."

Jack thanked him and was out the door. Greg and Chris on his heels.

As they started to get in the truck, Jack told Chris, "This isn't your fight. Why don't you stay here? You can head on to Asheville."

Chris shook his head. "Are you kidding? After everything you've done for me, I owe it to you. You might need me."

Jack didn't have time to argue, so he nodded and started the truck. He jerked the gearshift down and spun the Dodge around. He forced himself to calm down. He wouldn't do anybody any good if he wrecked the truck.

At the end of the driveway, he turned left. There was a road down this way that cut over to Little Cove, and he pushed the truck faster.

Two more turns and they were headed west on Little Cove.

Jack had been rapidly going over what he needed to do. When they nearing the Carroll's driveway, he came to a stop and cut the engine.

He looked over at Greg and said, "This driveway is lined with bushes. Give me five minutes to circle around to the back of the house. Then you drive down to the front. Larry said he caught enough of the conversation between Frank and Tony to realize something may have happened to the family. I don't think they're here. If they are, they're good people, so don't shoot them. If Frank's in there, it should flush him out the back, or he'll be distracted by the truck and come out the front door."

Greg nodded. Jack shoved the door open, then took off at an angle to the driveway. As he ran, he prayed that Emma was safe. For him to have come all this way, only to lose her like this. He angrily pushed those thoughts away and soon came to the back of the house. He pulled up short at the corner of the building and caught his breath.

Jack pulled his gun and eased to the front corner of the house. He darted a look around to the front and saw there were several saddled horses tied to the front porch.

He had his back to the house and was trying to decide the

best way to approach this, when he heard the Dodge slowly rumbling down the drive.

As it got closer, he heard the front door open and Jack snuck a look. It was a man in uniform. Jack was confused. He was familiar enough with the local police uniforms to see this wasn't any Pigeon Forge officer.

He decided to wait and see what happened.

Greg stopped the truck and turned off the engine. Jack was peeking around the corner and saw Greg open the truck door with a wide grin.

"I seem to be lost," he said. "I was looking for Emma Hudson."

Jack watched the lawman open his mouth but before he could say anything, a petite young woman with short hair almost pushed the man over to get out on the porch.

"Jack! Is that you, Jack Denton?"

Now Jack was really confused. Who was this woman? Then it dawned on him. This had to be the woman Larry had told him about, one of the people who had come up from Atlanta with Em. He saw Greg cut his eyes to him without moving his head. Jack put a hand up to tell him to stay there.

Jack stepped slightly away from the house and kept his gun leveled on the lawman. "Freeze right there!" he yelled.

The man froze and lifted his hands away from his gun.

The woman turned to stare at Jack. "What's going on? Please tell me one of you is Jack Denton!" she pleaded.

Jack saw no reason to lie. "I'm Jack. Do you know Emma Hudson?"

The woman vigorously nodded her head. "Jack, are we ever glad to see you!"

He saw a blond-headed man was behind her with a crossbow pointed at Jack over her shoulder.

The woman turned to the officer. "He's a friend."

Turning quickly back to Jack she said, "Jack, my name's Lori and this is Bryan. Emma took off on horseback about ten minutes ago chasing Frank, the sheriff. These officers are from Gatlinburg and are here to ask Frank some serious questions. They're the good guys. Frank didn't know Emma had seen him, and we don't know where he was going. We know he saw these deputies, and he's done some really bad things, so I assume he's trying to escape!"

She said this all in a rush and it took Jack a second to process it. He had just one question.

"Which way did they go, Lori?"

Lori didn't hesitate and pointed. "He went out the back and through the woods. They're both on horseback."

Jack looked the way she pointed and knew that Frank was trying to get out of town. He probably wanted to go by and pick some things up before he left. He realized it'd be quicker if he cut across on horseback.

Jack strode quickly to the porch. "I need a horse!" he exclaimed.

Lori quickly pointed to the last horse. "That's mine. His

name's Scooter. Please be careful and bring Emma back safe."

The man had lowered the crossbow and came out onto the porch. "Where do you think he's headed?"

Jack swung up on Scooter and motioned to Greg.

As he reached down for the AR-15, he answered the man, "I'm sure he's headed to his house for supplies before leaving town. Do any of you know Engle Town Road?"

Luckily, one of the officers inside the house stepped out and said, "I grew up here. What's the house number?"

Jack said, "It's 3111."

He was losing time. Turning back to Greg, he said, "Take that woman deputy with you and meet me at the house. I hope we're not too late!"

Greg wasted no words and just slapped the horse as it passed him on its way.

Jack mentally calculated the quickest way to Frank's house. He pushed the horse to race through the trees and over bushes. His mind was also racing as he thought about the irony of the moment.

Years ago, in high school, he had been driving home one night. It had been after a football game they'd won after beating their biggest rivals. Everyone had been celebrating and there had been several parties. Jack had only had a couple of beers, but Frank had been drinking heavily. Jack had started taking his own truck to those parties after Frank had left him once and he'd had to bum a ride with someone else.

After not seeing Frank for a while, he'd decided to leave

the party and head home. On the way home, he'd spotted the back end of Frank's car at a popular make-out area on a deserted road. He started to drive past when he noticed that the lights were on and the doors were open. Puzzled, he stopped the truck and watched to see if Frank was just taking a piss. When he saw no movement, he put the truck in reverse and turned in behind Frank's Camaro.

When he still saw no movement, he cut the engine and sat for a moment, undecided. That's when he heard a scream. He remembered snatching open the door and following the scream to the front of Frank's car. There he stopped when he saw a young girl in a flurry of motion come out of the bushes and hit a tree. He heard a distinct snap of bones as she struck her head and watched her slump to the ground. All of that had happened in a flash, and Jack stood motionless with the car lights shining behind him.

Frank staggered out, cussing angrily until he noticed Jack. Until now, Jack had always questioned the look he'd seen on Frank's face. His first impression had been that Frank had been furious. But as soon as Frank saw he wasn't alone, his face had morphed into anguish, so quickly that Jack was never sure if he'd really seen the fury.

Frank rushed to the girl's side and cried her name. Jack remembered that it had been Cathy.

Eventually, Frank was cleared of any charges after the young woman died.

Yet it had continued to bother Jack—those questions in the back of his mind caused he and Frank to drift apart.

While they had not exactly become enemies, they had never been close after that. Now, with all that he'd been told about Frank, his questions had been answered.

Arriving at the edge of a clearing, Jack pushed his memories aside and focused on the houses across the way.

His horse sidestepped restlessly as Jack searched for Frank's house. It had been awhile.

Just as he recognized the house, he saw movement on the other side of the clearing. He turned his head to focus directly on the figure.

It was a slender figure on a horse. Jack knew immediately it was Emma and his heart leapt. Just as quickly, he realized she was trying to sneak up on the sheriff, and felt a ball of fear tighten in his stomach. Gauging the distance to Frank's house, Jack knew he was too far away to stop her, and she wouldn't hear him if he yelled.

He saw her reach the back of the house and dismount. Jack dug his heels into his horse. The horse took off straight across the valley, and he bent close to its neck. He figured it would take him several minutes to reach the house, and he mentally urged the animal on.

He briefly thought about firing his gun. But, if he shot the rifle to get her attention, he would alert Frank as well. He gritted his teeth in frustration and pushed the horse to his limits. He would just have to see what happened.

Just as he was thinking this, he saw Frank easing around the opposite edge of the house, and Jack knew he must be aware of Emma's presence. Darting a look at Emma, Jack knew she had no idea what she was walking into. He knew he had to do something.

Reaching around to grab his rifle, he had a heart-stopping moment when his horse stumbled. Jack hitched a breath as he waited for the horse to regain its footing and continue on. But it didn't happen. Jack knew the horse was going down, and using all of the skills he had learned at the ranch, Jack pushed off with his legs. He had no time to roll. He could only hope there were no tree stumps where he landed. The high grass made it impossible to see any dangers. He only had seconds to think all of this before he landed on his chest and slid painfully to a stop.

He was stunned and lay still for just a second. Shaking himself from his stupor, Jack pushed himself to his feet and did a body check. He was thankful there were no broken bones, only bruises. He quickly swung around to look back at the house. He was about to yell for Emma to watch out, but saw it was too late and he was too far away. He saw his horse was unhurt but had run off. All he could do was take off running as he watched everything unfold.

* * *

Emma had her gun out and was concentrating on her footing as she eased to the corner of the house. She hesitated as she listened. Hearing nothing but the calls of birds in the trees behind her, she started to ease around the corner. At that moment, a brawny figure stepped around the corner and grabbed her neck. Emma started to bring up her gun but Frank was faster. He intercepted the upward sweep of her arm with his right hand and crushed her fingers as he squeezed her gun hand. He gripped it so tight she couldn't move any of her fingers. His left hand clenched her throat so tight, she couldn't breathe. Instinctively, Emma clawed at his hand with her own left hand. She needed oxygen. At first she was afraid, but now she was angry.

With wild, open eyes, Frank spoke through gritted teeth, "Well, well. Looks like I'll get to have something of Jack's before I leave. If you would have stayed away, I would have been gone and you wouldn't be in this position!"

He relaxed his grip just enough for Emma to suck in some air. Her vision cleared. She was pissed, not only for his assumption that she was defeated, but because she had let herself be caught off guard.

She was about to knee him in the groin and he sensed her movement. Frank used his weight to push her backward. He still had hold of her gun hand so that she couldn't get her finger on the trigger. She decided to fall backward. Maybe she could get him off balance and wrest the gun from his hand.

Emma relaxed her leg muscles and saw in his eyes that she had surprised him. Frank quickly shifted his weight and tried to keep them both from falling. Partly succeeding, they only stumbled back a small ways before slamming into Emma's horse. Frank's grip on her neck loosened again and Emma tried to jerk away. It didn't work, and the sheriff regained his balance.

Their faces were only six inches apart, and Emma could see that the big man was surprised at the strength and fight she was putting up. She saw him lower his brows in anger and knew he was about to shove her to the ground. She braced for the struggle when suddenly there was an explosion of fur from her bag where it was hanging from Leroy's pommel. Bella yowled as she jumped with claws outstretched and attached herself to Frank's face. The movement shocked them both, but it surprised Frank more than Emma.

He had to release Emma to get to the cat, and Emma sucked in a giant breath as he freed her throat. She coughed as she struggled to snatch her gun hand back from the sheriff, but he retained an iron grip on her hand. She saw the man reach up with inhuman speed and grasp the cat's fur with his left hand and then try to sling Bella from his face. He succeeded and slung the cat from him with a powerful snap of his arm. The cat didn't sail far before it slapped the side of a tree with a loud crack and then slumped to the ground and lay still.

Emma caught her breath in dismay, but only for a second. Frank reached for her throat again but Emma arched her back as she dodged his hand. With a seething anger unlike anything she had ever felt before, Emma whipped her gun hand around and broke the hold he had on her. He was over-balanced from reaching for her neck, and with the one move, Emma caught him reaching toward her.

Ducking under Frank's left arm, she spun with her right hand and with all her strength smashed the butt of the gun into the back of his head. He flew forward into Leroy and was unconscious before landing on his back.

As she staggered back, Emma couldn't believe that she had beaten the bastard. She was still catching her breath, and she paused for a couple of seconds to suck in some life-giving oxygen. She leaned forward with her hands on her knees before slumping to the ground next to Frank and feeling for his handcuffs. She had just found them and was starting to put the cuffs on his wrists when she heard something behind her.

She reacted and spun onto her butt, pointing the Glock at the man who showed up in her sights. She had put pressure on the trigger before she recognized who it was.

Jack. Her Jack. The Jack she had thought about night and day for nearly eight years.

Emma immediately lowered the gun. Jack was breathing heavily and quirked his top lip in a gesture she knew all too well.

"Jack?" she asked in a squeak. Due to the hand that had squeezed her throat, Emma could not speak properly, and she was still struggling to breathe. She saw the love of her life hover over her, and she smiled before passing out.

Jack slung the rifle over his shoulder and was still catching his breath as he reached down and tenderly grabbed Emma's shoulders. He had seen the whole thing. He eased the woman that meant the world to him over to the side and gently placed her out of harm's way. Turning back to Frank, Jack snarled as he finished putting the handcuffs on the big man and shoved him to the side. By the time he finished, Emma was stirring and Jack scooted next to her. Emma coughed and moved her head side to side but still had her eyes closed.

Pulling her close, Jack smiled gently and said, "Em, hey, it's me!"

Emma opened her eyes and looked around. Jack could see she was confused.

He didn't know what else to do, so he gingerly bent his head and touched his lips to hers. As he felt their lips touch, there was a familiar electricity that reached deep into his soul. The same electricity that he felt the first time they kissed. Jack reveled in the feeling of completeness that surged through his body. Good lord, he loved this woman!

He felt her respond and he knew she was there. She may be confused, but she knew him.

Jack's heart exulted even more as she came back and became animated. Emma pushed Jack back and opened her eyes wide.

"You're not supposed to be here for another week! What the hell are you doing here?"

Jack looked down at this little spitfire and grinned, "I decided to show up a little early. Is that okay?"

Emma looked at Jack with those impossibly beautiful green eyes that were so full of life and said, "Better late than never."

She finished this sentence and reached to him with both arms in a hug that never let Jack doubt for a minute that she had always loved him and always would.

After a moment, Jack felt her let go and quickly push him away. "Oh my God! Bella!"

She pushed against him and he let her up. "What? Who?"

Emma rolled to the side and staggered to her feet. "Bella. She's my cat and Frank hurt her!"

Emma steadied herself against Leroy. Jack stood behind her in case she were to faint again.

Jack had no idea what she was talking about, but he could tell it was important to her. He followed her as she walked to the tree next to the horse. He stopped and looked back at Frank to make sure he hadn't moved.

When he turned back to Emma, Jack saw she had slumped to her knees next to a pile of fur, and he held back, not sure what was going on.

Jack heard Emma stifle a gasp as she reached hesitantly toward the animal, gathered it into her arms, and started to inspect it. He felt kind of helpless, so he peered around at the backyard, but looked back as Emma finished checking the animal. He would protect her until the day she died, and anything that she loved would fall under that protection.

After a few moments, Jack asked, "Is she okay?"

Emma answered with a sob, "She's alive! Bella's breathing. She must have a concussion from hitting the tree."

Emma looked back at Jack. "She saved my life, Jack."

Jack nodded as he looked around and then asked, "How can we help her?"

He saw Emma shake her head. "Time. That's all we can do."

He watched as Emma took the ball of fur and gently placed her in the backpack.

Once she had the cat safe, Jack told Emma, "My friends should be just up the road." He handed her the Glock. "Keep an eye on this asshole until I get back."

Emma nodded and Jack pulled his rifle over his head.

"I'll be right back," he told Emma and kissed her on the cheek. Before he pulled away, Emma grabbed the back of his head and kissed him with all of her being.

Jack looked at her in surprise and saw tears in her eyes. "I will never leave you again," she said. As she said this, Jack could see something different in Emma. She was the same woman, but not the same.

He smiled sweetly and gently placed his hand on her cheek. "I'll be right back."

Emma nodded, smiled, and then leaned against the house. "I'll be right here," she said.

Jack glanced down at Frank to make sure he was still unconscious. Noting that he was, he winked at Emma then disappeared around the front of the house.

Emma realized her throat was still sore; she knew she'd have marks.

Still trying to calm her nerves, she started when she heard the sheriff groan. The bastard was waking up.

Pushing away from the house, Emma lifted her lip in an uncharacteristic snarl of near hatred. She backed away from the man and angled her gun at him as he turned to his back and his eyelids fluttered.

She kept quiet and let him come around.

After a moment, she saw that he remembered what happened. His eyes flew open wide, his hands jerked against the cuffs, and his back arched, all at the same time.

Emma briefly savored the feeling of revenge before stepping into the man's line of sight.

She saw recognition dawn in his eyes and she smiled sweetly as she said, "You almost made it, Frank. You almost got away with it all." Her smile dropped from her face as she continued, "So, tell me. How does it feel to get taken down by a woman?"

She saw absolute loathing cross the big man's face just before he lunged for her. Emma had expected this and sidestepped as Frank's cuffed hands brushed just past her midsection.

In his fury, he became overbalanced and fell hard to the ground again.

Frank had landed on his stomach and Emma quickly stepped over and brought her foot down hard on the back of his neck, pinning him to the ground.

She gritted her teeth as the images of Pete, Jeb, and the rest of his family flashed through her mind.

Leaning down, Emma put the barrel of her gun to the

man's temple and said, "I should just save us all a lot of trouble and blow your brains out. I hate bullying bastards like you."

She let him think about that a minute, then went on, "But then, that would make me just as bad as you. No, I think you should live, Frank. You'll have plenty of time, behind bars, to think about all the lives you've ruined."

She could hear him struggling to breathe as she spoke again. "I just have to ask. Did you kill Jeb's family? Or did you just tranquilize them like Jarvis said?"

Frank paused in his breathing and Emma knew he was surprised that she knew about Jarvis. He was probably wondering what else the man had told her.

She was about to say more when he surprised her with a hysterical-sounding laugh that made the hair on her arms stand up, "Kill them? I didn't kill them. I had plans for them. Especially Hawk's wife. She is one sweet piece of ass. A little feisty, but that just made it more enjoyable." He seemed to chuckle to himself at the memory.

As he spoke, Emma knew he was possibly lying to her to piss her off, and it worked. She couldn't help but think of Hawk and the anguish she had seen in his face as he thought his entire family, including his beloved wife, were dead.

Surprising herself, the anger drained away and she stepped back as the sheriff continued to indulge himself in verbally reliving the details of the rape.

She smoothly stepped down and straddled his left leg. With all her might, she pulled back her right leg and swung it forward as if she were kicking a football through the uprights.

He definitely wasn't expecting that, and as her foot connected with his genitals, it was as if she had stuck a cattle prod to his ass.

He shot ahead about a foot and howled at the top of his lungs in agonizing pain tinged with the sound of an angry bull. He was immediately incapacitated and reflexively curled onto his side in a protective ball. Emma could see, with satisfaction, that the man had his eyes squeezed shut, his jaw was clamped together, and the muscles in his neck stretched taut.

Emma knew from a medical standpoint that she had struck him so hard that she very well may have ruptured his testicles. She did not care. He had caused plenty of pain to other people without any repercussions to himself.

Knowing the man couldn't move, she squatted down next to him and in a soft but dangerous voice said, "As a nurse, I know what I have just done to you. It will be a long time, if ever, before you rape another woman. I hope that if you are ever able to have intercourse again, you remember this day and the fact that not all women are helpless."

Despite the undoubtedly excruciating pain he was in, she knew Frank heard her.

She had just started to rise to her feet when a low rumbling began to emanate from the earth. Soon after, the ground beneath her began to tremble. Emma staggered and tried to keep her footing. She realized at once that it was an earthquake and turned to Leroy, reaching for his reins.

The horse was already starting to whinny and rear. Emma managed to snag his reins as she was thrown against him by the violently shifting ground.

She laid her hands on him and tried to soothe him, and then it was over.

Emma hadn't even had time to become frightened. Back at the ranch, she'd felt small earthquakes all the time. Here in the southeast, however, it was unusual. And this had been a strong one. It had to do with the EMP, she was sure of it. It seemed to be escalating, and that worried her.

She had just gotten the horse settled, when Jack came skidding back around the corner of the house, frantically looking for her.

He saw her and looked visibly relieved. Jack glanced over at Frank and saw the condition he was in and then looked questioningly at Emma.

She ignored the look, holstered her gun, and asked, "Tell me how in God's name you got here so fast!"

Jack looked back at the sheriff, puzzled, before answering, "I drove here."

Emma jerked her head up, shocked. "Drove here? That's impossible! How?"

Jack grinned like a little kid. "I have magic fingers."

Emma snorted with affection, but backhanded him across the chest anyway.

He flinched and rubbed his chest with a playful "Ouch!"

Emma rolled her eyes. "No, seriously! How did you get a running vehicle?"

Jack smiled, then quickly told her the lucky circumstances.

As he was finishing, several people started to come around the corner of the house. Some were police officers with uniforms on, but two of the men had regular clothes on, yet had handguns.

Emma and Jack stepped back as the officers went to Frank and the leader read him his rights. Emma was surprised, but then, on second thought, she was glad that some things remained the same.

As the lead officer finished, he left Frank for the others and stepped over to Emma and Jack. "My name is Terrence. Len left me in charge, and when he didn't come back, we decided to come looking for him. Considering the reason he left, we thought something like this might have happened. May I ask who you two are, exactly, and what you have to do with all this?"

Emma opened her mouth to answer when there was a high-pitched sound behind her. "Em!"

Emma turned and saw Lori and Bryan sliding off two horses with other deputies who had let them ride double.

Lori ran to hug her friend, and Bryan followed at a normal pace.

Emma gratefully hugged her friend back and smiled at Bryan over Lori's shoulder.

She turned back to the lead officer and proceeded to give

a brief version of pertinent facts. As she spoke, she watched in amusement as the officers had to physically drag Frank over to a horse and hoist him across the saddle.

Emma finished by telling Terrence about Jarvis, where they could find his body, and that Jeb's family and Len were probably being held at the gem mine. The deputy had listened to her story carefully, but she could tell the man was getting angrier at every sentence.

When she was done, he thanked her and stormed away snapping orders.

Emma turned back to her friends and Jack's group who, apparently, had already made introductions and were chatting.

Before stepping over to them, Emma took a minute to take a closer look at Jack's two friends.

They were both armed, and the older one seemed to be looking everywhere at once. The younger man seemed to stand closer to Jack, and Emma swore the boy was protecting Jack. That was weird, but before Emma could think too much about it, there was another rumble and the ground shifted slightly beneath their feet.

Everyone held their breath and braced themselves, but it was just an aftershock.

As soon as it was over, Emma turned to Jack and said, "Are the earthquakes part of what's happened?"

Jack looked distraught, ran his hands through his hair, and nodded. "Yeah, the scientist that we brought with us says that the EMP is destabilizing everything. That's why we're getting the strange weather and earthquakes and God knows what else."

Emma nodded and then asked, "Who did this, Jack?"

He looked up at the green sky as he replied, "It's a long story, Emma, but it was the Chinese. I'll explain it all on the way."

Emma agreed. "That's fine. How long do you think it will take us to get home?"

Jack knew he needed to tell Emma and her friends what was going on and said, "Let's get out of the way and I'll tell you what's going on."

Emma started to ask him something, but Jack grabbed her hand and led her away from the house and out front to the truck. The other four followed them.

As they reached the Dodge, Jack released her hand and Bryan stood next to Lori with his arm around her shoulders. The other two men stopped a little ways away.

Jack turned to Emma and said, "First, I don't think I introduced you to my two friends. This is Chris; we picked him up on the way. He was trying to make it to Asheville and we gave him a ride. The other gentleman is Greg. He works for the government and is with me to try to help make this all go away." As Jack said this last part, he gestured to the green haze. Emma was slightly confused as she listened, and Jack saw this.

Heaving a sigh, he tried again, "Look, you know I worked for the government years ago, right?"

Emma nodded, but still looked clueless. She glanced at Bryan and Lori and saw they were baffled also.

Jack continued, "I'll try to give you the short version and fill you in later. My old boss, Jason Evans, showed up at the ranch shortly before the bombs went off. He knew this was going to happen. He came to ask my help to finish a shield that the government had been working on since they found out about this plot."

He looked to see if Emma was following him and she nodded for him to go on.

"The shield was at a facility here, near Pigeon Forge. They hoped to have the shield done before the bombs went off, and that it would protect us against the EMP blast. He also told me of a Chinese scientist that had defected and was on his way to America. That scientist was the one who created the bombs for the Chinese government. If there was anybody who could help finish the shield, it would be him. Unfortunately, the bombs were detonated way ahead of schedule and we ran out of time."

Jack had his hands on his hips and was pacing in agitation.

He glanced at Emma and her two friends and saw that they were beginning to understand.

He shook his head and continued, "Jason and I have brought the scientist, Greg, and two other agents for protection down to the facility in the hopes that we could use the shield to reverse the ongoing process of the blast. According to the scientist, it may be possible."

He had come to a stop and now looked at Emma and her

friends. They were clearly stunned. He looked at Greg and Chris and saw that Greg was watching their surroundings, but Chris was staring openly at Emma. That was strange. He watched as Chris saw that Jack was looking at him, and the boy blushed and turned away. Chris was probably struck by Emma's beauty and Jack brushed it off.

He returned his attention to the three as Lori was the first to speak, "China? Bombs? You mean there were more of these EMP thingies?"

Jack nodded. "Apparently, it was supposed to be worldwide. The Chinese had planned to incapacitate the rest of the world but at the same time protect their own country by using the EMP shield they had constructed for that purpose. Kuan, he's the scientist, said that was the plan. We convinced him months ago to sabotage the bombs and some nukes that were going to finish the destruction after the EMP bombs crippled the world's defenses."

Emma spoke up this time. "Nukes? There were nukes?"

Jack held up his hands and said, "The nukes and most of the EMP bombs were disabled, but obviously it wasn't a foolproof plan. At least one of the EMP bombs got through."

Bryan replied sarcastically, "Obviously."

Emma had been thinking and now asked, "Where is this facility, Jack?"

Jack said, "It's a few miles from here. I dropped Jason and the others there to try to get the shield working while we came to get you."

He chuckled as he thought about where he expected Emma to be. "I should have known you wouldn't be sitting there quietly waiting for me."

He grinned as he said this to Emma.

She snorted as she replied, "It wasn't for lack of trying. We made it to the cabin and tried to set up a place to wait, and trouble came to us."

He was still smirking as he answered, "Doesn't it always?"

Emma rolled her eyes and changed the subject, "So, instead of heading back to Wyoming, we need to go to this 'facility'?"

Jack's smile faded as he nodded, "Yes. I'm sorry, Emma, but I have to try to help."

He had a pleading look on his face as he looked at Emma, hoping she would understand.

Emma closed her eyes and rolled her shoulders, trying to take in the information Jack had just given her.

While he waited, Jack stepped over to Chris. He needed to let the boy go his own way. "Well, Chris, you've been a big help."

He stuck his hand out to shake the young man's own.

Surprisingly, Chris looked at Jack's hand, then glanced up into his face, "I-I don't really have any family in Asheville."

This surprised Jack and made him think about why the boy was here.

He let his hand drop and asked, "You don't have *any* family in Asheville?"

The young man was looking at Jack as he shook his head.

Jack asked, "Where *is* your family, Chris?"

Chris said, "I don't have any family, Jack."

This puzzled Jack. "What do you mean? What were you doing on that road?"

Chris held up his hand and shook his head. "It's too painful to talk about. You told all of us that if we wanted to, we could go back to your ranch in Wyoming. Is that offer still open?"

Jack hesitated. He had said that, and Chris was a good kid.

"Yes, I did, and I meant it. You're welcome to come back with us, but it's hard work. Everyone pulls his weight." He said this with a stern look on his face and was staring seriously at Chris.

Chris grinned with relief. "I'm a hard worker, Jack! You won't be sorry."

Jack nodded his head. "I hope not."

Turning back to Emma, he saw that she was now having a discussion with her friends.

"Are you sure you don't want to stay with Larry and Rita? I'm sure they wouldn't mind," Emma asked them.

Lori stepped forward and grabbed Emma's hands. "If it's okay with you and Jack, we'd like to ride with you back to Wyoming, and then we're going to head to California to find Bryan's mom and sister."

Emma looked back and saw that Jack was listening. She looked a question at him and he nodded.

Emma hugged her friend. "Jack says you're welcome to come."

Lori hugged her back and they followed Jack over to where Deputy Terrence was waiting to talk to them.

"We had time to look around Jeb's house a bit before we followed you here. There wasn't any blood so we think the family was just tranquilized like Jarvis said. We're heading to the Three Bears Gem Mine now to free the prisoners and get things back in order." He turned to Jack, "Is there any way to get other vehicles running like your truck? We sure could use some."

Jack shook his head, "I'm not sure, Terrence. You'd have to find older vehicles, ones that were made before they put microchips in them. They may run if they were parked in a heavily shielded place. My truck was in a cinder block building, which helped keep the pulse from getting to it. If you find a mechanic, they may be able to get an old car to run by changing out electrical parts that were shorted out. I just don't know what else I can tell you."

Terrence was bobbing his head in understanding and he stuck out his hand to shake Jack's. "I appreciate the information. Maybe we'll get things straightened out around here."

Before he turned away, Emma said, "Terrence, please tell Jeb and his family thank you for me. Let him know that Hawk protected us and that he's buried about a hundred yards southwest of the house. I wish we could have done more for him, but we did our best."

He nodded and started to turn away but Emma stopped him. "Oh, I almost forgot!" Emma was digging in her jeans and fished out some keys. "He had these in his pocket and Jeb might want them. Jarvis had this photo in his wallet. I think it's his wife and I don't need it anymore."

Terrence said, "Thanks, we'll return them."

Emma shook the man's hand and the deputies mounted and rode off. Terrence had searched Frank's house and found several duffel bags, which she noticed they took with them. If she had to guess, she'd bet they contained money. Hopefully, it would be put to good use.

Suddenly, Lori asked, "Hey, where's Scooter?"

Jack said, "I was riding hard across that pasture and he fell, throwing me. He didn't seem to be hurt, but he ran off."

Lori squared her shoulders and put her hands on her hips. "You lost my horse?"

At first, Jack smiled, but then realized she was serious.

His smile slid away, "Uh, no, I didn't 'lose' him. I'm sure he's around here somewhere. I'll find him. Sorry."

He noticed that Bryan and Emma were trying not to laugh at his expense and he glared at them.

Sighing, he headed off in the direction he saw the horse run and Chris went with him.

Greg was smirking as they walked past. "I'll be right

here, Jack, keeping an eye on things. Good luck!" He waved mockingly and Jack snarled at him.

Greg laughed openly at that.

After Jack and Chris walked off, Greg told Emma, "I left the truck out on the road. Jack gets a little nervous about the truck being too far away. I'll be right back."

Emma smiled at the man as he left.

Turning back to her friends, Emma heard a pitiful sound coming from her backpack. Lori and Bryan turned their heads in puzzlement as Emma rushed to Leroy. Her friends followed her and watched as she quickly flipped the top back on her bag.

A furry head popped up and looked around in a daze. Emma smiled and reached in, gathering Bella in her arms.

Bryan exclaimed, "Bella! What happened to her?"

Emma stroked the cat as Bella tried to purr. Tears gathered in her eyes as she answered, "She attacked Frank just as he was about to overpower me. I thought he had me beat, and Bella jumped out onto his face. If it wasn't for her, Frank would have won."

Lori asked, "Are you serious?"

Emma nodded as she checked the feline over again and noticed an indention in her ribs that she had missed before. Apparently Frank had cracked a rib as well as given her a concussion. She was one tough cat. Gently, Emma rubbed her face against the soft fur of Bella's head and silently thanked her for saving her life. The cat tried to purr harder and Emma smiled as a tear leaked from her eye.

She bent down and placed Bella on the ground to see if she could stand.

Emma held her breath as Bella staggered and then caught herself. She looked up at Emma in a perturbed manner, then sat and started to clean herself. Emma and her friends watched and saw her wobble a couple of times, but otherwise Bella seemed okay.

She'd have to keep an eye on Bella because of the concussion, but the rib should heal on its own.

Emma sighed relief and fished in her bag for some cat food and a bottle of water. She'd kept a used cat food tin as a water bowl and poured some in there. Bella gratefully drank the water, and then turned to the food. Emma handed the rest of the water to her friends, along with another bottle. She grabbed the last one for herself and they all silently quenched their thirst.

Emma looked in the direction that Jack and Chris went, and saw them walking back with Scooter in tow. As they got closer, she saw they were talking easily, and Chris laughed at something Jack said. Emma cocked her head, thoughtfully.

Something about the way Chris laughed tugged at the back of her mind, but before she could think more about it, they arrived.

Jack looked at Emma and said, "You know that we can't take the horses with us. I think we can leave them with Larry and Rita."

Emma nodded and said, "Yeah, I was just thinking about that. What about a trailer? Don't you have a hitch on the truck?"

Greg had just come around the corner of the house and heard what Emma had said and chuckled, "We did have a hitch and a trailer, but we kind of lost those in the Mississippi River."

Emma, Lori, and Bryan all looked a question at Jack and he sighed, "Long story, but, yes, we lost those a while back. Without a welder, we can't repair it. No hitch, no trailer, and the horses won't be able to keep up. I'm sorry, guys."

Emma sighed and shrugged.

Lori, on the other hand, asked, "How will Bryan and I get to California after we make it to your ranch?"

Jack was already waving his hand at them and said, "That's no problem. I'll give you a couple of horses from the ranch."

Lori looked stunned. "You'd give us a horse?"

Emma realized that Lori didn't understand the size of the ranch. She told her, "He has plenty of horses, trust me."

Lori just blinked in surprise, but Bryan had a question. "Wait. If you're supposed to fix things, with this device you have, won't everything go back to normal?"

Everybody went quiet and turned to see what Jack would say.

Jack was already shaking his head as he answered, "No, it doesn't work like that. When the EMP bomb went off, it released a powerful pulse that essentially fried the delicate parts of any electrical device. Once that's done, you have to replace or repair everything."

He looked sadly at the group for a moment, then continued, "The device that we're trying to get to work is a device that we hope will neutralize the ongoing electromagnetic effects that are trying to tear apart the earth. If we are able to get the device to work properly, it won't return everything to how it was, it will only stop the earthquakes and the crazy weather."

Jack placed his hands on his hips as he looked at the group. "The truth is, if we do succeed, we'll still have to rebuild everything. At least we won't have to worry about the world being destroyed."

Emma was staring at Jack. "And if you can't get this device to work? How long do we have?"

Jack's eyebrows were bunched up. "I don't know, Em. The scientist we brought may be able to answer that. I just don't know." He looked at her straight on and smiled ironically. If the device didn't work, he may not have long to be with Emma. It figured.

Everybody was quiet as they each mulled this over until Lori finally said, "Well, what the hell are we standing here for? We're wasting time!"

That motivated everybody and Jack said, "Greg, you take the truck and the others back to Larry's cabin. I'll take the horses and meet you there."

Emma said, "Hey! You don't think you're going to ride by yourself, do you?"

She turned to Lori and Bryan. "I'll see you two at the cabin." They agreed and she hugged them both.

Emma looked around and saw Bella lying in the shade at the edge of the house. Her tail was flicking in irritation, and Emma knew she had to be in some pain from the broken rib.

She walked over and gently picked her up. "Come on, furry butt, just a little while longer."

As Emma was about to place the cat in her bag, Emma saw Chris out of the corner of her eye and thought she heard him breathe Bella's name.

She stopped and looked right at the young man. That was impossible. He hadn't been here when Emma had taken the cat from the bag and she asked him now, "What did you say?"

Hearing the seriousness of her tone, everyone stopped and looked at Emma and Chris.

Chris hooked his head and said, "Nothing. I was just admiring your cat."

Emma looked searchingly at the young man's face, then decided to let it drop. He had turned and walked away anyway, so Emma finished placing Bella safely in the bag.

Jack walked over as the others climbed in the truck, and Greg started the engine.

"What was that all about?" he asked Emma.

She looked back at the truck as she finished tightening the saddle. "I don't know. Chris seems like a nice kid, but something's weird. I could have sworn that I heard him say Bella's name, but he's never seen her until just now. I don't know, maybe he heard someone else say her name." She lifted a shoulder. "Maybe I'm just being paranoid."

Jack had already gotten in the saddle and he patted the side of Scooter's neck. "I don't think you're being paranoid. I've had some weird things happen around Chris too." He waited as Emma got aboard Leroy, and then continued, "He always seems to be in the right place at the right time. He saved my life a couple of times."

Emma pulled up short and stared at Jack for a moment. He kicked his horse softly and she followed, catching up after a minute.

"Well, what do you make of it?" Emma asked.

She was caught off guard as he leaned across and encircled her waist with his arm. "Right now, I don't give a damn." He breathed this last word just before he pulled her against his chest and kissed her with all the love and longing he had for her. Emma felt the sweet burning spread all the way down to her toes and she kissed her handsome cowboy back with the same wild abandon.

After a few moments, the horses grew restless. Emma and Jack reluctantly released each other, and Emma grinned while trying to catch her breath.

"Well, sir, you have not changed a bit!" Emma's hand shook as she pushed back her black curls.

Jack chuckled low in his throat, but then became somber as the horses walked side by side.

Emma waited for what she knew would come next. She

didn't have to wait long.

"Why'd you leave, Emma?" Jack asked softly.

She looked ahead, but could feel his eyes on her from where he rode by her side.

Emma owed him an explanation, she knew that, but it didn't make it any easier.

Taking a deep breath, she began, "When we got engaged, I was so happy. I was already planning the wedding we would have and I saw us on the ranch with my family." She smiled as the memories of her excitement flooded through her mind. She glanced over at Jack and saw the hurt mingled with puzzlement in his expression.

She was still smiling, but it was now sad and apologetic as she looked back to the front, "I wanted everything to be done the right way. When we were on vacation at Larry's cabin that time, do you remember how we talked about having children?"

She looked at Jack and saw him nod as he remembered.

She looked away again and went on, "We'd laughed about whether the first would be a boy with your cowlick, or a girl with my long toes."

She took a moment to see if he remembered, and of course he did. She saw he had an amused look on his face as he chuckled.

She didn't give him a chance to interrupt. He needed to hear this, even though she knew he might not want her after she told him.

"Well, as I said, I wanted everything to be perfect, so I decided to go to my gynecology doctor and get everything checked out."

She stopped again to let him know the most significant part was coming, and then she told him in a very tender voice, "Jack, it was on that day that my doctor told me I can never have children. I didn't believe her, but she ran test after test and said time after time that I cannot and will never be able to have children."

She had stopped her horse and braced herself as she said the last word. She turned to Jack to watch his reaction.

She watched as the expected hurt and anger crossed his face. "Dammit, Emma! You should have told me!"

Tears welled up in her eyes as she said, "Yes, I shouldn't have left you hanging. I should have given you some closure. Maybe you would be married by now."

She felt herself withdrawing from him, and she started to nudge her horse into a walk.

Before she could, Jack reached out and smoothly grabbed and held her reins.

"Emma, please don't walk away from me again. I didn't say that you should have told me so I could have a reason to be through with you. I said it because if you had, we wouldn't have been away from each other for eight years." He continued to hold her reins as he watched his words get through to her.

As she realized what he was saying, she looked at this

rugged, handsome, disheveled man, and all the walls around her heart shattered and melted away.

She had to be sure, however; as she felt a tear slide down her cheek, she asked, "So, you still want to marry me, even though I can never have children?"

Jack pulled her even with him and softly cupped her chin in his hand. "I want to marry you even if the world explodes tomorrow, which it may do." He smiled crookedly, then went on seriously, "There will be so many kids running around from Danny and Scott, we'll have our hands full just being Aunt Emma and Uncle Jack!"

This got a chuckle from her, but overwhelmed with love, Emma threw her arms around his neck, and started crying in earnest.

Jack hugged her back, hard. He loved this woman so much, he couldn't understand how she could ever think otherwise.

After a moment, she shifted back in the saddle and wiped the tears from her eyes. "I am so sorry that I left and didn't tell you. I was young and in shock, Jack."

Jack gently squeezed her hand and said, "Water under the bridge. I'm just glad you still love me as much as I love you."

Jack released her and said, "I hate to say it, but we better get going before they come looking for us."

Emma nodded as she looked up, and noticed for the first time that it was getting late. She also saw that the wind had picked up, and she could see the edge of an ominous cloud just starting to show up over the top of the trees. As they watched, several flashes of lightning lit up the inside of the storm.

Emma and Jack looked at each other and felt a sense of urgency come over them. They kicked their horses into a gallop as they weaved through the trees, and soon they came to the cabin.

They slid to a halt next to the truck and heard the ticking of the engine. The others must be already in the house.

Emma and Jack tied the reins to the porch and knocked on the door.

Rita answered and motioned them in. Just as they crossed the threshold, there were several flashes of light and soon after, multiple booms of thunder.

Rita quickly closed the door and Jack looked around the room.

Larry and the others were sitting around and chatting.

Larry appeared cleaned up and looked like he felt better. He still had bandages on though.

Greg said, "Jack! Emma! Glad you two could make it! We just got finished telling Larry and Rita what happened."

Larry smiled as he said, "I'm glad that bastard got what he deserved."

Jack agreed, "Yeah, there are a bunch of things he needs to pay for. The Gatlinburg police took him away and are going to set things right in town. Listen, Larry, I hate to run, but we've got to get a move on."

Larry said, "Sure, sure, Jack. I know you need to go. Is there anything we can give you, before you go?"

Jack was already nodding his head. "As a matter of fact, there is. If we can get some water bottles filled we would appreciate it."

Larry replied, "Of course!"

Jack continued, "One other thing." He hesitated and Larry looked a question at Jack.

"We can't take the horses with us. Would you mind keeping them for us?"

Larry looked at Rita and the woman nodded.

"Sure, Jack. We'll keep them for you. If what you say is true, we'll probably end up needing them."

Jack agreed and said, "Greg, can you and Chris take the horses around back and unsaddle them?"

Greg saluted and Jack rolled his eyes.

Emma went out to get their things off the horses and Lori followed her.

Jack and Bryan went to get the water bottles to fill.

Lori had noticed Emma's red eyes, and when they were alone, she asked, "How did that go?"

Emma sighed as she removed her bag and said, "It went really good. He said if I would have told him, we could have talked things out and not wasted eight years apart. He said he doesn't need kids, we just need each other."

Lori batted her eyes, comically, and said, "That is so sweet!"

Emma snickered as they finished getting their gear and putting it in the bed of the truck.

Bella must have been feeling better. She popped out of the bag and stretched, gingerly.

Several more flashes of lightning and booms of thunder rolled and the smell of ozone hung in the air.

Bella cringed, saw the open window to the truck, and scrambled into the cab.

Emma watched and then hurried back into the house with Lori on her heels.

Emma saw that Jack and Bryan were out back filling the bottles, and she took the time to ask Larry, "I didn't get to hear what happened. I gather that Frank tortured you to find out where we were."

Larry nodded and Emma asked, "You know I'm a nurse. Can I look at your hand?"

Larry replied, "Actually, Rita knows first aid, and she fixed my nose and splinted the two fingers that were broke." He grimaced as he remembered the excruciating pain.

Emma felt guilty, even though she knew, technically, it wasn't her fault. "I'm sorry, Larry, is there anything I can do?"

He smiled through the two black eyes and said, "Yes, there is."

Emma immediately asked, "What?"

"You can marry Jack and make him the happiest man in the world. He's the best friend I've ever had, and that man loves you."

Emma smiled at the injured man, but couldn't speak for the lump in her throat, so she nodded instead.

She bent down and kissed the man on the cheek, and when she stood back up, Jack and the others were coming through the back door.

"Larry, we better get going. That storm's electrical and it's looking bad." Jack stepped over and shook the man's left hand with both of his own. "I can't thank you enough for everything you've done for me, friend."

Larry replied, "Just save the world, Jack, and we'll call it even!" He winked at Jack and Jack laughed.

He turned to Rita and said, "I'm sorry we met on such awful terms. I promise, when this is all over, Emma and I will come back and visit for a while."

Rita said, "Thank you." And hugged Jack's neck.

Greg had already opened the door and they all filed out of the house.

Emma started to get into the truck bed when Bryan stopped her. "Why don't you and Lori ride in the cab with Jack?"

Emma said, "Well, well. Chivalry is not dead!"

Bryan smiled and she patted him on the shoulder.

They all got in and Emma put Bella on her lap. Jack started the truck and looked at the fuel gauge. A quarter of a tank. That was plenty.

As he spun the wheel, he looked out the front window and examined the leading edge of the storm. It reminded him of those pictures he had seen a while back of hurricane Katrina, only this storm was shaded green. After he thought this, the blood drained from his face as the possibility hit him. How would they know if this wasn't a massive hurricane moving in from the Atlantic? There were no news or weather reports.

He kept his thoughts to himself as he pushed the truck a little faster. No sense worrying anyone else, when there was nothing they could do about it.

They were all lost in their own thoughts as Jack guided the truck to the main road.

As soon as he turned onto it, however, Emma asked, "I've been trying to piece together what you've been telling us about this device. You said there's a Chinese scientist that's trying to get it to work, right?"

Jack replied, "Yes. His name is Dai Ji Kuan, and he's an expert in electromagnetics and nanotechnology." He hesitated and glanced over at the two women before continuing, "He's actually the person who designed the EMP bombs for the Chinese."

Lori and Emma started talking at the same time and Jack held up his hand, "I know what you're thinking. Why would we trust this man and bring him to work on this device? Jason says Kuan had a change of heart before the bombs were finished, but by that time, there was no way the Chinese would allow him to quit. Jason and his agents approached him and gave him a way out."

Jack could feel the two women staring at him, unconvinced.

He sighed, "Listen, the best way to defend against a technology is to get the expert to build a mechanism that will counteract the effects of the device he built."

Lori responded, "And you trust this guy?"

Jack thought about the quiet scientist and then said, "I didn't get the feeling that he was being deceitful. He never says a whole lot, but he doesn't try to hinder us, either. From what Jason told me, about midway through the project, his wife was accidentally killed by the police during an uprising. He's been bitter toward them ever since."

The women seemed to relax and Lori said, "Well, that would certainly piss me off."

Emma asked another question. "Will it work?"

Jack gripped the steering wheel. "That's the million-dollar question. When we left, Jason and the others were just getting things started. I'll be honest. He told me that the thing was finished. The problem we have is that it needs a key, and he doesn't have it. We're hoping that Kuan can bypass the need for a key."

He looked over and quirked the corner of his mouth. "Kind of like hot-wiring a car."

Emma and Lori were both deep in thought.

After a moment, Emma softly asked, "What happens,

Jack, if he can't 'hot-wire' this device?"

Jack didn't look at the two women as he said just as softly, "Then there's every possibility that the world could tear itself apart."

He felt, rather than saw, the two women look at each other.

All of a sudden, the steering wheel started to vibrate in Jack's hands. The truck started to shimmy and Jack immediately let off the gas. Emma and Lori braced themselves, thinking they had a flat tire.

As the truck slowed, however, the trembling got worse. Bella dug her claws in to the top of Emma's thighs. Emma hissed, but couldn't do anything about it.

A tree up ahead of them crashed partway across the road. That's when they realized it was another earthquake.

Lori yelped as the truck started to bounce up and down, violently. Jack looked to the back of the truck and saw the three men hanging on for dear life.

Jack opened his mouth to tell them to leave the truck, when the shaking abruptly stopped.

Emma was breathing heavily and was still gripping the dash.

Jack shouted, "Everyone okay?"

There were various positive answers but Jack didn't wait. They were running out of time. He let off the brake and gunned the truck forward. Coming to the fallen tree, Jack slowed just enough to skirt around the edge of it and then shot down the road. He estimated they were about ten minutes away from the facility.

"Those earthquakes are a warning, aren't they?" Emma asked.

"Yes, they most definitely are," he replied.

Jack saw the turnoff coming up and slowed enough to take it safely.

There were no more questions as he headed up the mountain road.

Just as Jack was slowing down to find the yellow piece of cloth, fat raindrops started to fall and the lightning picked up the pace.

He spotted the trail, turned the big truck onto it, and turned on the lights.

Accelerating as much as he dared, Jack looked over at the women and saw they were still holding on.

After a minute, they arrived at the clearing and Jack pulled up as close to the granite wall as possible.

He started to reach for the door handle when Emma said, "Jack, it's just a rock wall."

"No, trust me," he replied quickly, "there's a hidden entrance."

The women clambered out on their side and Emma retrieved her bag from the truck bed. Bella might be disoriented, and she wanted her safely in the bag. As she turned around to get the cat, however, she saw Bella streak after Jack and the others. So much for disorientation.

Emma ran through the stinging rain and blustering winds as she caught up to the back of the group. A particularly bright bolt of lightning flashed, and they all automatically cringed as the deafening boom quickly followed.

They had almost made it to the wall and Emma still didn't see any opening. She sure hoped Jack knew what he was doing.

Just as this thought crossed her mind, she saw Jack and Lori disappear. She couldn't understand what was happening as she saw Bryan, Greg, and Chris also disappear just a few feet in front of her.

As she arrived at the spot where the others had vanished, it became clear that there was a dogleg to the left. She gratefully entered the sheltered area and paused. It was pitch black and she reached to find her flashlight before going further.

Someone else found one before she did, and artificial light bloomed in the enclosed space. She could see that everyone was bunched up waiting for the light, and they now started moving forward again. Emma finally gripped her flashlight and flicked it on. Before she moved on, she shone it around to look for Bella. The cat was sitting up against the granite with her tail wrapped around her feet and gazing back at Emma.

Emma smiled with relief and turned back to the group.

There was a high-pitched screech from a metal mechanism, and Emma saw the group start to enter a doorway into the mountain. She followed and soon was stepping through a metal hatch and into a brightly lit, cavernous room.

After staring in awe at the artificial lights, Emma turned off her flashlight. She joined the others who were gathered around Jack and two people she didn't know. Jack was speaking and Emma listened closely.

"Hey, Ray, how are things going?"

The big man shook his head slightly, "I'm not sure, Jack. Kuan has been working since you guys left. I heard them arguing about thirty minutes ago, but didn't want to bother them."

Jack took a deep breath. "Thanks, Ray. Where are they?" He was looking around the cluttered room and Ray pointed to the middle.

Jack nodded, then looked back at Emma and her two friends. "This is Atlas. I'm told it was protected from the EMP blast and has most of the former modern conveniences. I have to go talk to Jason, but feel free to make use of the facilities." He looked back at Ray and Cat and said, "Would you guys mind showing them where everything is? I'm sure you explored while we were gone."

Ray and Cat shrugged and nodded.

Jack thanked them and turned to walk off.

Emma quickly walked up and snagged the back of his shirt, "Excuse me, Jack. I, for one, would like to go with you and hear what's going on. I can shower later. This is just a tiny bit more important than a shower." Lori and Bryan were bobbing their heads.

Jack seemed briefly surprised, but then understood.

Smiling at them, and in a voice everyone could hear, he said, "Anyone who would like to, can come with me."

He wound his way through the machinery and soon came to a cleared area in the middle of the chamber.

Looking briefly over his shoulder, he saw that everyone had followed him—and he was not surprised. This was very likely the last shot they had at saving the world.

Turning back to the center of the cavern, Jack took a closer look. He knew the others saw it as well, when he heard several gasps and whispers. Then he distinctly heard Greg say, "Holy shit!"

There was a raised area about two feet tall and twenty feet across. Sitting on top of this pedestal was something that could only be described as otherworldly. It was about four feet high and covered the entire foundation. The object was a beautiful combination of art and machinery. It had curves in the material that looked like waves. Where the waves ended, there were spheres. There were small waves and large waves and the spheres were all manner of sizes and shapes. From perfect spheres to elongated ovals.

Intertwined throughout the waves and spheres were flowing lines that reminded Jack of Celtic knots he had seen in pictures. The entire contraption seemed to draw the eye in a mesmerizing track across the whole of the thing. Jack felt himself become calm and relaxed as his eyes traced the brilliant symmetry of the device. At last, it dawned on him that he had no idea what the thing was made of. Jason had been right. It had a bluish-gray cast to it, but shimmered like satin. Jack wondered what it would feel like if he touched it.

Realizing they had been standing there for almost a minute, Jack shook his head and concentrated. He heard Jason's voice coming from the device and soon saw his head pop up in the middle of the thing. Looking closer at the base, Jack saw that there was a path leading up to it from his right.

He turned that way and walked straight to the path. He heard the rest of the group whispering as they trailed behind him. He could tell they were as awestruck as he was.

Reaching the path, Jack shouted up to Jason, "Hey, Jason! We're back!"

He saw an opening in the device that the path led up to. As he got closer, Jason appeared in the opening and greeted him, "Jack! Did everything go okay?"

Jack could tell by his voice that Jason was frustrated. "Everything went fine. We're all safe and sound. How are things going here?"

Jack had reached the opening and Jason stepped down to talk to him.

He rubbed the back of his neck as he answered Jack, "I wish I could say it's ready to go and we're about to try it, but I can't."

He dropped his hand in futility, "Kuan has tried all day to find a way to bypass needing the key. There's just no way to do it!"

Jack could hear the annoyance in his voice as he saw Jason throw both hands up.

Jack hated to add to Jason's problems, but he said, "I guess you haven't gone outside lately."

Jason glared at Jack, "No, I've been a little bit busy here!"

Jack acknowledged that. "Yes, well, there's a really bad storm heading from the east, and it looks a lot like those pictures of hurricane Katrina. The earthquakes are getting worse too. I'm sure you all have felt those."

The blood drained from Jason's face as he listened. He seemed at a loss as he put his hands on his hips and dropped his head. "I'm all out of ideas."

Finally, Jason looked up and searched the group behind Jack. He saw Chris was moving up toward the front and he said, "I wondered if you had anything left in your bag of tricks."

Everybody turned as one to see who Jason was talking to. When they saw it was Chris, you could have heard a pin drop as they all froze.

Chris didn't look at Jack as he brushed past him to Jason's side, but he felt the man's gaze boring into his back.

"Chris?" Jack breathed in total confusion.

Chris looked up at the machine and saw that Kuan was standing there and nodded to himself in satisfaction.

He turned around and then addressed the group, "We don't have a lot of time, so you're just going to have to trust me for a bit. If what we're about to do works, then I'll answer most of your questions. If it doesn't, then your questions won't matter anyway."

He saw Emma step up next to Jack and slide her hand in his.

Chris smiled at this and went on, "What I'm about to say will seem unbelievable to you all, but I assure you, it's the truth. First of all, I have the key." As he said this, he tugged on a chain that was around his neck. He pulled it over his head and they could see there was something attached to the chain. Chris laid it on his open palm. They all drew closer and peered at the thing in Chris's hand.

Jack could see that it appeared to be a round plastic container. The container was transparent and held what appeared to be a round disc that was the exact same color as the device in the middle of the room. Jack thought it was a solid, until it moved. Involuntarily, he jerked back. The others had jumped too, and Chris grinned.

"I did that too, the first time I saw it move."

Emma asked, "What the hell is it? Is it alive?"

Chris shook his head and said, "No, I don't think so. Not in the sense that it needs to be fed or watered. But it moves on its own. I have to keep it in this case because it conforms to whatever shape it touches. That's why it's the only key that could work. You'll see in a moment."

Jack had recovered. He could hear the others talking excitedly. He dragged his eyes from the key and stared at Chris's smiling face. "Who are you? How did you get the key and where did you come from?" Jack felt deceived and was getting angrier by the minute.

Chris could see this and his face fell. "I'll tell you all that

I'm able to, just as soon as we try the key. Agreed?"

Kuan had come down the stairs and pushed through the group to see the key. He watched as the key moved ever so slightly in the container, and then he smiled.

He looked over at Jason and said, "I understand now! It all makes sense. The key makes itself!"

Jason looked confused, "What?"

Kuan, looking exasperated, plucked the key off Chris's hand and started toward the machine before anyone could move.

Jack yelled, "Hey!" And started to go after him to stop him.

Chris grabbed Jack's arm to hold him back. "Let him go, Jack. It's what he's supposed to do."

Jack pulled angrily on his arm, "We need to talk about this! What if—"

Chris smiled as he cut him off, "There's no time, Jack."

Jack looked back to see Kuan had gained the pedestal. He looked back at Chris in distress and saw Chris still had that smile on his face. Chris nodded slowly and Jack looked into the young man's eyes. That was when Jack's sixth sense kicked in. The tingle at the base of his neck and the slight ringing in his ears. He grew calm as he realized that everything Chris had said so far was true.

He smiled resignedly back at Chris. "It's okay. Let's go see what happens."

Chris nodded and dropped his hand from Jack's arm.

As the two men walked to the device, they saw that everybody was following the Chinese defector, Dai Ji Kuan.

Jason realized the scientist was going to try the key and he shouted, "Ray! Hit the lever!"

Jack saw Ray nod and dash off through the clutter. He had no idea what lever Jason was talking about. He felt that events were out of his control and he'd just have to roll with it.

Stepping up through the opening in the device, he saw there was plenty of room for everyone, and he moved up beside Emma. She sensed he was there and grabbed his hand again.

Just as she did, Jack heard a deep rumble from overhead.

Looking up, they watched a portion of the cavern sliding apart to create a rectangular opening. Beyond it, they could see the angry sky as lightning bolts almost continually skittered across the green clouds. Rain and debris were floating down to the chamber floor, and Jack turned back to the scientist.

Kuan had opened the container and hesitated as he looked at a hand-sized indention in the machine. Jack saw that it was in an area of the device that projected out at about waist height. The indentation was about half an inch deep and completely covered with minute and intricately detailed whorls and spheres. These matched the designs on the outside of the device. Jack also saw that there were several small pinholes in the depression.

Jack was completely befuddled. How was a key supposed to fit in that?

Kuan was grinning now as he smoothly reached out and turned the plastic container upside down over the indention.

Jack's eyebrows drew together as he watched what happened next.

At first, the key seemed to flow slowly through the depression like syrup. It soon covered the entire area and became still.

Emma shifted beside him. "Are we safe here?" she asked Kuan.

He was still smiling as he said, "I am reasonably certain we will be okay."

That didn't exactly comfort Jack, but it was too late now as he watched what happened next.

The key had covered the entire depression and filled up the pinholes. Then it became still.

Suddenly, they saw tiny sparkles start to glitter inside the key. The glowing, tiny specks began to get brighter. They also started to move. Slowly, at first, but then faster. Soon, they became a blur and the whole key was glowing white.

Jack quickly glanced at the others and then back at the key.

Now, the glow shot into the pinholes and there was an immediate humming that surrounded the whole group. They all looked around at the device and noticed that it was starting to glow as well.

Before they could think about it, there was an unpleasant tingle, and then a brilliant blue light emanated from the device. It came from the surface of the machine and completely encircled the group as it shot skyward in a cone.

There were gasps from the group as they all tilted their heads back and stared in amazement.

As the dazzling blue light made contact with the green sky, it immediately began to send out a circular, expanding wave that appeared to consume the green haze.

Jack knew it didn't make sense, but it was the only way he could describe it.

It was an incredible sight. He watched as the lightning from the storm seemed to be attracted to the blue light like a lightning rod. The lightning would strike the beam and disappear.

It was all happening so quickly. All of this had occurred in less than thirty seconds.

Soon the blue light spread across the sky and out of the group's sight. All they could see now were clouds and gently falling rain. The beam of blue light lit up the gray underbelly of the clouds.

Everyone looked around like an audience that had just woken up from being hypnotized.

Jack looked at Chris and started to say something, but Kuan beat him to it.

"Chris," the scientist said, "I believe it's done its job. Is it safe to remove the key?"

Jack looked over at Chris as the young man nodded, "Yes, you can remove it now."

Kuan hesitated and looked back at Chris.

Chris quirked the corner of his mouth and stepped up to Kuan. Taking the container from the Chinese man, Chris reached into the depression and grasped the key with the kind of care a person would use to pick up a tissue off the floor.

Holding it about three inches above the container, Chris released it. Jack's jaw fell open as he watched the key cling almost fondly to Chris's fingers before letting go reluctantly. It seemed to defy physics as it dropped slower than normal and, simultaneously, assumed the container's shape.

Chris closed the container and lifted his eyes to Jack's.

Holding the chain out to Jack, he said, "It's yours now. I'm supposed to give it to you for safekeeping."

Jack was about to burst with questions and Chris could see it. "Ask away, Jack."

Everyone was listening with rapt attention. Jack gestured to the device. "Did that really work?"

Chris nodded, "Yes, it did. It will take several hours to circle the globe and remove it all."

Jack had so many questions, he didn't know which one to ask next.

Emma had no such qualms. "I think you better start by telling us just who in the hell you are, and how you knew all this." She flung her arm up to encompass everything.

Chris's smile got a little bigger. "I am from twenty-six years in the future. As for how I know all this," he turned to gaze back at Jack, "You told me, Jack, when I turned twenty-three."

Staring back at the man, Jack bunched his eyebrows together and tilted his head to the side. Chris could see he was trying to figure it out. Jack still hadn't taken the key. Chris slowly stepped forward and took Jack's hand and turned it palm up. He dropped the key in the upturned palm and closed Jack's fingers over it.

Behind Chris, Greg suddenly spoke, "Time travel? You expect us to believe that? If time travel was possible, we would have already figured out how to do it!"

Dai Ji Kuan replied, "It is possible. It was my pet project I was working on after my wife died." He said this softly, but with fervor.

He stepped up now and continued, "I have it all worked out up here." He tapped the side of his temple. "My peers thought I was foolish and the Chinese government didn't want me wasting my time, but I worked on it anyway. I almost had the plans complete when I had to leave."

Jason agreed, "Chris came to me before I started Atlas and told me he was from the future. He knew so many personal things about me, it finally convinced me that he really was. He was the reason this all came about."

Jack sucked in a breath. "That's why you recognized him on the road back in Missouri!"

Jason looked disconcerted. "Yeah, I'm sorry I lied to

you, Jack. Things had to happen exactly as planned. Chris wouldn't let me tell you anything."

This made everyone return their attention to Chris, and he spoke, "Everything had to happen exactly as it happened in the past. If just one thing had changed, no matter how small, this ending would not have occurred as it had. For example, I had the key when we arrived here this morning, and I could have used it then. But if I had, the past would have been changed and there's no telling what would have happened. I had to follow the script, Jack. There were two important things that you gave me on my twenty-third birthday. One was the key. The other was your journal. When you leave here, you will write a very detailed journal. Complete with dates and times. It will be the script. The script that I follow twenty-six years from now."

Jack looked down at the key and knew that from everything he had just heard and witnessed, time travel was very possible.

But something bothered Jack, so he asked, "Why would I send someone who was so young? And where did the key come from?"

Chris glanced at his watch before answering with a shrug, "We don't know where the key came from. You give it to me in the future and I give it to you in the past. It's like it's stuck in some kind of loop. That's the thing about time travel. We haven't got all the answers, but we're getting there."

Chris had been searching for something behind Jack. Jack reflexively looked over his shoulder just as an oval appeared about ten feet back down the path. Jack was so startled, he jumped. The rest of the group gasped their surprise.

Chris eased his way through the group toward the oval. It was about seven feet high and three feet wide. It had a white, misty appearance to it. The group was caught up in wonder as they followed Chris to the oval. As they drew closer, they could see little tendrils of mist escaping from the oval and disappearing.

Chris stopped at the oval and turned back to Jack. "This is the portal. We knew exactly when to set it for, thanks to the details in your journal. Don't forget the details, Jack."

They all were staring in amazement. If they hadn't completely believed Chris before, the portal definitely did the trick.

Chris looked down at Emma's feet as something caught his eye. Bella had sauntered up to see what all the fuss was about.

He smiled affectionately as he went to one knee and caressed the feline's head. "As for why you picked me," he said, with tears in his eyes as he faced Jack and Emma, "you see, Bella and I go way back. She followed me everywhere when I was little." He paused. "I am your son. My last name is Denton, not Black. Christopher Jack Denton."

Emma inhaled sharply as her hand flew to her mouth and she staggered backward. Jack caught and steadied her. There were multiple outbursts from around the room, and Emma heard Lori shout, "Oh my God!"

Emma knew from the moment she heard the words, that it was the truth. That niggling little something. It was now apparent he had Jack's walk but her hair. His grin reminded her of her brother Scott, and his quietness was definitely her other brother Danny. The whole combination was perfect.

She rushed to Chris and almost knocked him over as she hugged him.

He hugged her back just as hard as he whispered, "Momma."

Jack knew it was true, too. That thing he couldn't put his finger on all came together. He stepped up behind his family and encircled them both with his arms. He got a lump in his throat as they hugged for a long time. He could hear sniffling in the background as a tear rolled down his own cheek.

After a moment, Emma pushed Chris back to arm's length and asked breathlessly, "How? The doctor's told me there was no possible way! None!"

She was crying openly now and Chris took both of her hands in his, "You, of all people, should know that doctors aren't perfect. They're like weathermen; they can't be right all the time, and they aren't God. I am your son and I like my name. So don't forget it. I have to go now, but we'll meet again real soon." He quirked his lip just like Jack always did. Pulling her close, he kissed her warmly on the cheek. He released her hands and grabbed Jack in a bear hug, "I love you, Dad. Don't forget. The journal and the key. Twenty-third birthday."

Chris released his father and stepped toward the oval. He hesitated and turned, "One last thing. Keep Kuan safe. He builds the time machine." Addressing the scientist directly, he went on, "It's the main reason we needed you. Your wife would be so proud of you."

Jack had his arm around Emma. They didn't want to let him go, but they knew they had to. They knew *he* had to. Chris looked around at them all one more time. Then with a smile, he turned toward the oval and was gone. The moment he stepped through, it shrank to a pinpoint with a hiss, then vanished.

Everyone stood frozen for a moment. Emma was the first to move as she turned in Jack's arm. "We're going to have a son!" she breathed in shock.

He smiled down at her. "Looks like it."

Lori ran to Emma and Jack was forced to release her as Lori smothered her friend with a hug. "Oh, Emma! This is awesome! You even know what to name him already!" Emma laughed at her friend's enthusiasm.

Bryan had followed Lori over and shook Jack's hand. "Looks like congratulations are in order. It feels strange, though, to congratulate you before the conception."

Jack snorted a laugh and thanked him.

As the excitement wore off, Jack looked around for Jason. He saw the man a few feet away, surrounded by his agents.

He walked over to join the conversation. Emma and her friends followed him.

Jason acknowledged them, then he said, "When Chris visited me, he let me in on a few things. This is where Kuan builds the time machine. I have to go to Washington and see what is left of the government. Greg, I really need you to go with me. It'll be a rough journey and I'll need your help."

Greg shrugged and said, "Sure, Jason, I don't have any big plans."

Jason replied sarcastically, "Why thanks, Greg. I'm glad it's not going to cut into your busy schedule."

Shaking his head, he turned to Ray and Cat, "This facility has to be protected." He looked over at where Kuan had returned to the device, doing…something. "I assume Dai Ji will want to stay here and work with the device. I would really like for you two to stay and protect Kuan and Atlas. It's well stocked with food and all the conveniences of home."

Ray and Cat looked at each other with a smile, then told Jason they would.

Jason smiled knowingly at the two, "I'm not stupid."

The two agents had the grace to blush and Jason continued, "Alright, I guess that's it for now. Take turns keeping watch tonight, and Ray, do you mind hitting the lever? We don't need that open anymore."

Ray nodded and moved off through the clutter.

Watching Cat follow the big man, Jason stepped up to Jack and said, "They make a good couple. I didn't see that coming."

Jack replied, "You can't predict everything."

The double meaning was not lost on Jason, and the man hung his head. "Yeah, I know. I truly am sorry, Jack. I knew he was from the future, but he didn't tell me he was your son.

I found that out the same time you did. That's a real shock to me. Once he said it, though, it made sense. He's just like you. Congrats, by the way."

Jack chuckled, "Thanks in advance. It all feels unbelievable."

Jason agreed, "It took him quite a while to convince me, but he did."

Jason grew serious and asked, "What are you going to do now, Jack?"

Jack raised his eyebrows and breathed deeply, "I'm going to take Emma, Lori, and Bryan back to the ranch." He looked at Emma's friends and nodded, "Bryan has family in California that he wants to go find, so I'm going to give them a couple of horses."

He looked down at Emma. "As for us, it looks like I have a journal to write and a child to conceive."

Emma backhanded his chest, hard, and blushed.

He leaned away and smiled lovingly at her.

Jason cleared his throat and changed the subject. "That's exactly what Chris said you would do. When I'm done in Washington, I'll come by and check on Kuan. There are some other things at area 51 that Chris says I need to show Dai Ji, things that will be crucial for building the time machine. Then, we'll have to figure out how to get those things here. When I'm done with that, I'll come see you and we'll make our plans."

He sighed as he continued, "It's going to take years, but I'll be knocking on your door one day. Chris wouldn't give me any other details. He said it will all happen as it should."

Jack replied, "Well, I guess that's it, then. We'll get a good night's sleep and leave in the morning."

Jason nodded then pointed to the back of the cavern. "The living quarters are back there. There are several rooms and it should be easy to find the food. They even ran plumbing for a couple of bathrooms. Make yourselves at home."

Jack said, "Thanks, Jason. I'll check it out in a minute. Right now, we're going outside to look at a normal sky with no green haze."

He smiled at Emma and she nodded her head.

Ray was back and when the whole group heard him, they all buzzed about wanting to go.

Jack beckoned them to follow and he led the way to the hatch. He had to let Emma's hand go to turn the handle, and the door screeched as it opened.

They made their way single file through the dog leg. As they came to the opening, they fanned out and slowly came to a stop. Emma felt something against her leg and looked down. Bella was gazing up at her. She bent down and carefully picked her up.

The lightning was gone, and even the rain had stopped. The clouds were still there, but that didn't bother the group. They looked at the sky and saw that there wasn't even a hint of green. For the first time in weeks, they gazed upon a sky straight from their memories.

A soft breeze caressed their faces as they were all lost in

their own thoughts. It had been a turbulent journey that had forced them all to experience feelings that spanned the whole spectrum of human emotions. They had witnessed people at their worst, but also had their faith restored by seeing others go above and beyond to help their fellow man.

Jason and the agents were thinking of duty and a list of things that had to be done. Bryan and Lori were thinking of love and their journey to California in the hopes of reuniting with his mother and sister. Jack and Emma were still stunned to find out that they would be having a son.

All of them, however, had a renewed sense of hope for themselves and all of mankind. It was time to rebuild.

They could only hope that a lesson had been learned. The world had nearly been destroyed because of greed and arrogance. Maybe this time things would be different. The possibilities were endless…